CHASING AFTER YOU

A YORK BEACH NOVEL
THE CAPPELLI FAMILY

NICOLE VIDAL

COPYRIGHT

Published by: Jasper Media, LLC
Copyright © 2023 Nicole Vidal
Cover images © Doug Lemke (lighthouse), and Volodymyr
TVERDOKHLIB (models).

Cover design by Designs with Sass
Developmental Edit by Virginia Cantrell of Hot Tree Editing
Final Edit by Jamee Thumm of Hot Tree Editing

ISBN 979-8-9863925-3-0

TABLE OF CONTENTS

KEEP IN TOUCH WITH NV

Visit me on social media or online to learn about my newest releases:

Facebook (http://fb.me/NicoleVidalAuthor)

Instagram (http://instragram.com/nicolevidal_author)

My website (www.nicolevidal.com)

Goodreads (https://bit.ly/NVGoodreads)

Amazon (https://amzn.to/2XCLSlR)

Pinterest (http://pinterest.com/NicoleVidal_Author)

PROLOGUE

LILIANNA

TWO MONTHS AGO

The heaves haven't lessened since I pulled away from the bar. I turn into a spot and throw my car into park. Our bench. I didn't know where else to go. We came here so many times over the years, a spot we found near the end of high school. Almost every visit was to celebrate an amazing milestone, like graduation or when his team won the state championship. We celebrated here about a month after he was drafted to play professional football as well. The only time we were here for a sad moment was when his grandmother passed about ten years ago. Now, there is no "we." *We* aren't here. I am. Alone. By choice, but still…. He'll go to my house first. Hell, he has a key and a cushion molded to his ass on my couch. I exhale and ignore the tug of the past for a short time.

It's the right decision—sever all ties. I know it is. Well, for him anyway. He's happy, at least he appears happy. For him, I would take a bullet, assuming I could shove him out of the way. For him, I will wallow in heartbreak and stride forward a tiny bit each day without my almost lifelong best friend.

Our unlikely friendship started in third grade when Leo yanked my ponytail hard while taking a step backward. The memory makes my heart constrict.

"Let go you big oaf!" I recall shouting at him. It only happened once. He didn't expect me—barely a whiff of a girl—to stand up to him and his towering size. Even then his size was imposing.

He laughed and released the ponytail that reached to my waist.

I turned to face him. "How dare you? I don't even know you!"

"It was either grab your hair or let him tackle you." Young Leo pointed to a classmate sprawled at my feet.

My mighty protector, a role he filled a few times over the years. "Well, thank you. I'm Lilianna." I extended my hand to him.

His hands were gigantic and enveloped mine. "I'm Leo, short for Leonardo. I guess our parents like long names." A sadness filtered into his eyes when he said "parents."

I shrugged. "Everyone in my family has long names, except my big brother."

"How many of you are there?" Leo asked with his head cast down toward the ground.

"I have three sisters and a brother. I'm fourth in line. You?"

"It's just me and my—"

The recess bell rang and cut off our first conversation. It was the start of a beautiful friendship spanning most of my life.

The trill of my phone pulls me back to the present again. A friendship that is now over. I ignore the text message; I know it's from Leo.

I'm alone after the final confrontation I'm willing to have with the enigmatic Danica. His girlfriend comes and goes from the bar and Leo's bed when it suits her. Apparently, she travels frequently for her job. Even though she's rarely present for more than four or five nights a month, she has demands of her boyfriend—demands that include an engagement ring and never spending time with me alone. She'd prefer he spend no time at all with me, even though our monthly movie nights have been in place for the last six or so years. She clearly doesn't know Leo as well as I do. He would never betray her. He's loyal to a fault. It's not how he's built. Additionally, he isn't interested in me as more than his best friend, who happens to be a woman. As far as I know, he never has been.

He's found family. Choosing to end our friendship impacts more than me and him. It affects my entire family, and it isn't going to go over well at all.

Without thinking, I answer the call that comes through instead of rejecting it. I can already hear him talking. *Ugh!*

"Lilianna, talk to me please."

"I can't. I love you."

"I love you too."

The ache in my heart is difficult to bear, yet I force out the words. "No, you don't understand. I'm *in love* with you."

I imagine him scrubbing his beefy hand down his face like he does when he's frustrated. "Where are you? I want to talk face-to-face."

"Don't. I didn't want you to find out like this. You're dating someone else. It's not who I am. I'm not a home-wrecker."

His tone sounds more forceful and pained. "Where are you, Stella? We need to talk. I refuse to allow you to make this decision for me—for us." He gave me the nickname sometime in high school after he learned my middle name is Stellaluna. At a later point, he shared he selected it because I'm his North Star.

"There is no us. There can't be." I don't need to bring up Danica's ultimatum. He's well aware. I'm sure he's as torn about losing our friendship as I am.

Me on the other hand, "devastated" and "heartbroken" barely describe the hollow darkness I feel. You would think we've kissed or been together, but I've never tasted his whiskey-laced lips and likely never will.

I hear the telltale sounds of my alarm and my new puppy barking. Also, I'm certain, despite his haste, he'll let Lola out of the crate and let her out before leaving.

After a few minutes pass, he continues. "I know where you are. Please wait for me. I'm coming to you."

"Leonardo, please don't. I can't handle more right now." My words are disingenuous because the only thing I want is a huge bear hug and assurance he could be mine. His hugs are epic and can fix almost anything wrong in my life. *No! Not this!* It'll only make the raw wound gape more.

"Stella, it makes me crazy you're hurting right now, and it's my fault. Stay there, please. This conversation needs to be in person."

"Please don't. This is hard enough. I won't make you choose." A silence falls over the line. *I love you,* I whisper in my soul. I pull the phone away from my ear, the call still connected. "Goodbye, Leonardo. You're the best friend a girl could ever ask for."

I end the call and force my lead-laden feet to move toward my car. He'll be here within the next five minutes. As I crest the hill and stop near the exit, I glance back at our bench once more. It was a special place. I will never come back here again. I reminisce a bit too long, until Leo charges into the lot and parks. I take that as my cue to leave.

CHAPTER ONE

LEONARDO

PRESENT DAY

It's been two months since Lily ended our friendship. The details are still vivid in my mind as I sit in my private office. Lily was sitting at the bar chatting with Miguel, my bartender, when Danica breezed in. Danica is Lily's physical opposite in every way. She's blonde, bubbly, and has an athletic build. She works in construction sales and travels the mid-Atlantic and New England states for work.

I didn't see it, but my staff indicated after the incident, she wasn't pleased with Lily's presence. Danica expressed her disgust to my best friend loudly and without regard for me or my customers. I heard most of her words as I made my way into the bar area.

"You don't belong here. Leo is my boyfriend," Danica spewed.

"I'm aware. He's my best friend, and this is a public place," Lily calmly replied.

As I rounded the corner, I saw Danica hovering with her lips near Lily's ear. From my position, I couldn't hear what she said or read her lips. Whatever her words were, it was enough for Lily to throw back the remainder of her drink and storm out of my bar.

Spotting me, Danica sauntered over and threw her arms around me before I could fully process what just happened.

"What did you say to Lily?"

"The truth," she replied.

I yanked her arms away from me, and all but dragged her into my private office. "What is the truth?"

"You don't want her like you want me. If you did, I wouldn't be here. I mean, she's been following you around like a lost puppy for the last.... It doesn't matter. You're mine, and she has no place in your life."

Has she listened to anything I've shared about myself? It's absolutely the other way around. "No, you're wrong. She's the reason I'm where I am. Along with her family, she saved me from life circumstances and poor decisions more than once."

"I don't care. It's her or me. I meant what I said, Leo. I want her gone, and I want a ring."

"I'm not having this discussion with you again. We haven't been together long enough for me to consider marrying you. Hell, I don't love you. More importantly, I will not give up my friendship with Lily or her family for you."

"Are you sure you want to choose her over us?"

"It isn't that simple, Danica."

"Yes, it is," she bit back.

"Then, yes, I'm choosing Lily and her family over you."

When I didn't add more fuel to the argument, she stated, "Fine, I'm done." Without another word, she turned on her stilettos and walked back out the way she came.

I pulled my phone from my pocket and thumbed a text to Lily. Doubting I would get an answer, I grabbed my keys and hustled to my truck. I sent a few more texts, demanding to know where she was. On the way to her place, I took a chance and called her. Much to my surprise, she answered. I keyed open the front door to find her not home, but Lola, her new fluffy puppy, was whining in her crate.

The conversation that ensued was nowhere near what I expected. The faster I want to move, the more time it took to get Lola back into her crate. By the time I made it to our spot—our bench—all I saw was her taillights.

These last two months since she ended our friendship has been close to the worst time of my life. The only other times I was this miserable was when my dream was stolen with one unfortunate tackle and when my grandmother died. I've tried everything I could think of to get her to talk to me. I even stooped to reaching out to Mama Cappelli for assistance.

Like Lily's sisters before her, Mama told me to keep trying. "Leonardo, I love you as if I birthed you. Only you can fix this with Lilianna. You have too much history to give up so easily."

"I won't give up."

"Good" was all she said before ending the call.

I refuse to give up the only true family I've ever known, aside from Gran. My early life story, which I've gleaned over the years from anecdotes and cautionary tales, includes my mother, who was an alcoholic, leaving me with my father at eight months old. It only took him a few months of single parenthood to leave me with Gran. We moved to York Beach the summer before third grade.

Lily has been beside me through it all. From the time we met, she and her family became my family. Mama and Papa Cappelli never looked down on the kid who stole food from their pantry. Once she realized I didn't have enough to eat at home, Mama prepared extra plates for me every Sunday to take with me. Lily would have extra food in her lunch for me if I needed it after that point too.

Over the years, Lily has had two relationships of note. Her relationship with Matt, during college, required some intervention from me. Matt never treated her well, and I caught him with another girl at a campus hangout after practice one evening. It was helpful my teammates were present at the time. As the other girl and my teammates watched, he called Lily and dumped her. I strongly suggested he lose her number. He did, and the other girl left him as well.

Her second relationship was with Oliver. I mentally refer to him as "the suit." On paper, the two of them were an excellent match. Lily is book smart, funny, and gorgeous. She's a bit taller than average, but her curves belie her height. Objectively, Oliver met the societal standard of good-looking and smart. He seemed to treat her right, so I didn't interfere. Nor did I share my interest in pursuing a relationship with her.

Danica hasn't been around to see me since I chose Lily, but she has sent a few texts and left messages. I haven't responded to any of them, nor do I intend to. Not only did my former girlfriend expect me to end my relationship with my family, but she didn't trust me with Lily either. I'm not the one who travels often. If anyone should be concerned about faithfulness, it should have been me.

Wrestling with losing Lily has been abject torture. When Lily spilled her deepest feelings to me, my gut churned. Lily knows all my dreams and secrets. No one else knows me as well as she does, not even my girlfriend—well, my ex-girlfriend. There was a time earlier in our friendship when I thought Lily and I could be great together.

The more I considered us as a couple, the more I felt it would never work. I couldn't risk our friendship or my family if our relationship didn't work out. Now, having not spoken to Lily for nearly two months and the prospect of seeing her at Frankie's wedding this weekend, I may have underestimated my feelings for her. The constant nagging ache in my chest and the urge to call or text her hasn't diminished. In fact, it grows stronger each day. Perhaps I've been in love with Lilianna my entire life. I didn't realize what real love was until I lost it. More accurately, Lily took it back.

Unsure of how to handle my emotions, I bury myself in paperwork. When I reach the bottom of the pile, I notice an envelope with Lily's signature stamp in the upper left corner. *When did this arrive? Was she here?*

Though she refuses to talk to me or see me, she's still working for me. Sort of. When I was drafted, I asked Lily to manage my signing bonus, salary, and investments, much to the dismay of my agent at the time. She agreed despite her position as a portfolio manager for Upton Gerber. It's one of the largest brokerage companies in the country. Each month, she provides a report of my financial status. I tear into the envelope, hoping to find her usual cheerful note. Unfortunately, I find only the report. The fact she continues to help me but refuses to talk to me widens the divide in my heart. In the wee hours of the morning, I trudge upstairs to my apartment and try to sleep away the major missteps I've made in my love life.

Normally, a potential suitor would have a best friend to enlist in the pursuit of a woman he desires. In my case with Lily, I am—was—no, I am the best friend, which leaves her sisters, who are basically my sisters. They have adamantly and fervently done everything in their power to avoid helping me. Outside of saying, "Talk to Lily," from Lia, Frankie offered, "Force Lily to talk to you, but don't hurt her more," and my personal favorite from Lina, "Get your head and your heart right, then chase her. She's absolutely worth it, and you know you can't survive without her," my *sisters* have been unhelpful.

Each of them is undoubtedly correct. I don't know what else to try. Lily isn't a grand-gesture type of woman. She's private and reserved with her affection to everyone… except me. It wasn't until Danica's edict that Lily regressed to our teenage "no touching each other at all" stance. I don't mean in a sexual way. It wasn't abnormal for her to curl up against me during movie night, curl her hands around my bicep, or seek comfort in my arms when something went awry, like her douchebag ex-brother-in-law being released from prison, albeit for a brief time.

I consider my options while fitfully chasing sleep. I fail miserably.

Over the rest of the week, I haven't made any progress in deciding the best way to mend my relationship with Lily. I've been going back and forth trying to decide if I'm still welcome at Frankie's wedding. It wasn't my choice to end our friendship. I weighed the pros and cons numerous times before deciding all I can do is use my invitation as an avenue to show up for my family. While I'm there, I can only hope to steal some time with her on the dance floor or a private moment after the ceremony. Her sisters may not want to intervene, but Frankie asked me to partner with Lily for the introductions due to the size of her bridal party. With that in mind, I foresee a scenario where Lily and I have no choice but to speak to one another later today.

After I tug on my suit pants, dress shirt, and shoes, I grab my ticket to getting Lily to talk to me. She knows nearly everything about me. This box may be the only thing of mine she doesn't know, because it's all about her—the box and my tattoo, I guess. I sift through the contents and smile, hoping this will be enough to entice her to listen. With my jacket and tie slung over one arm and my box for Lily under the other, I make my way downstairs into my bar.

I opened Endzone Draft and Barrel within six months of my career ending. The tackle looked textbook no matter how many times I replay it in my mind or watch the footage. However, a third significant concussion in five years was enough for me to wise up. The building was a dump when I bought it. With some professional assistance and a lot of sweat equity, I turned it into a successful sports bar with a craft whiskey distillery on the side.

"Morning, Miguel," I greet my bartender as I enter the main area. Miguel has a similar background to me. We were teammates in high school. The only difference between him and me is I was afforded the chance to go pro for a short time. He wasn't.

"Morning, boss. Looking spiffy. Wedding today, huh?"

I glare at him. "Yes. No, I don't want to talk about Lily."

"Can I admit I miss having Lily around, but Danica not so much?"

"You just did."

He shrugs. "Good luck winning back our girl."

I miss her to my marrow. "Not mine or yours."

"At least one of us has a shot though," he admits.

"Maybe."

Confident in my choice to attend the wedding, I wave at Miguel and head into the parking lot. I set my jacket and tie on the seat and the box in the footwell on the passenger side. Realizing I left last night's deposit in my office, I hurry back inside. After stashing the deposit into my bag, I sling it over my shoulder and make my way back to the bar. It's then when I smell it—the telltale scent of rotten eggs.

"Miguel, get out!" I yell.

When he doesn't answer, I search for him in the main area but come up empty. I stow my bag the near the coat room and resume my search, checking the storage room, then barrel room. As I move toward the basement, a loud boom reverberates, and the floor beneath my feet shakes. It's the last thing I remember.

CHAPTER TWO

LILIANNA

Brave face, Lily. Smile and get dolled up. Today is about Frankie and Tommy. We're getting ready in the bridal suite at the hotel near the Hartley Mason Reserve. It's the same location Luca and Willa used for their wedding. It's stunning, and both Frankie and Tommy have an affinity for the water. Truthfully, I do as well. All the Cappelli women, plus Ellie, my soon-to-be official niece, are almost ready. I was doing fine until my sister Lina asked if Leo was still coming.

"I don't know. I haven't talked to him in a couple months."

"Oh, Lily." Lina judges me with two words and a disdainful tone.

"Do you know something I don't?"

"No, but you can't ignore him forever." The look on her face says something else entirely.

"Spill, Lina," I demand.

"Nothing to tell exactly. He asked me for advice since your heated exchange with Danica at the bar. He said you've been distant."

"And?"

"I told him he needed to get you to talk to him."

"I'm miserable and heartbroken. He's the only person who can repair the damage. Except, he doesn't want me."

"Are you sure about that?" Lia, my youngest sister, asks, joining our conversation.

"Nothing he has said or done since I shared my feelings indicates he does."

"How many times has he called or texted?" Frankie interjects.

No reason not to share the truth. "At least twice a day."

"Lily!" Lina shrieks. "You need to hear him out."

"Do I? If he loved me, he would've told me when I divulged my feelings to him."

My sisters gasp collectively.

"You told him the truth?" Frankie whispers and takes my hands in hers. She looks gorgeous. Her Kelly Barnett original is a fitted, silk gown with covered buttons down her back and train.

"Yes, I told him the complete, unvarnished truth, and he didn't respond in kind. I'll be fine eventually. I'm sorry I messed everything up for all of you."

The rest of my sisters swarm and hug me close. They understand the type of relationship I want with my future husband. Each of them wants it too. Our parents have been married forty-plus years. They love hard and completely, and still disagree, make up, go on dates, and dote on us, our brother, and our children.

The hardest part of choosing myself is Leo loses his family too. No matter how much it pierces my soul, I can't go back to before I shared my feelings, even to give him his found family back. At least... it won't be anytime soon.

Once each of us is photo ready, we take the bridal party photos beforehand. We move to the ceremony location while Ellie does a first look with her dad before Frankie does one too.

Frankie walks down the runner on our dad's arm. Tears stream down his face like I've only seen once before—in his own wedding video. My father was the epitome of an overcome, emotional groom. He may have been overcome when Lina married Derrick, but I was younger and not paying attention to those details. Once Tommy takes her hand, I cautiously scan the crowd row by row and come up empty. I restart from the opposite side this time. Still no Leo.

Frustration blooms in my chest. *This is all my fault*, I admonish myself. He should be here despite our current status. I consider checking again, but I know the result will be the same.

Frankie gifts Ellie a beautiful necklace to symbolize the three of them as a family. Tess, Ellie's mom, is here and smiling. Their relationship took some time to settle. Now Tess sees Frankie for what she is... an amazing bonus mom for Ellie.

The justice of the peace disturbs my thoughts, saying, "You may kiss your bride."

Tommy dips Frankie as they share their first married kiss. Almost simultaneously, every cop in attendance—including Smithson, Davis, and Captain Ramirez—check their phones.

I've seen this scene before. Each one kisses their wife or significant other and rushes away. Unfortunately, after Smithson kisses his fiancée, Scarlett, he moves beside me.

"Lily, there's been an explosion at Endzone."

Leo. No, this can't be happening.

"Is he...?" My voices cracks as I speak, and I grab his forearm to prevent myself from keeling over. It takes monumental resolve to remain on my feet.

"I don't know."

"Where should I go? There or to the hospital?"

Smithson considers his answer. "I would suggest York Memorial. By the time you get to the scene, EMTs will likely have started transport."

Logically, he's right. It would take me twenty minutes to get to the bar—what's left of it anyway—whereas it'll take ten to get to the hospital from here. "Thank you, Smithson."

"You good?"

"Not even a little, but go."

He turns and rushes to his vehicle.

Mama and Lia converge on me. Lia thrusts my phone and purse into my hand and takes my flowers.

"Call us when you know anything. We'll talk to Frankie," Lia informs me.

"Mama—" Tears flood my eyes.

In a strong, stalwart tone, Mama interrupts. "No, Lilianna. Do not even consider it as a possibility. You don't have enough information. Leonardo needs you. Go now! Willa already left."

I pluck off my heels and run to my car faster than I did in the state track championship race in high school. The route to the hospital is blurry as I fight back tears and break every speed limit to arrive as quickly as possible. I shove the shifter into park before rushing to the emergency room.

The ambulance bay doors slam open. My stomach is in knots as the EMT starts to speak. "Twenty-year...."

I stopped listening after hearing the age of the patient. I pace back and forth until the doors crash against the wall again.

"What have we got?" a nurse I don't know asks.

"Male driver, unknown age, pronounced on scene."

Not Leo. I can't handle losing him. It's one thing for him to be alive and happy with someone else. It's something else for him to be gone.

My phone pings in my hand.

Willa: Where are you?

Me: Waiting in the ER. Do you know something?

Willa: I'll be right there.

My sister-in-law's position as director of nursing affords her access and faster updates. The fact she didn't answer doesn't ease my anxiety right now. Within a minute, she's beside me.

"Willa, do you have any information?"

She loops her arm around mine, leads me forward, and says, "Two victims were brought here from the bar. Leo has a serious head injury and Miguel didn't make it."

Fear, anger, and anguish hit me at once. My knees start to buckle, but Willa is stronger than I give her credit for despite being markedly pregnant. She props me up against the door of a hospital room. My eyes dart to the monitor. A steady heart rate scrolls along the top of the screen. Then my gaze drops to the bed. The mixture of emotions coursing through me is inexplicable. I've never been ecstatic and distraught at the sight of his scruffy beard and imperfect nose at the same time. Tears rush down my cheeks as I attempt to enter his room.

Willa stops me cold with her next question. "Lily, who is his medical power of attorney?"

I push out a harsh breath. "Me."

"Who is his neurologist?"

"Dr. Rothstein."

"Okay. I'll inform the on-call neurologist to contact Dr. Rothstein given Leo's history. You need to deal with the blonde ball of fury in the private waiting room."

My head drops of its own volition. The last person I want to see right now is Danica. "Can I?" Willa knows what I'm asking.

"Keep it brief. Only family is allowed to visit."

Willa's words make my stomach drop to my toes. I step inside his room and approach the bed slower than you would think. The nurse shifts to her left. My hand shakes uncontrollably as I reach for his. I cover his hand with mine and will every ounce of strength I have into him. Aside from the fact he's unconscious and lying in a hospital bed, his outward injuries appear minor. There's a small gash near his left eyebrow and some minor abrasions on his hands. Reaching deep for resolve I didn't know I possessed, I step outside.

I don't need to search for the number; I have it programmed in my phone. Leo went to a follow-up with Dr. Rothstein three months ago. Like every appointment since his first concussion, I was beside him. I leave a message with his answering service, indicating my call is urgent. There isn't anything else I can do at this point except wait for the specialist to call me back. I send a message to Lina with an update.

Me: Leo has a head injury. Called his neuro. Need to deal with
   Danica.
Lina: Thanks. I'll inform everyone. Good luck. LY
Me: LY2.

I steel my resolve and make my way to the private waiting room. With a deep breath, I knock and enter the room.

"What are you doing here?" Danica states.

Through gritted teeth, I reply, "The last thing I want to do is fight with you. I made the hardest choice I've ever had to make for Leo by walking away. Current circumstances dictate I'm back for now."

"I want to see him," she demands.

"No. They are only allowing family for now."

Danica points her bony, unmanicured finger at me and spews, "You aren't family."

It takes deep strength not to break her finger. We are family in every way that matters. "Technically, no. However, I know how he earned each scar on his body, the name and contact number for his doctors, and I'm also his medical power of attorney, and he's mine."

She's momentarily stunned silent. "What am I supposed to do? I want him back."

Now it's my turn to be speechless. As much as I would like to dig into her statement, I don't have the time or gumption right now. "Danica, I'm sorry but you can't see him right now."

More venom spills from her lips. "It must be a heady experience to have all the power back, isn't it?"

Be the bigger person, Lilianna. "The power was never mine or yours. It was always Leo's." I consider my words carefully. "I don't know what happened between you and Leo since our heated discussion at Endzone. I don't want to know, especially from your perspective. The best I can do is agree to let you know if he's allowed nonfamily visitors and if he wishes to see you."

She doesn't dignify my statement with a reply. Turning on her heel, she leaves the private waiting room. I take a few settling breaths before returning to Leo's side.

Nothing has changed since I left, other than Willa—clad in her bridesmaid gown showcasing her bump—looking out the window.

"Thank you, Willa," I offer.

"Least I could do considering I sent you to deal with the she-devil."

Containing a laugh is impossible. "She wasn't happy to see me at all."

"I gather she didn't take the news well."

"More like she wasn't pleased I'm here and she can't be. Although she did mention they aren't a couple anymore."

Willa raises an arched eyebrow. "Really? Not something she should share if she truly wanted to get in here."

"She shared after she demanded entry."

"That makes more sense," Willa observes. "Dr. Rothstein is on his way."

"Thanks. Can I lay with him?"

"Be careful of the tubes."

I nod. "Willa?"

"Yeah?"

Palpable sadness constricts my heart. "When Miguel's brother arrives, please let me know."

"I will." She leaves the room.

As carefully as possible, I lie on the edge of the bed beside Leo and set my hand on his chest lightly. "Leo, I don't know if you can hear me…. When you asked me to be your medical decision maker, I didn't intend for it to be so soon." While I gather my thoughts to share more, Dr. Rothstein arrives. With slow and precise movements, I push to my feet.

"Miss Cappelli, I would have preferred to see you again under different circumstances."

I take his extended hand. "As would I."

He scans Leo's chart and makes a few notes. "His chart indicates he likely suffered a blast injury from the explosion but wasn't a primary victim. The results of his CT scan are pending. Once I review it, we can determine next steps."

"Thank you. Does his chart indicate whether he regained consciousness at all?"

"Only indication is he kept repeating 'Stella.' He's sedated right now."

Oh, Moon. He leaves the room, presumably to request the test for Leo, and I sit on the edge of the bed again.

Before I speak to Leo again, Willa knocks on the doorframe. "The rest of the family is in the large waiting room."

"Thanks, Willa. I'll be out soon."

"Okay. I'll let them know." She closes the door as she retreats.

My gaze settles on the man I love more than words could ever properly express. If only he loved me back…. Yet there's no place I would be than right here. Maybe, after Danica's admission, we might have a chance for an "us."

A technician appears in the doorway to transport him for his scan.

I swipe the stray tear and press a kiss to his forehead. "Don't quit on me, Moon. We have things to discuss."

He wheels Leo down the hall, and I make my way to the waiting area with my family—our family.

CHAPTER THREE

LILIANNA

Every family member is still decked out in their wedding attire, except for Antonio. He shed his tie and dress shirt already. Frankie and Tommy are here as well.

"I'm sorry, Frankie."

She pulls me into a hug. "Nothing to be sorry for." My sister releases me.

"You should be packing for your honeymoon in Turks and Caicos."

"We have time," the bride replies.

"Promise me you'll go."

"We will," Tommy assures me.

"Auntie, is Uncle Leo going to be okay?" Em asks with her arms wrapped around me tightly. They have always addressed him as "uncle" though we aren't a couple.

Lying isn't my intention, but I don't have a good answer for her. "I hope so, sweetie."

"Me too. He builds amazing forts, and I love him lots."

Same, Em. Same.

"We brought you some food and a piece of cake." Mama shoves the Styrofoam carton into my hands. "Eat," she demands.

There's no room for me to dismiss her. I take a seat and dig in to the food. Surprisingly, it's tasty lukewarm.

"Do you have an update?" Lia asks cautiously.

"Not really. They're running tests. Considering his older injuries, Dr. Rothstein is checking everything before making a recommendation. I can't fathom a guess as to what he would suggest as a treatment. The last time Leo had a concussion, he needed to get glasses and decided to quit the game he loves." I can't imagine making a life-altering decision for him. Yet it's exactly the position I may find myself in.

"How you holding up, *piccola*?"

My father has been calling me tiny since I was a young girl. "I'm doing the best I can, Papa. He's…."

"Your other half, and you're hurting because he doesn't see it."

I'm rendered mute. Of course my father would see my love for Leo painted on my face.

"My darling, Leo will figure it out eventually. For now, we focus on his health and then the rest."

"Thanks, Papa." I finish the food and join Em and Antonio at the small table to color.

"Uncle Leo will be fine, Auntie. He's a big, strong dude. He's got this," Antonio assures me.

From your lips, little buddy. "Thanks, bud."

He shrugs. "Anytime."

There's a strong knock on the door about an hour later. "Miss Cappelli, Dr. Rothstein would like to speak with you."

"I'll be right out." I rise from the floor and take a sharp inhale. The nurse leads me into a private room a few doors away.

"Lily, please have a seat." Dr. Rothstein motions to the chair on the opposite side of the square table in the sterile, nondescript room. It's devoid of wall art as well.

I settle myself and hope the news he has isn't tragic. "Give it to me straight please."

"Leo has a tertiary blast injury. He has an acceleration bruise on the front of his brain. The good news is the location of this injury is different from the concussive injuries he's had in the past. I strongly recommend putting him into a medically induced coma until the swelling goes down."

My heart feels like it's in my throat, and I can't breathe. "What are the risks?" I manage.

He steeples his fingers before replying, "Blood clots, infection, and atrophy."

"How long do you expect the treatment to last?"

"It's hard to say. At least a few days, but it could be as long as ten days. If I had to make an educated estimate, I would say three days. However, his previous concussions could impact the timeline."

"What's the likelihood of deficits when he regains consciousness?"

"It's hard to determine. It appears most of the swelling is in his frontal lobe, which—"

"Which controls concentration, judgement, etc."

"Yes. Do you have someone to discuss this suggested treatment plan with?"

I nod tightly. "Yes, our family is in the next room."

"Please take some time and talk to them. I'll have the nurse prepare the paperwork for you. Let me know if you have more questions after you discuss it with them."

I push to my feet. "Thank you. I'll let you know as soon as possible." On the exterior, I'm calm and collected, and I will be until I make it into the room with my family. On the inside, however, my heart is pounding, my chest aches, and I would give almost anything not to be in this position. When I reenter the room, everyone stops talking and stares in my direction expectantly.

Surprisingly, it's Tommy who speaks first. It's a shock because he doesn't know me well. My family knows I'm a thinker, and they're giving me time. "What did the doctor say, Lily?"

His newly minted wife attempts to silence him with a hand on his forearm.

"It's okay, Frankie." I share with my family the information and ask for their opinions. No one offers one. Silence blankets the room until I have the courage to speak again.

"Willa?" She's a nurse and a damn good one.

"Dr. Rothstein is one of the preeminent neurologists in the world. I would follow his recommendation if it were my decision."

The only other input I receive is from my mother. "Leo is like another son to us. Please heed the doctor and consent to the treatment."

I drop my head and will the tears away. It's my turn to be strong, not that I've asked the same of Leo yet. Ideally, I'll never need to. An army of limbs surrounds me while I gather my composure. Sufficiently placated for now, I consider what's next, but Lina beats me to it.

"What do you need from us?"

"I need someone to take care of Lola."

"Can I do it, Dad?" Ellie asks almost immediately.

"Let me ask your mom." Tommy pulls out his phone and presumably texts his ex-wife, Tess.

"I've got next," Lia offers a little levity.

I crack a smile and continue. "I need my laptop and charger, phone charger, and some clean clothes."

"We can gather those items," Lina offers. "Anything else?"

"Nothing you guys can do. I'm sure Captain Ramirez will be by eventually."

After another round of hugs, my family scatters. Lia and Willa hang back for a little longer.

"Where's Luca?" I ask.

Willa glares at me. "Where do you think he is?"

I shake my head. "At the scene. I'm sure he wrangled special privileges."

"I'm sure he did." Willa laughs softly. "I'm going to head home."

"Thank you."

Willa leaves the waiting room.

Lia slings her arm over my shoulders. "Can I see him?" Lia and Leo have a special quasi brother/sister relationship. She was a toddler when I met him.

I hug her and lead her back toward Leo.

Dr. Rothstein is also approaching at the same time. "Hello again, Lily. Do you have any additional questions?"

Lia links her hand with mine.

"No, I don't have any more questions."

"Did you make a decision?"

"Yes, please proceed with the treatment."

"Very well. Please sign here, and I can get things started."

I take the pen from his hand and pause, poised over the signature line. *I need to do this for Leo. He would do it for me.* In addition to my inner pep talk, Lia squeezes my hand. I scribble my name before continuing to his bedside.

"I don't think I've ever seen Leo this still." Lia attempts to cover his hand with hers. The sheer size alone is a close comparison to my hands. It's obvious my sisters and I are siblings. Lia and I, however, could be twins outside of our height difference.

It's hard not to laugh. Leo can't even make it through an entire movie without moving around. "Only when he's sleeping, and he doesn't sleep for very long." At most, Leo sleeps five hours a day.

Lia hangs out for a bit longer and orders Leo to rest and heal up quickly. Near eight, my sister hugs me tight and leaves.

"I'll verify Lola is set with Ellie."

"Thanks." I retake my spot beside Leo. Lifting his beefy hand, I set one of mine on the bed palm up and make a sandwich. I rest my head on top of the pile and close my eyes.

A few hours later, Millie, his night nurse, nudges me. "Miss, perhaps you would be more comfortable on the pull-out bed."

Groggily, I nod and shift to the bed. It isn't until the next morning I startle awake and find my requested items were delivered. Lina not only brought the items, but she wiggled my phone from my hand and plugged it in.

CHAPTER FOUR

LILIANNA

It's been less than twenty-four hours, but it feels more like a year. I've been coordinating a few things, like restoration of the building as far as water removal and damage remediation where possible, in between one-sided conversations with Leo. I keep the topics light, usually about our favorite books or movies. We agree the *Lord of the Rings* is greater than *Harry Potter*. Our taste in music is vastly different. He prefers classic rock, which I can get behind. However, he hates country music, which I would mix in every few songs.

I shouldn't be surprised, but my family has clearly created a schedule to not overwhelm me or the staff. So far today, Mama and Papa have been here to visit. They indicated Lina would stop by later this afternoon and Lia would bring dinner. Leo was moved to a critical care floor very early this morning. The good news, for me at least, is the overnight guest accommodations are a bit better and there's a shower I can use.

Just before lunch, I meet with Miguel's brother and nephew. "I'm sorry for your loss. Miguel was a great worker and, equally as important, a better friend to Leo."

"*Gracias*. My brother was grateful for the chance Leo gave him to prove himself. He found a good footing with Leo and the other staff members," José replies, and his son Tito nods.

"Can we visit Leo?"

"Unfortunately, no. They are only allowing family members to visit at this time."

"*Si. Yo entiendo.*"

"Please let me know when the services will be," I request.

"It won't be until next week sometime. We have family travelling here."

If I recall correctly, Miguel's parents moved to southern Florida in the last few years. "I understand."

After a brief embrace, both men exit the hospital. I curl up again with my laptop. I've barely made progress when Captain Ramirez, Smithson, Detective Jones, and my brother consume the threshold of Leo's room.

"Can we come in?" Luca inquires.

I nod and step into Luca's arms.

"How are you doing?" he asks before releasing me.

"I'm doing the best I can. Do you have an update?"

Captain Ramirez defers to Detective Jones and newly promoted Detective Smithson. "I'm merely here for support. Jones and Smithson are handling the investigation for our department. Lieutenant Foster from the YFD may be by later as well."

Detective Jones speaks first. "Good afternoon, Miss Cappelli."

"Hello."

"Early reports indicate the explosion was intentional. The report from the utility company shows the property drew extra gas in the last thirty-six hours. Further, Mr. Santos turned on a light, which sparked the explosion."

"Do you know of anyone who did work at the property? Was there a malfunction requiring repair?" Smithson asks.

"No. Leo and I…. I could check the company's digital records for invoices to see if Leo requested any repairs."

"Much appreciated. Does the bar have security cameras?" Jones inquires.

"Yes. I can provide the security firm's information and contact them, allowing you access to the footage for your investigation," I offer.

"Does Mr. De Gaetano have a partner, silent or otherwise?"

"For the bar? No. He's the sole owner."

Smithson asks, "You have access in your capacity as…?"

"I handle his personal and business books. I have access as a second key for unfortunate situations like this."

"Leo is family," Luca adds, although Smithson already knows this information. His prior service with the YPD and the fact he's my brother should be enough for Detective Jones to accept my assertions.

"Who has unfettered access to the building?" Jones continues.

"Leo, Miguel Santos, and me," I respond honestly.

"The deceased victim?"

"Yes."

"When is the last time you used your key to enter the premises?" Jones asks.

"About four months ago was the last time I was in Leo's apartment and used my key. Two months ago was the last time I was at the bar as a patron. I also dropped off his statement last month during business hours." *If you would like the time I left, I can provide that on the nose as well.* The snark in my mind is high and harsh. I would never jeopardize Leo's dream despite the status of our personal relationship.

"Where is your set of keys?" Jones asks.

"In my purse." I'm surprised he doesn't ask to see them.

"Where are Mr. De Gaetano's?"

"I assume with his keys as well. Let me check." I make my way to the closet in his room and sift through his personal belongings. I push down the bile rising in my throat from the sheer notion Leo could've done this on purpose. He would never.

Leo was drafted by the regional team in New England. When his injuries caught up with him, he sold his modest home near the stadium and bought the bar. He made peace with the end of his career and instead runs a highly successful bar and craft distillery.

"His key to the bar is this one. The square is for the exterior entrance to his upstairs apartment." I point out and slip my index finger through the ring. A pang of sadness hits me when I see the faded football keychain I gave him on draft day.

Seemingly satisfied with my explanation, Detective Jones moves on to more indelicate topics, although he wouldn't know. "Is Mr. De Gaetano dating anyone?"

I clench and unclench my fists at my sides before wrapping my arms around myself. I forbid myself to look over at Leo to gain my composure. "His most recent girlfriend was Danica Ryder. She works in sales for Midland Construction." *Well done, Lily.*

"Are they still dating?" Jones asks.

"She was here last night, insisting to visit. After I informed her only family was allowed, she indicated a desire to win him back. I don't know exactly when they broke up or who ended their relationship." Deep down, I hope Leo made the choice, even if we don't end up together.

"How long were they together?"

"A little more than a year," I supply.

"Do you know how to reach her?" Smithson asks.

"No, but if I recall correctly, she has an apartment in Portsmouth near the airport."

"Thank you. We'll be in touch. If you think of anything else, please reach out." Detective Jones extends a card in my direction. "For now, the building is off-limits."

"I assume his apartment is uninhabitable?"

Jones replies, "Correct."

"Thank you."

Detective Jones and Captain Ramirez exit Leo's room. Only Smithson and Luca remain.

"Sorry about the stiffness, Lily," Smithson apologizes.

"No worries, Smithson. You're doing your job. I appreciate it actually."

He nods. "What else will you tell me about the girlfriend? You left something out."

I raise an eyebrow at him. Smithson may have been recently promoted, but his instincts are finely honed. "I have no idea how she would know to come here. If they broke up, how did she know Leo was here? I certainly have no means to contact her."

"Understood. What else? You and Leo have been joined at the hip since elementary school."

"About four months ago, Danica demanded an engagement ring and for Leo to stop spending time with me. Fast forward a bit, she and I had a loud but violence-free, verbal spat at the bar. It was the last time I saw Leo before last night."

"I'll use that information as discreetly as I can. I have no concern you or Leo tampered with the gas line. Call if you have questions or if something strikes you."

"Thank you. Will do."

He and Luca bro hug, and he leaves.

Luca glances behind me to look at Leo. "How are you really?"

"I'm pushing aside my emotions and focusing on things I can control."

"Not the healthiest of options," he accuses.

"True, but he would do this for me despite our current state of flux."

"Accurate. Anything I can do for you?"

I twist a key off Leo's ring and extend it to Luca. "Can you bring his truck to my place? He won't have anywhere else to go for a while."

"Sure. Are you getting enough to eat?"

I laugh. "Mama is on top of it. I have a guest every few hours with food and comfort supplies."

"We stick together when things go sideways."

"I know, Luca. Go. I'm sure Willa would prefer you to be by her side right now."

"Love you, Lily."

"Love you too."

I return to Leo's personal items haphazardly thrown into a plastic bag. His messenger bag with his intact laptop is inside, as well as a deposit meant for the bank. I remove his wallet and the chain he wears with a small star charm. I set my hand on my neck for my chain. We exchanged these chains sophomore year of high school. The ache in my heart renews. I took it off four months ago. I haven't worn it since. Before I think better of it, I text Lia.

Me: Can you grab my chain for me?

Lia: I'll bring it tonight.

Me: Thanks. Love you.

I ignore my overflowing text and email inbox and secure Leo's chain around my neck. The rest of the items are clothes, including pinstripe charcoal pants and a crisp, white shirt. Imagining him in a suit isn't hard to do. However, he hasn't worn this one since the day he signed his football contract. I put his keys, broken phone, and his wallet in my purse and retake my position beside Leo.

As best I can, I text with one hand, clear out my inbox, and watch the monitor repeat his stats for almost an hour. Lia breezes in with dinner, an update about Lola, and my chain as requested.

"Are you sure about putting that back on?" she asks softly.

"Yes." I tug down on the hem of my shirt and reveal his around my neck. "It wasn't a gift of romantic love. It was a gift of enduring friendship and platonic love."

"He still wears his even though…?" Lia wonders aloud.

"Yeah, apparently." I don't have it in me to unpack the meaning behind it, so I shelve it for now. We chat about her summer break before Nurse Millie kicks her out.

Each segment of my day is exactly the same. The nursing staff here is amazing, and they rotate on a set schedule. They manage his medications, monitor his vital signs, and move his limbs to avoid bedsores. My family has been trying to get me to leave, but I refuse. Willa offered to sit with Leo so I could go home for a few hours. I appreciate their love and support, but I won't leave his side. As the days pass, I have been working, pausing deliveries for the bar, fielding calls from his employees, and ordering some clothes for Leo to be delivered to my house, including a new suit. The staff informed me Danica has been turned away twice since Leo was admitted. At this point, three days later, I know what time it is by which nurse is tending to Leo.

"Morning, Carly," I greet her. She's blonde and bubbly but not annoyingly so.

"Hi, Lily. How are you?"

"Hanging in there."

"Someday, when I find the right man, I want our family to be as strong as yours and Leo's," she muses aloud.

"I hope you do."

She smiles and whispers, "Me too." Carly checks his IV and notates his chart. "Dr. Rothstein should be here in the late morning to give you an update."

"I appreciate the information."

Carly exits quietly. I have about twenty minutes before Mama shows up with more food than I can eat. Since I unloaded my feelings, albeit inopportune, it has been torture on my heart. I don't imagine an unrequited broken heart heals quickly—if ever—but somehow this is worse. The man I love with my entire heart is incapacitated in this bed, though purposefully. The ache is somehow worse than when I knew he was romantically happy without me in his life. Knowing he's single again makes me wonder *what if* more than I ever have before.

It dredges up the trepidation too. Did he not want me beside him as a love interest or was our timing simply off? I realize he can't answer me and force my emotions down again to settle before Mama arrives. If anyone other than Leo can see right through me, it's her.

I seem to be getting a reprieve today. Dr. Rothstein arrives before Mama. "Morning, Lily. How's our patient?"

I appreciate the attempt at levity, but I'm not a doctor. "You tell me, Doc."

"All indications are favorable for reversing the treatment." A rush of air infuses my lungs. Before I can ask, he continues. "We slowly decrease the drugs used to induce the coma and monitor him."

"What can I expect when he wakes?" Ever the optimist Lilianna—for his health and our relationship.

"The brain is a complex organ. He could be completely fine since it was a different area of the brain, or he could have issues with concentration or short-term memory loss."

"Wait and see, huh?"

He cracks a small smile. "Exactly."

"How would we handle short-term memory loss? He needs to learn how he ended up here, right?"

He looks at me over his wire-rimmed glasses.

"Got it. Wait and see."

He answers my question anyway. "We'll answer any questions our patient has with the truth. If he experiences any memory loss, it could return. The severity of this injury is significantly less than the others. In his case, the overall number of concussive injuries is key."

"I understand."

"The reversal will take some time for the drugs to work their way out of his system. I would suggest getting something to eat." He makes some notes and has Carly adjust the medications.

"Mama is waiting not so patiently in the hallway with my next food delivery."

"My apologies."

"None are necessary. My family has been coming with food at regular intervals."

"I'll be back when he wakes. If he becomes agitated, tries to pull on the tube, or attempts to speak, call his nurse."

"Thank you. I will."

Mama rushes in with my food as if I'll waste away from starvation by waiting an extra fifteen minutes. "Morning. What did he say?"

"He's reducing the medication. Now we wait for Leo to wake."

"Wonderful news! How about you?"

"I'm worried, but all I can do is wait a bit longer."

"Everything will work out as it's meant to, Lilianna."

A twisty knot of fear tightens in my belly. "What if an 'us' isn't meant to work out?"

Mama pauses to consider her words. "I have never pried, but I'll make an exception. Has anything romantic happened between the two of you?"

"No. We kissed once under the mistletoe sometime during high school, but it was a chaste peck."

"I see. It's up to the both of you whether the risk is worth the reward. You have decided the reward outweighs the risk. Leonardo needs to do the same."

"Thanks, Mama. I hope you're right."

Mama forces me to eat while we chat about the happenings outside the hospital. I appreciate her straying away from the subject of me and Leo. When she takes her leave, and I remain glued to Leo's side. Nearly two hours later, Leo's hand squeezes mine.

CHAPTER FIVE

LEONARDO

I'm uncomfortable. My throat is dry and feels rigid. I shift my right hand slightly against a scratchy surface. My left hand feels warm and heavy. I attempt to speak, but I can't. My eyes fly open, and I turn my head to the right.

"Easy, Leo." Her voice is like an angel. It soothes all that ails me most of the time. Flawless porcelain skin and perfect, pouty lips appear in my hazy view. She looks exhausted.

I attempt to draw her closer, but she resists.

"I'm right here. Breathe for me."

I do as she instructs. I'll do anything for Lily, and she for me. Incrementally, sounds and smells flood my mind.

Softly, she repeats, "I'm right here. Breathe for me."

Then there's a rush of activity. Two more people are beside me now.

"Nice to have you back with us, Mr. De Gaetano," a man in a white coat greets me. He listens to my heart and my lungs before making notes. Then he checks my reflexes at my toes, confirms I can feel the metal against my foot, and asks me to squeeze his hand.

I'm in the hospital. *Why?* I attempt to dig into my memory but don't recall how I got here. With as much strength as I can muster, I squeeze Lily's hand.

Her eyes dart back to mine. "It's going to be okay." Lily has never lied to me. She's been beside me since third grade. I can't imagine a day without her.

The doctor speaks again. "You were in an accident that caused a tertiary blast injury. You're coming out of a medically induced coma. Nurse Carly is going to remove the tube from your throat. Do not try to speak immediately."

I drop my chin in acquiescence. The tape pulls on my beard as the nurse removes it. The pain is nothing compared to what's in Lily's eyes. Anguish and relief are an intriguing and concerning combination.

"Take a deep breath," Carly instructs and slowly draws the tube from my throat. After removal, she raises my head a bit more.

The entire time, my gaze is locked on Lily. Her expression gives me no information about how I got here, yet I'm confident whatever happened is manageable. Lily releases my hand and moves away. The comfort I lose is markedly obvious.

"Slow sips." Carly brings a straw near my mouth.

I do as she asks.

"Good."

My vision is still hazy, but I don't have my glasses, so it makes sense. As if she heard my thoughts or, more accurately, anticipated them, Lily sets my dark-rimmed frames on my face and returns her hand in mine. Never until now have I allowed myself to notice how soft her skin is and how perfectly her tiny hand fits in mine. "Lily." Her name comes out hoarse and quiet from my lips.

A single tear falls down her cheek, which she swipes away almost instantly.

I glance at the doctor, and I'm able to read his name. What is my neurologist doing here?

"What year is it?" Dr. Rothstein asks.

"2023."

"What month is it?"

I pause. "April."

Lily's eyes widen and dart to the side at my answer.

"Not too bad, Leo. You've been here for almost four days. With your concussion history, I advised Lily a medically induced coma was the best course of action to reduce the brain swelling."

"What happened?" I inquire.

"What is the last thing you remember?" Dr. Rothstein asks.

"A disagreement with my girlfriend."

Lily's head drops, effectively hiding her reaction from me.

"About?" the doctor prods.

"Lily." I turn my gaze toward her, but she doesn't look up at me.

Dr. Rothstein shifts to his other foot. Clearly not the answer he was expecting. "Can you pinpoint how long ago?"

"No."

Lily attempts to pull her hand out of mine, but I tighten my grip. Something significant occurred between my last memory and now between Lily and me. I don't remember it at all, at least not yet.

"That will be enough for now. Do not attempt to force your memory back. It'll come back when it's ready. Soon, I'll have the staff get you up and moving," Dr. R advises.

"Thank you for coming all this way. It's above and beyond, Dr. R." My voice emerges scratchy and low.

"She's quite persuasive. You're welcome, Leo." He leaves the room.

"I'll be back in under an hour with more muscle to help you out of bed," Carly says with a grin.

Lily chuckles softly as Carly exits.

I tug Lily to sitting on the edge of the bed. "What day is it? How did I get here?"

"It's June seventh."

"How did I get here?" I repeat.

Lily shakes her head. "As much as I would like to cobble everything together for you, I'm going to heed Dr. Rothstein. His advice hasn't failed us yet."

"Fine," I grumble. I'm as surprised as Lily is at my agreement not to push. "Will you lay with me?"

Her hesitation is slight, but I see it. I don't miss much when it comes to her. It comes from years of expertly honing my Lily radar. She turns and carefully lies beside me with her head on my shoulder. This isn't the first time we've been in this position, but I don't recall cataloging her against me before. She fits like a precision-cut puzzle piece. The silence between us is deafening.

Lily's phone vibrates in her back pocket. I reach down and pull it out and hand it to her. Before she checks it, she asks, "Do you want visitors, or do you want me to ask them to hold off?"

"Have they been coming all along?"

She tilts her head back to look up at me.

The urge to kiss her breathless overcomes me. Then confusion takes its place. Where is this coming from if I have a girlfriend who isn't Lily?

"You know better than to ask. Everyone has been here almost daily to check on you and bring me food."

"Have you left here?"

"No."

She has been beside me for the last four days. I would do the same for her if the situation were reversed. "I'm open to visitors."

She nods and checks her phone. With a few texts, she settles back against me, her eyes anywhere but on mine.

My mind is spinning. I recall fighting with my girlfriend about Lily, but the person is faceless in my mind. "Do I have a girlfriend?"

Lily shudders against me. Lucky for her and perhaps me, Carly and some extra muscle arrives.

"Let's get you up," Carly states. She's about the same size as Lily. By sheer height alone, Carly is too short to support me. I understand why she would want assistance, given I haven't stood on my own in almost a week. She introduces Matt and Jimmy. Both men are tall and fit.

I push to sitting before twisting to dangle my feet off the edge of the bed. Carly adds some socks with nonslip grips on the bottom. After some instruction, I rise beside the bed with assistance and gather my bearings. On my right, Jimmy loosens his grip and slides away.

"A few steps toward the door, then turn and walk back to your window," Matt instructs from my left.

I successfully walk to the door with limited assistance. When I turn toward the window, I catch Lily's reflection in the window.

Whether she catches me or regains her composure, Lily turns to face me. Her shoulders are strung tight with tension and worry, but there's a smile pasted on her face. I know her as well as I know myself. Her expression isn't genuine.

Fuck! I hurt her deeply somehow. As I attempt to recall, my steps falter a bit.

"You good?" Matt asks.

"Yeah, lost my focus for a moment." I make my way to the window and turn purposely toward Lily.

She lifts her gaze and takes a step back to allow me to continue.

"Good. A few more laps in here, then a break and some food," Matt encourages me.

I take a few more turns around my room and resettle in the chair instead of the bed.

Matt and Jimmy leave.

"I'll send up some food for you, but I don't believe it'll be necessary," Carly indicates.

I nod despite not understanding her statement about the meal. Within minutes of her leaving, Mama and Papa Cappelli make their way into my room with food and dessert for Lily and me.

"Oh, Leonardo! You gave us quite a scare," Mama admits as she kisses my cheek and hugs me lightly.

"It wasn't intentional, I'm sure, not that I recall anyway. Doc says to hold off on trying to remember. I have a gap of about two months," I offer.

Both freeze in place briefly. Whatever happened between Lily and me centered around the mysterious argument I had with my girlfriend I surmise.

Mama fusses around me and sets up food on the table and slides it in front of me. "Eat, Leo."

I smile. "Yes, Mama." I don't recall when I started addressing her as "Mama," but it has been quite some time. As I dig in, Lily takes a seat in the window and does the same.

We chat for a while after I finish Mama's delicious lasagna and cheesecake before they make their way home so the others can visit. The rest of the afternoon includes visits from the rest of my family, except for Frankie and Tommy and Willa. Luca stops by for a quick visit at Willa's urging before rushing home to wait on her until their baby decides to grace us with his presence.

Near seven in the evening, it's only Lily and me. Despite all the guests, my mind has been spinning with ways to figure out how our relationship can be repaired. The problem is I don't remember where or when we broke. "We need to talk, Lilianna."

"We do. Not now, not here. You need to remember on your own."

"What if it takes too long?"

The pain on her face is difficult to watch. "You need to remember yourself. I can't go through it again, Leo."

I drop my head. Without waiting for assistance, I make my way to the bed and climb in. When I open my arms to her, she hesitantly climbs into bed with me. Remembering and fixing us is my highest priority. I never want Lily to hesitate around me ever again.

I wait her out. It isn't until her breathing is shallow and steady that I close my eyes and allow sleep to claim me as well. My respite is short-lived. My brain is overactive, and sleep is elusive. Snippets of a conversation filter into my mind.

"Can I admit I miss having Lily around, but Danica not so much?"

"You just did."

He shrugs. *"Good luck winning back our girl."*

I miss her too. *"Not mine or yours."*

"At least one of us has a shot though," he admits.

My chest constricts, and my eyes fly open to her angelic voice.

"Leo, wake up."

CHAPTER SIX

LILIANNA

Curling into Leo's arms to sleep is not the best plan for my heart, but I did it anyway. Truthfully, it's where I need to be. The sliver of possibly from Danica's slipup is nice, but not once has Leo ever given me a single shred of hope we could be more than friends.

A few hours after I sidle against him in the narrow bed, he's talking in his sleep about "our girl" and "not mine." I push up onto my elbow and nudge him. When that doesn't work, I call his name. "Leo, wake up." Calling him also fails. I shift more, raise the top of the bed a bit, set my palm against his scruff, and call him again.

His eyes open rapidly, and he inhales sharply. "Lily?" His green eyes seize mine like never before. "Why aren't you mine?"

The dagger to my heart is excruciating. I want nothing more than to be his, completely his, but the pain runs deep and wide. The pain of not being enough. The pain from him never choosing me. I take a moment before sidestepping his question. "What did you remember?"

"Are you going to answer me?"

"Yes, but not here."

"We have never been unable to talk to each other, Lily."

"I'm not sure that's accurate, especially recently. What did you remember?" I urge him to share. Maybe it'll spark the rest.

"I recall a conversation with Miguel at the bar. He admitted to missing having you around, but not Danica."

I drop my head in tacit acknowledgment.

He continues, "Miguel said something about winning back our girl." His entire body starts to shake, and his hands turn clammy. The monitor spikes, and alarms blare.

I hop off the bed and retake his hands in mine. "Leo, look at me. Take a deep breath."

"What happened to my bar?"

A tear runs over the ball of my cheek and falls onto our linked hands.

Millie rushes into the room.

"Leo, what do you remember?" I ask again to keep him talking and inform Millie why his alarms are blaring.

He shares about getting ready for the wedding and how, after preparing the deposit, he smelled rotten eggs. "The last thing I recall is searching for Miguel. Is he here too?"

I glance over at Mille who nods in preparation. "Miguel didn't make it." My grip tightens, and Leo's eyes clamp closed.

He fails to speak for a decent amount of time. Millie watches the monitor until his heart rate returns to normal. "If it spikes again, I'll be back."

"Thank you, Millie," Leo grumbles without looking at her.

I acknowledge her, and she leaves.

"Please tell me what you know about my bar," Leo begs. The anguish in his voice is devastating to hear.

I settle between his knees with my legs crossed yogi style and take his hand into mine. Starting from the morning of Frankie's wedding, I share what I know, facts only including the excess gas and Miguel's death. I also include what Luca and Smithson believe. In fact, they're due to provide an update today.

"Can you contact José and tell him I'll cover all of Miguel's final expenses?" he asks.

"I already took care of it."

"Why?"

"You know why." Silence falls between us, and I can tell he wants to talk about what happened between us. However, he moves on. I'm sure my reprieve will be only as long as he's here or until the rest of his memory floods his brain.

Choked up, he asks, "When are the services?"

I glance at my watch and note it's the wee hours of the morning. "Tomorrow. They were waiting for his family to travel here."

"I need to be there."

"I know. Dr. Rothstein will be here later this morning to see you. You need to heed his recommendations. We'll see what he says first."

"It isn't a choice, Lily. I may not be at fault, but it was my building. He's my responsibility. He was my responsibility."

There's nothing for me to say. Leo is an exceptional boss, and he gives people second chances. Losing Miguel is deeply personal and painful for him regardless of how it happened.

"I make no promises."

"I need to be there. It's the least I can do." He gathers his composure again before asking, "How bad is it, Lily?" His voice is strained and concerned.

"I don't know. I came here from the reception and haven't left. All I know is you can't go into the building right now."

"What else have you done?"

The initial tone makes me defensive, but I ignore it. He isn't angry with me. "I paused all the deliveries I could, verified the payroll for Miguel, Butch, Cassidy, and Taylor, as well as the kitchen staff, and paid the outstanding invoices due last week."

"You didn't have to—"

"Yes, I did. If the situation were reversed and you could do my work for me, you would."

"I would."

"We should try to get some more sleep before it's actually morning."

"I don't see that happening, but I'll try." He tugs me upward, and I settle back where I was before. Only this time his hand is branding the skin at my waist and his other hand is covering mine. Until now, any skin-to-skin contact was brief and unintentional.

He has no idea the turbulent emotions flowing through me. While cuddling with Leo isn't abnormal, like this, as if we're a couple, absolutely is. I will my body to relax. I'm not very pleasant without enough sleep. Although I thought it would be more difficult, I succumb to the pull of dreamland.

Hours later, I hear talking. I claw my way to awake and open my eyes.

"Hey, Lily," Luca greets me.

"Hey. What time is it? You don't usually arrive until lunchtime."

A huge, glorious smile grows on my brother's face. "I've been here for hours."

"Is he here?" Leo asks.

"Luciano 'Luke' Vincent Cappelli was born about three hours ago. I came to check on Leo and see if you wanted to be the first to meet my son."

"Yay!"

"Go, Lily. I'll be fine on my own," Leo urges.

"No, you should come too." I push the call button and implore Carly to allow me to bring Leo upstairs.

Within ten minutes, Matt agrees to take a longer walk with Leo, which happens to go up to the maternity ward. Despite my giddiness, I watch Leo warily. The roller coaster of emotions he's likely on can't be fun. One minute he learns Miguel is gone, and soon thereafter, his nephew has made his grand entrance into the world.

Willa's room is the one in the corner. She finishes changing Luke's diaper and immediately hands him to me.

"Congratulations, Willa. How are you feeling?" Leo asks her.

"Thank you, Leo. I'm okay considering no pain medication was involved by choice. How are you feeling?"

"Physically, I feel… not too bad. I feel better than I did on Mondays when I played so…. The rest is going to take some time to sort out."

"I understand. Please let us know if we can assist in any way."

"Thank you."

I only half listen to their conversation. I'm mesmerized by my nephew. He's perfect. A tiny bundle of hope for the future.

Luca moves closer to me. "How is he doing really?"

"He remembered some parts but not everything." I share the extent of Leo's memories with Luca. "Do you have an update?"

"No, I've been out of the loop for the last few days because I was on a call. Now I'm on leave with my amazing little family."

"I'm crazy happy for the both of you."

My brother whispers, "Me too," and smiles.

Leo makes his way beside me and extends his arms toward Luke. I set our nephew into his arms. The little boy looks even smaller tucked into the crook of Leo's muscular arm. I've never seen Leo holding a baby before. The shot of hormones coursing through me is infinitely beyond anything I've ever felt. Motherhood was always in my plan, but I needed to find the guy first. A man who would love me like my dad loves my mom. Deep down, I only ever wanted a child with Leo, I don't know if it's a possibility anymore or if it ever was.

Cheers erupt from the doorway. It appears Aunt Lily time is over. My parents step into the room and greet Luca and Willa. Leo dutifully hands Luke off to Mama.

"We'll be down after our visit, Leo," Mama assures him.

"Thanks, Mama." He kisses her cheek and makes his way to the door.

We take a circuitous route down to his room to eat before Dr. R arrives. Leo opts for the chair and clears the breakfast tray. I sit cross-legged on the bed and eat as well.

Carly arrives with Dr. Rothstein within the hour. Carly checks his vitals while the doctor reviews his chart.

"Morning. How much have you remembered?"

"I remember from the night before until the morning of the explosion," Leo replies.

"Anything before that?"

"Not yet. When can I get out of here? I need to attend Miguel's funeral tomorrow."

"I don't see any reason for you to stay here. However, you can't be alone and need to take it easy for the next two weeks. I'll schedule a follow-up then."

"What does 'take it easy' mean exactly?" I ask.

"No weightlifting, no running, and no driving for the first week."

"Understood. Thank you for everything you've done. We greatly appreciate it."

We? There isn't a "we."

"You're welcome. I'll have Carly get you out of here this afternoon."

A small smile curves the corner of his mouth. If I wasn't looking for his reaction, I would've missed it. It isn't until after they leave that Leo truly reacts to the news. He rises from the chair and hauls me into his arms.

"I don't have appropriate words to thank you and show how grateful I am to you."

"None are necessary. You would do the same for me."

"I would without question, but I'm sure it wasn't easy to make those decisions on your own."

I shake my head against his chest. "No, it wasn't. I would do it again if necessary."

"Thank you, Lily."

"You're welcome. I would much prefer not to make any more medical decisions on your behalf for a long time."

"Deal. Will you do a few more things for me?"

Anything. "What do you need?"

"Clothes to leave here, my suit for tomorrow, my phone, and—"

"Slow down. There are new clothes in the cabinet. I ordered you a new suit, and it was delivered to my house two days ago. Your phone is in my purse, but it's broken. The replacement will arrive tomorrow or the next day."

"When did you have time to do all of that?"

"Four days of worrying wouldn't work for me. I kept myself busy handling my work and yours."

"I don't know what I would do without you." He kisses the top of my head before moving to the cabinet.

I'm rooted to the linoleum floor. He doesn't realize he's never kissed me before.

"Lily, what's wrong?"

"It can wait."

"Tomorrow night, you and I are having an open, honest conversation about our relationship. I don't care if you have to break the rules Dr. R. set forth and fill in some gaps. I'm not waiting any longer."

"Okay." My voice is shaky in response.

Instead of dressing, he steps back into my personal space and cups my face. "It can only get better between us."

My words catch in my throat as he presses a tender kiss to my forehead before disappearing into the bathroom. The swirl of emotions sets me on edge. Luckily, my parents arrive to visit Leo after meeting Luke upstairs, so I don't have time to dig into what he means right now. My wait won't be long, but still. The pressure and tension wrack my nerves.

"Hi, Mama. Papa." They both greet me and hug me tight.

As they release me, Leo emerges from the bathroom, freshly showered and wearing athletic pants and a cotton tee stretched over his massive chest. If I didn't know he was a huge teddy bear, his stature would concern me. Instead it makes me feel safe and protected, at least physically. My heart is another story.

"Does this mean what I think it means?" Mama asks him.

"Yes. I'm going home…." The sadness in his voice is heart-wrenching despite not seeing the damage firsthand.

"He's staying with me until he's fully released by the doctor," I offer.

Papa claps his hands together. "Wonderful. Would you like us to pick up Lola and some groceries for your house?"

"Yes, thank you."

"Need anything specific, Leo?" Papa asks.

"No, thank you for your help."

"Of course. We're family. Lily, can I have your key? That way we don't have to go home first. I'll leave it on the island."

I fish my keys out of my purse and twist off my house key. "Thanks, Papa." They leave quickly to get the groceries and my puppy before we arrive.

His room has been a revolving door of people since we woke this morning. While I pack up, Detective Jones and Smithson arrive.

"Mr. De Gaetano, pleasure to see you up and about. I'm Detective Jones. I believe you and Detective Smithson are acquainted."

"Hey, Leo. Nice to see you awake."

"Thanks. Do you have an update?"

They fill Leo in on the details again. He doesn't interrupt, though I shared all of it before. Then it starts to get sticky when they get around to Danica.

"It's our understanding you are or were dating a woman named Danica Ryder who worked for Midland Construction. Is that correct?"

"Yes, that's her name and her place of employment. I don't recall if we're still together at this point. My memory has only been recovered to the night before the explosion."

"I understand. The issue we're having is she doesn't exist."

"Excuse me?" His face turns ghost white.

"No one named Danica Ryder works at Midland Construction. Could you provide us with a phone number for her?"

"Not off the top of my head. All I recall is the 603 area code. My phone is broken and inaccessible at the moment. You can pull my phone records to expedite your search." He rattles off his phone number for Detective Jones.

"Thank you. Have you ever been to her apartment?"

"No. She always came to the bar because of my late hours. She mentioned she lived in Portsmouth though."

"Do you have a photo of her?" Smithson asks.

"Maybe on my phone, but again, it's not fixed yet. Are there photos on the website for Midland?"

"Unfortunately, not," Jones replies.

"She was here," I remind them. "Can you pull the footage from the ER camera for the day Leo was admitted? I also understand she has stopped by each day attempting to get information and visit Leo. The staff thwarted her though."

"Did you prevent her from visiting?" Detective Jones inquires.

I resent his implication, but I was only following instructions. "No. Dr. Rothstein was clear his visitors were limited to family only."

"Understood," Detective Jones replies. "We'll put in the request for your phone records. When your phone is repaired, please forward any information you have to me."

"I will."

"Where can we reach you?" Smithson inquires.

"I have two weeks of house arrest under Lily's watchful eye."

Smithson laughs, but Detective Jones doesn't. I provide my address and phone number again.

"If you recall anything or find any useful information, specifically about Miss Ryder, please reach out," Detective Jones instructs.

"I will." They shake hands and leave Leo's room.

He lowers himself into the chair I vacated before muttering, "What the hell is going on?"

I turn my gaze from out the window in his direction. I'm not sure if he's truly asking, so I wait him out.

"I'm not crazy. She was a real person, right? Never mind, Miguel met her and so did you. I'm getting worked up for the wrong thing. Why was she lying to me? More importantly, why didn't I see it?"

"Let's focus on getting you out of here for now."

"Okay. Can you see how much longer?"

"Sure." At the threshold, I turn back.

Leo has his head in his hands with his elbows propped on his thighs.

"Leo," I call out.

He turns his head to look at me.

"The police will figure it out. If they need assistance, I'm sure Captain Ramirez knows someone who can help." Unlike some people, I have faith in the police department, especially since ours has fine people who work there.

CHAPTER SEVEN

LEONARDO

The last time I stepped foot in Lily's bedroom was when she had the flu last winter. She refused help from anyone for two days. Her sisters felt I had the best chance of making it past the threshold.

Lily earns a significant salary. She doesn't splurge on red-soled shoes or high-end handbags. Her car is sensible as well. The only thing that reflects her salary is her home. She owns a huge, renovated colonial with five bedrooms and a separate office. It's decidedly too large for only her. Her kitchen is top of the line, as is her master bath. The remainder of her home is comfortable and stylish but not stuffy. I don't worry about putting my feet up on her tufted ottoman. However, she has an affinity to the water like her sisters. Not just water, the ocean. Her home offers spectacular views on three sides with a wraparound porch on the first floor. The master bedroom balcony has a stunning view of the ocean.

"You going out or…?"

"Sorry, it's been a long time since I saw this view."

"I know." She disappears into her massive closet.

I wander outside and take in the salty breeze. The sun is falling slowly toward the horizon and won't set for another few hours. With everything going on in my life right now, this is soothing. In the last week, I've had my brain scrambled again, my employee has died, my bar is in shambles—though I haven't seen it with my own eyes—and my ex-girlfriend is a liar, manipulator, and I don't know what to call her. Then there's my strained relationship with Lily, which I would give anything to figure out how I broke it. I gave her until tomorrow, and I will honor my word, but damn! Can't a guy get a break?

There has never been a time where Lily wasn't part of my life until apparently two months ago. I still don't recall what went wrong, but I'll fix it no matter what it takes.

"Are you hungry or ready to sleep?" Her voice surrounds me from behind. She may be upset with me, but she's determined to take care of me.

"I could eat something."

"I'll make something for us. I set up your suit and the other clothes I bought on the left side of the closet. I replaced all your toiletries," she informs me.

I don't know what I did to deserve her as my best friend, but I refuse to let her go. Hell, I want more. Yet she isn't mine. It doesn't make any sense in my confused mind. "Thanks. I'll be right down."

I throw on a thin hoodie after snapping off the tags and join Lily in the kitchen. In the short time she's been down here, she has two leftover plates from Mama's kitchen warming in the microwave.

"Water or iced tea?"

"Water, please," I reply. I skirt around her and grab some forks, a knife, and some sliced bread from the fridge.

We eat in relative silence. As much as I want to talk about us, it requires undivided attention, and we need to rest before tomorrow. We clean up the kitchen, and she flicks on a movie we've seen numerous times. Within the first thirty minutes, Lily is out cold beside me. I could easily carry her to her bed, but I don't want to risk her safety right now. With an alarm set, I draw her closer and let sleep claim me too.

The next morning, we scurry around to get ready after snoozing too many times. Everything Lily has done for me since the explosion is perfect. I shouldn't be surprised. The suit is tailored perfectly. She managed to find comfortable dress shoes and every other article of clothes I could possibly need for today. I'm sure it boils down to Lily's need for order. Handling these details helped her manage the chaos from the explosion and my medical decisions.

She reaches the bottom step. The navy wrap dress accentuates her curves exquisitely. Yet complimenting her today probably isn't wise given the occasion. The sight of the chain I gifted her around her elegant neck is a shot to my heart and other unmentionable places. I noticed she was wearing mine at the hospital but opted to wait to discuss it with her. The last time she wore both chains was a horrible day as well.

"How are you feeling? Any headache or dizziness?"

From her, not my concussion. "No, but the lights are a tad bright. I can deal with it."

"I have a pair of dark glasses in my car."

"Thanks."

"Ready?" she asks.

"As I'm ever going to be. I haven't been to a funeral since...."

"I know. I'm here for you now, like I was at Gran's services."

We make our way into her garage. "How and when did my truck get here?"

"You didn't notice it last night?"

"Nope."

She smiles. "I asked Luca to bring it over when Detective Jones told me you couldn't stay in your apartment. Did I overstep?"

I laugh heartily. "Lily, you have done so much. Why would you think this is overstepping but checking the tags on my boxer briefs to order the correct size isn't?"

The faint blush on her cheeks is intriguing, and I yearn to explore what else will make her body respond.

"Fair point."

Now isn't the time.

She pulls into the church and parks near the rear of the lot. Mourners are walking up the front steps into the church. We make our way to the staircase and are joined by Mama, Papa, Lia, and Lina.

"Thank you all for coming. It wasn't necessary."

"Oh, Leo, when are you going to learn, we stick together when times are good and tough?" Lina reminds him.

I give her a side hug and take a seat in a pew near the front of the church. The service is short and simple. Miguel's family opted for a Christian service with burial in Florida at a later date.

"You can do this," Lily bolsters me as Miguel's parents approach, sliding her hand into mine. Ignoring the shot of heat and comfort it provides has me pausing midstep. "Alma and Manuel are their names."

Working a business is my thing. Knowing the names of my employee's parents and handling details is Lily's. "Thank you," I whisper.

She squeezes my hand.

"Please accept my condolences for your loss," I offer them and accept a hug from Alma Santos.

"Thank you for giving Miguel a second chance. When you learn who is responsible for the error, please make them pay," she requests. When Miguel wasn't drafted, he made a slew of poor choices from aggravated assault and petty theft. I gave him a job and the support he needed to get back on his feet.

I hadn't considered this could be anything other than an accident. I don't have any enemies. Quite the opposite actually. I give back to my community here and where I played. I pull my mind back to the conversation.

"Miguel was a great worker, and he proved me right. I'm profoundly sorry for your loss. Have a safe trip home." Manuel, José, and Tito each shake my hand before leaving me in shock near the vestibule. I'm shocked because they don't blame me like I blame myself for Miguel's death. After some more time to gather myself, I turn to leave and find my family waiting patiently at the bottom of the staircase.

"You good for now?" Lily murmurs, casting her chocolate eyes upward to meet mine.

"For now, yeah."

We descend the stairs, and I accept condolences from Lily's family. Aren't they my family too? They're the main reason I've never shared my true feelings with Lily. The risk could be catastrophic for me and them, not to mention Lily.

"You will be at dinner on Sunday, yes?" Mama commands.

All I can do is agree. If I don't show up, she'll hunt me down. She's done it to Luca more than once and Frankie too. "Yes, Mama. I'll be there."

She casts a stern look at Lily, hugs me again, and leaves with her arm tucked around the crook of Papa's elbow. *I want enduring love with Lily. Is it even possible? The risk though.*

"Is there anything you need to do before we go home?" Lily asks with her delicate hand on my forearm.

"I need to see it with my own eyes."

"Are you sure you're up to it?" Her question is a whisper laced with concern for my well-being.

"I'm not prepared to see my second dream in shambles, but I need to see the damage. Then I can figure out a path forward."

"Do you want me to get some backup?"

"I assure you whatever the condition of the bar, I'll remain on my feet."

She smiles tightly. "Good, because I can't hold you up."

"You already are, Stella."

Her grip on my forearm tightens, but she says nothing. I lead her to the driver door. I can't help but admire the glimpse of her toned thighs as her dress rides up. Lily is gorgeous. I'm not blind. My teammates both in college and in the NFL made sure I knew if she wasn't my best friend, they would've chased her relentlessly. Thankfully, bro code won out and no one ever pursued her. I would've needed to confront the disconnect in my heart about our relationship much sooner if they had.

The ride to the bar is silent. The radio is off, and Lily hasn't uttered a word. Honestly, I'm not sure if it's because we're coming here or my words. She parks in my spot at the bar and opens her door.

I steel my nerves and push to my feet. Lily is beside me while I take in the condition. I reach for her hand, and she allows me to take hers. Again I wonder, *Why isn't she mine?*

Yellow police tape surrounds the building. There are also two-by-six boards nailed over the main entrance. The south corner of the building over the boiler room has crumbled down to the first floor.

My living room and kitchen were crushed under the weight of the roof. I force my feet forward around the east façade of my brick building. The extent of my knowledge about architecture and structures is dismal. However, as I turn to the north side of the building, I see it's still standing. There's a chance my barrel room is intact. I hope it's a promising factor in my rebuilding timeline.

I trust Lily's business acumen. My insurance will likely cover the rebuild. The more pressing issues are my employees and the bottling contracts that are going unfilled the longer it takes for me to get into my building.

"Step away from the building," a booming voice warns. "The building is off-limits." A heavyset man rounds the corner and stops in front of us.

"Who are you?" Lily asks despite his jacket indicating he's likely with the fire department.

"Good afternoon, ma'am. Lieutenant Foster of the YFD. We received a report people were attempting to enter the premises."

"It's my building, Lieutenant. I was surveying the damage," I inform him.

He pulls a small pad from his pocket and flips a few pages. "Mr. De Gaetano?"

"Yes."

"My apologies, sir. We were concerned given the nature of the incident."

"I understand. I would like to arrange a walkthrough of the property. Is that with your department or building and zoning to assess the necessary repairs?"

Lieutenant Foster fishes a card out of his pocket. "Please reach out to Iris in my office. She can schedule with you once YFD has completed their initial investigation."

"Thank you."

Lieutenant Foster returns to his vehicle, and I finish walking the perimeter of the building. When I arrive where I started, my gaze locks on crumpled brick and building materials. Grief, anguish, and anger rush through me. The problem is I don't have one person or thing to set my desire for revenge on.

A fragment of a discussion with a Danica filters into my mind.

"You don't want her like you want me. If you did, I wouldn't be here. I mean, she's been following you around like a lost puppy for the last.... It doesn't matter. You're mine, and she has no place in your life."

"No, you're wrong. She is the reason I'm where I am."

My heart rate increases, and my hands start to shake.

"Leo, talk to me," Lily demands. "Did you remember something else?"

"Yes."

Lily waits me out.

"I'm not sure where it fits, so I'm going to wait to share, okay?" It's a white lie. My memory is filling in rapidly as we speak.

"Of course." Her response is too quick for my liking.

I pause at the passenger door and survey the building once again. With Lily's help, I can fix this. Rebuild my second dream and focus on the next one at the same time.

"What's next?" she asks, pulling out of the lot.

"We're going home to talk. I want an answer to my question."

"Which is?"

"Why aren't you mine?"

She pushes out a harsh breath, and her hands grip her steering wheel tighter.

I'm part of the answer, but I didn't know until my memory returned over the last ten minutes or so. "What are you afraid of, Lilianna?"

She stops at a traffic light, turns her head in my direction, and our eyes lock in silence before her succinct, gut-punch reply, "Losing everything."

Horns blare behind us. Lily takes a right turn toward home but doesn't say another word. She parks and retreats to grab a package near the garage door. She casts her heels aside once she's in her house, which isn't like her at all.

CHAPTER EIGHT

LILIANNA

I pluck my heels off my feet and toss them near the door. I set the package and my purse on the console near the door and deposit my keys in the bowl. After a few long strides, I set my hands on the edge of my waterfall island facing into the kitchen. Leo paces behind me.

I've wanted to have this conversation for the last year at least.

"What am I afraid of? Losing everything I've ever wanted for myself. Ruining what we already have. You chose her, and I chose me. It was the hardest thing I've ever done." I squash the tears threatening to fall.

Leo stops behind me. "Did I?"

"Yes."

He slides my hair over my left shoulder and traps me against the cold marble with the length of his body. His hands cover mine. He dips his head, his lips near my ear.

Holy hell! The fire scorching my skin is unparalleled.

"No. I asked you to stay put at our bench, and you drove away. You refused to wait for me."

Tingles course through me. I never allowed myself to react to him physically because he's my best friend. I would never disrespect him or his relationship with someone else despite my deep-seated disdain for Danica.

"I literally had an intense argument with your girlfriend at your bar. She threw some hefty accusations my way and disrespected you. Danica and I are nothing alike. All I want is for you to be happy."

"What did she say?"

I cringe and take a moment before speaking, replaying her words in my mind. "She—"

"No, I don't want to know. I remember everything, Lilianna. Your admission was a surprise. It made me realize I was wrong about us. You also refused to talk to me. Honest communication is one thing you and I excel at. For the last few months, we failed miserably. I lost count of how many times I reached out to you. I chose you and your family. I choose you."

I consider turning, but it may lead me to act on the pressure building between my thighs—an ache that has been present for quite some time. I've loved Leo almost my entire life. I couldn't possibility pinpoint when I fell in love with Leo, but the moment I knew I wanted to taste him is easy to define. At the end of my last relationship, I knew no man would ever meet the standard I created for my future except Leo. "Could you repeat that?" My voice is shaky.

"I chose you and your family. Any woman who doesn't see what you mean to me, isn't the one for me. Being unable to talk to you or see you forced me to realize no one could ever be everything to me... except you."

I exhale slowly and drop my head forward. "Not once have we ever discussed being more than friends."

Leo lowers his lips to the curve of my neck before taking a step backward. His hands slide off mine, settling on my waist. The loss of him against me causes a shiver to overtake me. Slowly, he turns me, my body teasing his as he sets me on the edge of the island. I catalog how his hands feel bracketing my waist and the intense sparks from our proximity. I've been this close to Leo plenty of times, but we have never discussed us as a couple.

He lifts my chin with his forefinger. "How long, Lily?"

"What?"

"How long were you hiding your feelings and reactions to me?"

Unvarnished truth is the only way to go here. I would expect the same. "Since you made Matt dump me in college."

"You knew about that?"

"Not until a few months later when Mika came to me and apologized. She claimed she didn't know about me until you confronted Matt."

"No more hiding, Stella."

I set my hand on his cheek and close my eyes. The warmth of his skin beneath my hand is as wonderful as I imagined. "No more hiding. What about you?"

He turns and kisses the inside of my palm before lowering our linked hands between us. "The risk is heavier for me than for you."

"I won't hurt you."

He shakes his head. "I know, but that's not what I mean. Your family accepted a lost, starving boy and gave him love and stability. They helped me become who I am. So did you. Choosing to chase an us may put my family—our family—at risk."

"Oh, Leo. They would never cast you aside if we don't work. It's one of the reasons choosing me was so difficult. I know how much you mean to them and what they mean to you. I realize now it was a bit selfish too. Choosing me put a wedge between all of you. I'm sorry."

"Not your fault."

"You didn't answer my question."

He scrubs his hand down his face, returns his gaze to mine, but fails to speak.

"Moon, there isn't a wrong answer."

She hasn't called me that in a long time. "There has never been a time when I wasn't attracted to you. You're crazy smart, funny, and way out of my league in the looks department. What's the saying? I outkicked my coverage."

I set my head against his chest and chuckle softly. Only he would make a football analogy.

"To answer your question, I made a conscious choice when Gran died to shelve my romantic feelings for you. I couldn't fathom losing the only family I had left or ruining our friendship."

"You have been pining for more than a decade?"

He shrugs.

Then the obvious dawns on me. "Were all of your girlfriends completely opposite of me on purpose?"

Leo has never dated a brunette, someone with curves, or someone who challenges him intellectually. His dating history isn't overly extensive either. He had a semiserious girlfriend in college. Gina couldn't handle the significant amount of time Leo spent training and preparing for games. They were together almost two years before she asked him to give up football. He politely declined and broke up with her instead.

"Yes."

I'm almost afraid to ask, but I manage. "And now?"

Leo lifts my gaze to his and cups my jaw. "Now… I need to know if you and I are meant to be everything to each other for the rest of our lives." He eliminates most of the space between our mouths.

My belly is fluttering and twisting in knots at the same time. I'm equally terrified and ecstatic about the prospect of kissing Leo. "You said it yourself, it can only get better." The reminder is all it takes.

Leo draws me closer and skims his thumb over my lower lip before he tentatively presses his lips to mine. The fear of losing him disappears as my desire to grow closer increases exponentially. He pulls back enough for me to wet his lower lip with my tongue. I angle my head and grip his shirt. The heat of his tongue delving into my mouth is more than I expect. We kiss and kiss some more until we're both panting. Resisting the urge to progress faster because it's Leo, I slow our pace. No man has ever made me feel so deeply with the touch of his lips… only Leo.

"Now what?" I ask, having barely caught my breath.

"All I know is I was a fool, and I want to kiss you repeatedly."

I wink at him. "I'm game. Dinner first?"

"Sure." He attempts to move away from me, but I tug him back by his shirt.

I set a tender kiss, or five, on his lips before allowing him to walk away. Ignoring the heat between us is difficult, especially knowing I don't have to anymore.

We round the island and prepare to cook. Leo cuffs the sleeves of his dress shirt, and I watch with wide eyes and a slack jaw.

He glances in my direction. "My forearms, really?"

"Hell yes!" I reply, feeling my face flush. I move to the sink to wash my hands. The small reprieve allows me to handle my admission to Leo and settle my nerves. Leo. I'm dumbfounded. The man who has been beside me my entire life is my… best friend, confidant, biggest supporter, and, as of a few minutes ago, boyfriend. The title isn't enough to encompass what we are.

"What are you thinking over there? I can see the smoke rising above your head."

I grin at him over my shoulder. "Reveling and mulling. Good things, all good things."

"I want to know it all, Lily."

"You already do." *Almost all.* I fill the pasta pot, set it to boil, and steal a quick kiss before returning to the sink to clean the shrimp. Leo is halving the tomatoes and starting the cream sauce.

Aside from our kiss a few moments ago, nothing about this is abnormal for us, at least before Danica's edict. We plate our dinner and each take a stool at the island. A weird silence falls between us. I push it away and polish off my food.

"Is this weird?" he mumbles.

"Yes and no."

He waits me out.

"No, because we've eaten dinner countless times over the years. Yes, because we opened a door that has been closed tightly with numerous locks on both sides for the entire time we've known each other."

"It feels right to have the door open."

"Completely."

He turns on his stool, sets his hands above either knee, and turns me so we're looking at one another. "My request is fifteen years late, but... are you free on Saturday night?"

He knows I am. It's our standing movie night, but I answer anyway. "Yes."

"Lilianna, will you accompany me on a date?"

I smile at him. "Yes." I lean forward and brush my lips across his. After sitting in silence with the gravity of my answer, we clean the kitchen and change into comfy clothes.

"Was the package my new phone?" he asks when we return to the living room.

"Yeah. It's on the console table near the door. Are you sure now is a good time to listen to your voice mail?"

"No, but it needs to be done."

"Okay. Want some company?"

"Always." He grabs the package and my purse from near the door.

I pluck out his old phone and hand it to him. We settle on the couch, and he swaps the memory card. While we wait, I turn on the television and search for a baseball game.

After Leo inputs his password, his new phone lights up, and a slew of notifications ping for a solid minute.

"Damn! Twenty voice mails, sixty texts, and fifty personal emails. This is going to take a while."

He inputs his password again and starts to listen on speaker.

"Baby, I need to talk to you. I was wrong. Asking you to give up your friendship was a mistake. Call me." The time stamp info plays, and Leo deletes the message.

"Baby, I'm going to be in town tomorrow. I want to talk. Call me." This message is from the night before the accident. Leo deletes it.

I look over at Leo. His face shows no reaction to Danica's pleas. It's oddly comforting.

"Brother, calling to check on the plans for the reunion. Hit me back." Leo saves this one.

"Mo?" I ask. Mo was his teammate in college, and they were even drafted together. Football was a way to set up his family for life.

"Yup." He starts the next message.

"Ohmigod! I'm here. Baby, Lily refuses to let me see you! How could—" He deletes the rest of the message without hearing the rest.

"As much as I appreciate not hearing those, perhaps you need to listen. I can leave if you would prefer. There may be information that may be helpful to Jones and Smithson."

He clenches his fist and restores the deleted message. "I was purposefully ignoring the issue."

"I'm sorry, but there's a lot going on right now, and part of it includes Danica lying to you about who she truly is."

"I'm more worried about my employees than her."

"Your sentiment makes you an amazing man, boss, and business owner. However, something is sketchy about her, and I'm not judging her because you're mine now."

He sets his phone on the ottoman and hauls me into his arms. "Say that again."

Leo holding me isn't new, but the emotional aspect is consuming. Until now, I never considered the placement of his hands. Not once were his hands too low on my back or too far around my rib cage before today. In this moment, however, one arm is around my back, and his huge hand spans the curve of my hip. The other is on top of my thighs warming me through my leggings.

"Lily, say it again," he demands.

I push aside the visceral reaction to him touching me and replay my words in my head until I get to what I think he wants to hear. "You're mine now."

He presses a kiss to my forehead and whispers, "And you're mine in all ways." Leo glides his hand up to my jaw. "I will find each spot that makes you lose your words, even if it takes the rest of my life."

I set my forehead against his and agree. The unsettled feeling I have in my chest dissipates into lust and desire after cataloging Leo's hands on me. Acting on those urges right now isn't the way to go. "Thank you."

"We may have waited too long, but a little longer to do it right isn't going to kill us."

I press a kiss to his mouth and move back beside him, closer this time. We spend the next two hours culling his emails and texts. There are ten from his former teammates looking for updates about the reunion and another ten asking how he is. He doesn't go back to the voice mails though.

Near eleven, we walk to my bedroom. I tug my hoodie overhead and deposit it in the hamper. It's then I notice he hesitates at the threshold.

"Do you want me to sleep in the guest room?" he offers.

"Why would you do that? I slept on top of you last night on the couch."

"True, but… we're different now."

"Yes. We're better. Please stay here," I implore.

He tugs his shirt off and sets it on the dressing bench.

I fly through my memory, trying to recall the last time I saw Leo shirtless, and come up empty. Long enough that I don't have a frame of reference. It's one thing to fall asleep with him fully clothed. It's happened countless times. It's an entirely different situation when it's purposeful and his broad chest is exposed. He's always been fit and clearly didn't slack much on gym time since he was forced into retirement.

"I'll put it back on if you need." His words interrupt my thoughts. He was obviously waiting for me to gather myself.

"No, just processing. What's the point? You already showed me."

He grins. "You kind of like me, huh?"

I love you. I arch an eyebrow at him but say nothing. He knows how I feel about him. It isn't the time to voice it out loud again. Not yet.

He throws the sheets from my side open for me. I slide beneath them and curl against Leo. Tentatively, I set my head on his shoulder and my hand in the center of his chest. His breath hitches the instant my cold hand touches his warm skin. I consider moving it, but he covers my hand with his before I'm able.

He kisses the top of my head. "Night, Lily."

"Good night, Leo."

CHAPTER NINE

LEONARDO

Unlike Lily, I don't sleep much. She was out cold within ten minutes of snuggling against me. I listen to the rise and fall of her breathing until sleep claims me. My mind has never been a calm place except when she's beside me.

Early rays of sunlight mark her ceiling. I've been awake for the last hour, diligently memorizing each freckle, dip, and slope of her lush curves. I've been this close to her numerous times, but I've never allowed myself to capture each minute detail that is uniquely Lily. She hasn't moved much since she fell asleep last night. Her hand is still on my chest, only a little lower. Her soft, long tresses are fanned over my arm.

Maintaining a hard line between romantic love and friendship wasn't as difficult until she shared her feelings with me. The prospect of waking up with Lily beside me daily makes my heart swell. My fears weren't misplaced, but our timing was off. I smile and start planning our date in my head. Our friendship gives me more insight than any other man would have. It'll make it virtually impossible for me to screw up our first date—the last first one we will ever have.

"How long have you been awake? How are you feeling?" she murmurs, looking at me through her long lashes.

Amazing and terrified at the same time. She means my head. "A little while. Fine, so far."

I see the instant she realizes the position we're in. Before she can overthink, which Lily is notorious for, I roll and trap her beneath me. One of her hands is against my flank, and the remains on the center of my chest. Although this position might be more precarious with my rock-hard length against her. "Morning."

She inhales sharply and slowly exhales. "Morning. Our kiss wasn't in my head, was it?"

Lily and I waking up together isn't an anomaly, although I don't recall the last time it was in a bed. Usually, we wake on one of our couches. "No. It was very real and worth waiting for like everything else we'll share in the future. I can certainly refresh your memory if you would like."

A sexy smile curls at the curve of her mouth. "I mean, it isn't a terrible plan to solidify my memory, is it?"

"Not at all."

As I lower onto my forearms, she draws in another deep breath in preparation. The action has her cotton-covered breasts grazing my bare chest. I press my lips against hers, and strong, steadfast Lily melts into the woman only I'm privileged to see. The woman who put her feelings aside to assure my happiness and made a heart-wrenching decision to put me into a coma. The vulnerable woman who wants a marriage like her parents—a marriage spanning decades with a houseful of children. A woman who wants a man to stand beside her when things go well and, more importantly, when things go terribly wrong.

Palpable passion zings from my lips to my toes. Kissing Lily is more than my imagination ever conjured up. Waiting until now was the right choice, but taking measured steps forward is going to be arduous, especially since I want to explore every inch of her and watch her shatter with pleasure from my love. I tug her lower lip between my teeth. Rewarded with a soft whimper, I loosen my bite and repeat it again.

"Leo." My name comes out as a desperate plea for more.

I drag my tongue along her jaw to the shell of her ear. "Yes, Lily?"

"My memory wasn't this fantastic."

I grin at her. "Good, we're just getting started. We may know everything about each other outside of this room, but in here, not so much."

"Now please?"

"No, you need to get to work, don't you?"

She frowns. "I would rather keep exploring us in here instead of reviewing spreadsheets and market projections."

I raise an eyebrow.

"Out there is going to take some learning too. You should know, I'm demanding in here."

"Are you?"

She pushes up onto her elbows, drags her tongue along the skin she can reach, and wets my lips before kissing me deeply, possessively. If her definition of demanding is bestowing hot, sultry kisses on my body, I'm in. We may set fire to her home when we come together as one if a kiss or ten makes my entire body ache with need.

Reluctantly, I add space.

"You're going to force me to be responsible, aren't you?" she grumbles, pouting.

"Yeah."

"Meany."

We've reverted to third grade. I chuckle. "Lily, I'm not going anywhere. We don't have to rush through the flutters of a new relationship. Are the lines a bit blurry given how much we know about one another? Sure, but demolishing the door we unlocked yesterday isn't wise."

"But—"

I skim my lips across hers lightly to refocus her attention. "Every second of the wait will be worth it like it was for our first kiss. Don't mistake my need for time to pursue us properly with a lack of desire to strip off your clothes, savor your gorgeous curves, and make you shatter for an entire day."

Lilianna Stellaluna Cappelli stunned speechless is a remarkable sight. Her eyes close briefly, and she exhales softly. "We've waited, albeit separately and unknowingly, for a long time. What if we ruin us?" Her voice decreases as she gets to the end of her thought.

"Impossible. We built a stable foundation of friendship forged in pain, happiness, sorrow, joy, and platonic love since the day we met. Allowing ourselves to explore our deeper feelings will only make us stronger, separately and as a couple."

"I'm scared. You are... everything I ever wanted. You're the only person who knows and unconditionally accepts all of me. I can't go back to being without you in my everyday life if this doesn't work."

"The fear makes the leap worth it. The reward—us—is worth it. I won't let you hide or run away from me ever again. I will chase after you for as long as I live."

She slides her hand around my neck and pulls my mouth down to hers. Before I consider the ramifications, I roll us back over. Her hair falls around our heads like a curtain. As the heat of her settles over my length, I groan into her mouth and grip her hips with both hands to keep her still. My resolve won't last if she grinds against me. As if a pliant and willing Lily on top of me isn't enough, her ample breasts nearly spill out of the tank she slept in.

Panting with swollen lips, Lily adds a sliver of space between our mouths. "I could easily get carried away right now."

"Same. We should slow down a little."

She looks away for a moment before returning her gaze to my face. "You promise?"

I sit up and reposition Lily in a less precarious spot before taking her hand and setting it over my heart and mine over hers. "I promise. I will chase you until my last breath."

With our arms crossed between us, Lily rests her head on my shoulder. A few minutes later, she kisses me tenderly and starts getting ready for work. Luckily, her office is downstairs.

The last thing I want to do is move, listen to my voice mails, and deal with the bureaucrats to fix my bar, but it must be done. I tug on my shirt and pad to the kitchen to start coffee for both of us and breakfast for Lily. Less than fifteen minutes later, Lily rounds the corner. She's dressed in leggings and a running hoodie, and her wet hair is in a loose braid over her shoulder.

"You didn't have to do that."

"I know. I wanted to." I hand her coffee and avocado toast.

With a short kiss, she retreats to her office. Given it's nearly nine, I'm guessing she's almost an hour late this morning. I polish off my coffee, shower, and dress. With no other way to procrastinate, I start back with my voice mails, starting with the one I restored.

"Ohmigod! I'm here. Baby, Lily refuses to let me see you! Why is she in charge? I need you back. I miss you."

I shake my head and delete the message and move on.

"Leo, I'm getting worried. I stopped by the hospital, and they won't let me in. Said family only. I need to know if you're okay."

I tamp down my brewing anger at Danica and focus on the date and time. She was at the hospital each day. I make a note of the time stamp for Smithson and keep going. The sooner I listen, the better.

"Baby, it wasn't supposed to be this way. Please call me. I need to know if you're okay. I'm getting worried something terrible happened to you."

I check the time stamp. This is from two days ago.

The last one was from yesterday.

"Leo, it's me. I got a new number. I need to see you. I was so wrong. We were supposed to be together forever. No one was supposed to get hurt. Please call me back."

No one was supposed to get hurt. I replay her words in my mind a few times in succession as I scroll through my gallery and find two photos of Danica. Oddly, neither show her entire face. I clear out the rest of my voice mail inbox and make a list of calls to return to my teammates. When I'm finished, I head out to find my girl.

As I approach her office, I hear her speaking and can tell the phone call isn't going well.

"Why now? I've had my remote work schedule for the last five years." Whoever she's talking to says something else. "Well, I'll give it some thought." She pauses, presumably listening to the person on the other line. "As I said, I'll consider if your proposed amendments to my employment contract are acceptable, sir. Have a nice day."

Standing in her doorway, I see her head fall forward, her shoulders slump, and she grabs the back of her neck with her empty hand. I consider waiting until later, but I need to assist Smithson as soon as possible.

She turns back toward her desk and sees me in the doorway. "Hey."

Rounding her desk, I pull her against me without a second thought. My body absorbs some of the tension radiating from hers. "Who was that?"

"My boss."

"Not a fan of your work-from-home structure anymore?"

"Well, technically it's the new VP who isn't a fan. He wants everyone in the office every day."

"I may not be a financial whiz like you, but it costs him less for you to work from home and less stress with the commute to Boston."

"I think you sell yourself a little short. Either way, the new head guy wants me in my office by the end of the month."

"Or?"

"He didn't really give me an 'or' option."

"You had a remote schedule before it was even a thing."

"True."

"Do you know who the new head guy is? Is it actually a guy?"

She laughs. "No, I don't know who it is, male or female. But the new VP for the Boston office is from Chicago."

"What is your plan?"

She takes a deep breath as best she can flush against me. "I'm good, Leo, but not that good."

I kiss the top of her head. "Now who is shortchanging herself?"

"Thanks. I'll come up with a brilliant plan... I hope."

"I have no doubt."

"Was there a development?"

I shrug. "Sort of." I consider withholding the information, but it isn't who we are as best friends or a couple. I love how that sounds. I play the voice mail for her.

"What was supposed to happen?" she wonders, lifting her head off my chest.

"Don't know. Smithson has to find her first. I considered calling her back to ask that exact question but decided to talk to the detectives first."

"Good idea." Lily rises on her toes and kisses me lightly before pulling away and grabbing something from her desk. She hands me the cards for Jones and Smithson. "I would call Smithson. He's more receptive to finding her and getting an answer."

"I will. Then I'm going to schedule a time with the building inspector. Can you join me? Do you still have the contact information for the contractor who did the buildout? Scott something."

"Of course. Let me know when. I'll pull it up for you."

I kiss her again and leave before I can't. As much as I would like to get the appointment scheduled, I call Smithson first.

"Hey, Leo. How are you feeling?" he asks.

He was just promoted to detective recently. No offense to Jones, but Smithson is extended family, so I would prefer to talk to him, new or not.

"Not too bad. I made it through my voice mails and found two photos for you. Where can I forward them?"

He indicates the number on the card is good for the voice mails but to email the photos. I provide him a quick synopsis of the content of the voice mails. "Do not call her unless we ask you to. If she shows up, stall her and call me."

"I will. She has no way to find me. At least I don't think she does. I'm at Lily's since my apartment is uninhabitable for now. Danica and Lily were barely civil to one another."

"Which explains why Lily didn't have her number when we asked."

"True. Any reason for me not to get started on the estimate for repairs?"

"Hold on. Let me look," Smithson requests. The sound of him typing comes through the line. "The report isn't final yet. We sent it back to YFD for their final assessment. Give Lieutenant Foster a day or two."

"I understand."

"Good luck, Leo."

"Same to you."

He chuckles and ends the call. I reach out to Iris as Lieutenant Foster requested and set up an inspection early next week. Later, after a quick lunch, which Lily doesn't stop for, I make the call of dread… to my insurance company. As expected, they need the complete report before processing my claim.

I rummage through the fridge and get started on dinner. Once everything is cooking in the oven, I plan my first real date with Lily. Initially, I considered going simple. Then I decided I'm going to court her as if she weren't my best friend and person. I place a few calls and request some assistance. Each person I speak to is eager to assist.

Lina is on top of the items I need for Saturday. The only thing left is food and flowers. Lia is gathering the supplies for Friday. Frankie and Tommy will be arriving home sometime late Saturday. The only one I was a tad worried about was Luca. As the only brother, I expected a stern warning, but it never came.

"How are Willa and Luke?"

"Amazing. Being a dad is phenomenal. Being an uncle is fun and fulfilling, but when you and your other half are the sole provider of each emotional or physical need, the depth of love is unfathomable. So, you're finally taking Lily on a date. How can I help?"

I explain what I need for my two-day date.

"Leo, be sure before you open the door to more than friends."

Too late. "I'm sure."

"I'm happy for both of you."

Near six, with a glass of 2018 Mayacamas Chardonnay, I knock on her office door. "Almost done?"

"Sure. Is that for me?"

"Yeah. I should hold off until doc clears me."

"Thanks." She takes a healthy sip and curves her arm around me.

I tuck her beneath my chin and clasp my hands at the small of her back. I breathe her in. Subtleties I purposely ignored during our friendship, such as the softness of her hair, the vanilla and floral scent that surrounds her, and how well she fits in my arms, I sear into my mind. Unfortunately, the timer for dinner sounds, and I need to release her. We eat dinner and relax for the rest of the evening.

CHAPTER TEN

LILIANNA

My drive to work given my boss's request and a newfound desire to remain in bed with Leo has taken a dramatic hit. The next morning, I wake my laptop and scan my inbox, finding nothing out of the ordinary. The week end report and three funds to examine top my to-do list.

There's virtually no chance I'm going to heed my boss's request. Early next week, I plan to draft a counterproposal. If it isn't accepted, I'll turn in my notice. What I plan to do after that, I don't know yet. I have over six weeks of accrued vacation time. That plus my two weeks' notice gives me two months to figure out what to do next with my career. I have plenty of options and experience. Given my savings, I can sustain my lifestyle for a few years without working—a luxury nearly few can claim.

Halfway through my second fund, my phone vibrates with a text. Grabbing up my phone, I realize I've received texts from two of my sisters.

Lia: Hey there. How is Leo? I don't want to annoy him.

Me: It wouldn't be annoying. He's good.

Lia: Got anything juicy to share?

Me: Oh, Lia! All I'm willing to say is we talked.

Lia: I won't push, for now. Love you.

Me: Love you too.

Next is Lina.

Lina: How are you? How are things with Leo?

Me: I'm okay. Still worried about Leo. What is going on?

Lina: What do you mean?

*Me: You and Lia are asking about Leo. The only one who hasn't yet is
   Luca.*

Lina: Oh, just wondering.

Me: Uh-huh. What is he up to?

Lina: Whatever it is, can you allow him the chance to do it?

On one hand, it's sweet he's including my siblings. On the other, I
would prefer to keep our relationship only between us for a little longer.
Lina is right. I need to let him handle our date like he requested.

Me: Okay. I give.

Lina: You won't regret it. Love you, Lil.

Me: Love you too.

The icing on the cake would be a text from Luca. I decide to head him
off.

Me: How is my newest nephew? How is Willa?

*Luca: He's amazing. I can't believe I get to be his dad. She's a rock
   star. I already knew before he was born though.*

Me: Luke is lucky to have the two of you.

Luca: How are you and Leo doing?

Me: You're in on it too?

Luca: I don't know what you're talking about.

Me: Fine, I won't push. We talked, and we're figuring us out.

Luca: I won't push either. Love you, Lils.

Me: Love you too.

I smile. Whatever Leo is planning for our date, he needs assistance, and he didn't want it to come from me. It makes me fall a little more, as if there was still some deeper abyss for me to plunge into.

Just before lunch, Leo knocks on my office door. "Hey. How was your morning?"

"Fine. You?" I ask.

"I made an appointment for Monday at lunch to meet with the inspector and the contractor. I forwarded the report to the insurance company, and they're working on my claim."

"Any news from Smithson?"

"Not yet. They're searching for her. She hasn't called again either."

I wasn't going to ask, but I appreciate the unsolicited information. "Thanks."

"Are you going to eat lunch now or wait until dinner?"

Curious question. "I'm waiting, why?"

"Could you stay away from the kitchen and garage until dinner?"

My heart squeezes. "I can if you bring me a water and a snack for later."

"Consider it done." He rushes away and returns with two waters, a packet of half and half iced tea mix, and a snack bar. With my requests arranged neatly on the sideboard, Leo extends his hand to me and draws me close. His hands slip beneath the hem of my shirt, around my back, and grip my sides when his arms collapse around me.

I love how his hands feel on my skin. I sigh softly and melt into him. The ability to completely let my guard down and just be is a state I never felt with anyone else. It dawns on me in this shared moment, I've never completely and unconditionally trusted anyone like I do Leo. It's why choosing me hurt so deeply—more so now knowing I didn't have to choose at all.

I've dated two men seriously—actually, more like one. Matt, in college, wasn't a keeper, I knew within a month. Yet I stayed until he cheated on me. After him, I dated Oliver for nearly three years. He checked off all the boxes: smart, decent looking, and a good career. He earned a promotion and a transfer to the second-largest office in the company and invited me to come along. The problem, he wasn't inviting me for the long term. He invited me to warm his bed while he conquered our collective professional world. Giving up my professional aspirations then wasn't going to work for me.

Now, jumping headlong into a relationship with Leo, I know it won't matter if I work in my chosen profession again. He wants me for the person I am, not how I look on his arm.

"Whatever you're thinking, stop. We're moving forward together." He adds some space between us, slides one hand up to the side of my face, and tilts my head upward. The control he's exerting over me is thrilling.

The warmth of his lips on mine mends a fissure I created when I chose me. I succumb to the pull of us and meet his desire with the flick of my tongue. His arm around my waist tightens as he lifts me and, with three strides, settles onto the love seat on the other side of my office. My knees fall on either side of his powerful legs, and my needy core rests flush against his hard length.

How did I not notice towering, hulking Leo is well-endowed until now? Easy, I was ignoring the fact I wanted him to be mine. Now, I'm not. I mentally shake my head and rock against him. As I grind harder, wetness floods between my thighs.

"Lily," he groans. My name sounds like a warning.

I add a sliver of space between our bodies as I press the tip of my nose against his. "Do you want me to stop?"

"No. Hell no!"

With his response, I tug my shirt overhead and then his. It takes him a few moments to gather his words.

"You're more gorgeous than I ever imagined." He places an open-mouthed kiss near my collarbone and continues down along the edge of my bra and over the swell of my breast. "I always wondered what your thing was." His voice is muffled against my skin.

"My thing?" My voice sounds strained with lust and a mixture of fear and curiosity. The tantalizing streaks of heaven coursing through me are from Leo. *Leo.* The feeling of him nestled under me and the heat of his mouth on my body is a heady experience.

"Some women like shoes or purses, you opt for sexy-as-fuck lingerie."

I think back to dressing earlier. I chose my dark blue La Perla set. I giggle softly. "If you love this one, the rest are better."

He growls and draws the strap of my bra down my arm, baring my breast to his hungry mouth. His warm tongue draws a circle around my taut nipple before he bites lightly.

A shudder of pleasure spikes through me as I rock faster over him.

"I'm making a mental list of each thing that brings you pleasure, Lilianna."

Containing a desire-laden whimper is impossible. Rarely does Leo call me by my full name. I didn't realize how much I love it. "Same." As the word escapes my lips, Leo unclasps my bra and draws it from between us. His large hands cover me and knead in turn. My head drops backward as I seek to ease the ache between my legs.

With his hands gripping over my shoulders from behind and his head buried in my chest, Leo meets my downward thrust with upward ones. The waves of my orgasm surge from my lower back down to my core. I collapse against Leo's broad chest and revel in the receding tingles of my first step into carnal anything with him.

My mind is cataloging how I feel and how I can't wait to experience so much more. I hear Lola scampering around as if we have a guest. Then I hear my sister's voice.

"Lily, where are you?" Lina asks.

"Lina, we're in my office. Do *not* come in here. Leo will be right out."

In response, I hear a chuckle, retreating footsteps, and nails tapping against my hardwood floors.

Leo presses a kiss to the top of my head and then my lips. "To be continued."

"I wasn't done now," I whine and reluctantly slide to the right to allow him to stand.

"Neither was I." He locates his shirt, tugs it on, and kisses me again before slipping out the door.

I drop my forehead to the back of the couch and recalibrate myself. I fail miserably. My heart is racing, and my mind is spinning. As crude of a measurement, I'm flustered from second base plus a dry-hump orgasm. *I'm screwed.* Knowing Lina will want to see my face, I redress and take a seat at my desk.

I don't have long to compose myself before there's a knock on the door. "Come in, Lina."

"Good afternoon, sis. Have anything you would like to share?"

"Nope, not sharing. I don't ask for details about you and Gugliotti. I don't want them."

My older sister has her hands on her hips and a surprised look on her face. "Fine, but are you kicking yourself for not telling him sooner?"

"Yes and no. Our reasons were different, but I understand why he kept his feelings to himself. I may have in his position as well." It's not my story to share. If Leo wants anyone other than me to know, he should be the one to do so.

"I won't push. Will you both be at dinner on Sunday?"

"Yes. Mama politely demanded our presence."

Lina smiles. "Good. Then the rest of us will have time to grill you. Plus, Frankie and Tommy will be back from their tropical honeymoon. Have fun on your dates."

I drop my head. I know she's right. "Bye, Lina."

Dates, plural? I consider storming into the kitchen, but I promised Leo I would stay put. What is he up to? With nothing else I can do, I refocus on my work. By the end of the day, I have a rough outline of my counter proposal for my boss. I'm perfectly content walking away from my job. My productivity has remained level or increased since my shift to remote work. I attend all required meetings at the home office. I don't see why the new head honcho needs to see my face across the floor to know I get my work done.

Near six o'clock, a single, red-tipped, pink rose slips through the crack in my office door, followed immediately by Leo. "Ready for our date?" He extends the flower to me and takes my hand.

"Our date is tomorrow," I challenge him.

He shrugs. "We're having one really long date with three parts, and it starts right now. You in?"

"I'm in. Why three parts?"

"Our date is for a few stages of our friendship. Experience a few things as a couple instead of best friends. The first date tonight is to remind us of our teenage days."

"Okay, what do I need to wear?"

"Another layer should work. I won't let you get cold."

"You never have." We may not have been a couple, but Leo always gave up his hoodie or jacket for me.

A small smile graces his face. "I never will." He ushers me to the bedroom for a sweatshirt and shoes.

"You're going to have to tell me where we're going."

"No driving required." For the first time, he threads his fingers with mine. It's a simple act of connection, but with him it feels long overdue. He leads me down to the garage. I peer inside, hoping to get a glimpse of what he's hiding. No luck.

My patio is set up for a bonfire, complete with roasting hotdogs and s'more fixings. Well, a firepit-style bonfire with a cozy pile of pillows and blankets for a picnic. "How did you decide on this for our teenage years?"

Leo hands me a hot dog on a roasting wand and joins me near the fire. "I decided on this one because it was the last thing we did before graduation."

"Senior beach bonfire and campout." It was a great night. Truthfully, my invitation was solely because I was the best friend of the captain of the football team. Nothing about high school me was popular-kid event worthy except Leo. We built two massive bonfires, roasted hot dogs, and made s'mores. Some of our classmates drank, most of us didn't. It was a chance to let loose together one last time.

"Yup. I failed you that night. I should've protected you from Adam."

I stop rotating my hot dog and set my free hand on top of his forearm. "No, you didn't. I put myself in a position to be alone with him. Both you and Luca taught me to take care of myself."

Leo grins at me. "True, but I should've followed sooner."

"I appreciate your protect-my-girl mode more than you know. I wanted to be alone with Adam. I wasn't planning on having sex with him with a bunch of our classmates within earshot. He had other plans. When he didn't take no for an answer, the shiner was the least of his worries. You've blamed yourself for me having to defend myself all this time?"

"Yeah, it was my job."

"No. Please forgive yourself. You have never failed to show up for me when I needed you."

He raises an eyebrow at me and steps over to the table. "Not accurate either, Lily."

"It is. At any time, you would've come to assist me if I asked, despite your self-imposed wall. Don't dig in your mind for examples. You have never let me down, not once in my entire life."

He sets down his food and hauls me into his arms. "Really?"

"Truly, not once."

Leo sets a fierce, hard, and possessive kiss on my lips. I rise on my toes and clasp my hands around his neck. Our lip-lock continues for so long, we both need to reheat our dinner. With newly warmed dinner, we slide into one of the chairs and eat. Well, Leo sits and I settle on the arm with my legs over his and hooked under the other arm.

The sun is lowering toward the horizon, and the colors are amazing. More so when we were younger, Leo and I shared numerous sunsets and a few sunrises. Those were when we were in college though. This one is special. It's our first one as an actual couple, and I'm taking in every streak of color and ribbon of sunlight in the evening sky. Once Leo finishes eating, he sets his skewer on the stone patio and draws me into his lap.

"What's on your mind, Lily?" he asks, his mouth moving along the curve of my neck.

I snuggle deeper into his chest, and his arms tighten around me. "I was thinking about us overall. Now though, I'm reveling in how fantastic I feel with you touching me however and whenever you want to."

"I'm a huge fan too. For the longest time, I focused on keeping my hands to myself, especially after choosing our family over you."

"Don't say that. I understand why you felt more loss would be devastating."

He continues, "There were so many times I almost broke, but I refused to risk my family—any part of it."

"Like when?"

"Are you sure you want to know?"

I drop my gaze to our intertwined fingers. "Yes."

"The day you told me about Oliver's promotion, his invitation for you to move with him, and you turning him down. First, I wanted to physically harm him for hurting you. No one should ever feel like an accessory for someone else's success. You're so much more than arm candy. You're successful, gorgeous, and sexy. I volunteer to be your arm candy."

"Do you now?"

"Absolutely!"

"Oh my God! I'm completely on board with it, but please finish the story."

He brushes his lips along mine and continues. "Hell, you could've applied for the same position if you wanted it. Then I wanted to kiss you until you forgot his name."

"That was almost four years ago. What stopped you? What's different now?"

"You were exceptionally adept at hiding your true feelings for me. Every now and then, you would take my arm or linger a little longer than a woman who is only my friend, but it was rare, and I never allowed myself to examine it deeply. Now though, you shared how you feel. You showed me by choosing to put my feelings before your own and making difficult medical decisions for me when you could've protected yourself more. I was choosing to stay away from our family over the last few months. It would've felt wrong without you there. I didn't want you to choose either. Now, as a couple, neither of us has to choose. Nothing can break what we have."

I shift, slide my hand up along the scruff of his beard, and lower my lips to his. Effortlessly, he stands from the chair and carries me to the comfy pillow pile on the other side of the patio.

CHAPTER ELEVEN

LEONARDO

I lower Lily onto the soft, fleece blanket and hover over her. The amber color from the fire dances across her flawless skin. Her chest rises and falls with a few deep breaths.

"You too?"

"A little." I narrow the space between us more. "Lily." There's no reason for me to be nervous. We've already gone past where we are in this moment. Yet the moment I kissed her, everything changed. My world shifted on its axis to revolve around her.

"Kiss me again, Leo."

Her demand is all it takes.

I drag my tongue across her lower lip and then sweep into her mouth like I've been kissing Lily for years instead of a few days. The more I kiss and touch my best friend, the more I crave. Only she has ever made me yearn for the softness of a woman's touch. It took me far too long to realize she would never make me choose between her and our family. Now I'm never letting her go. Her hands snake beneath the hem of my shirt and climb my chest.

"This needs to come off."

I drop onto one forearm, and she lifts half my shirt off. Crossing over her, she repeats on the other side.

"Better?"

"For now." There's a twinkle in her eye that I've never seen before, and it sends heat streaking down my spine.

Lily may not have been overstating when she indicated she was demanding. She unzips her hoodie and wiggles out of her tee beneath me. At least she is allowing me some fun. When I lower my mouth to her earlobe and nip slightly, Lily bows upward, and her heated center is against my hard length. A desire-addled moan escapes her pouty, pink lips. I work my way over the corner of her jaw, along her neck, and down to the sweet-smelling valley between her ample breasts.

Her fingernails burrow into my shoulder blades. *Noted, Lilianna.* I slip the strap of her bra down her arm and take her aroused nipple between my teeth while working the silk and lace away from her curves. Determined to draw whimpers of pleasure from her, I bring her closer and shove two pillows under her. I cover one breast with my hand and roll her nipple between my fingers, while I suck the other into my mouth.

Her hands glide down my flanks and dip under the waistband of my joggers and boxer briefs, pushing them over my hips. I freeze the instant her small hands surround me. A mixture of emotions fly through my mind. First on the list is Lily is topless and her hands are pumping me with equal, precise movements. The flush in her cheeks is from my mouth exploring her lush body. The mere fact she's still wearing any clothes is a testament to the inner battle going on in my mind. As much as I want to make love to Lily, I don't want to skip the other steps either.

Her hands glide over me with increasing speed.

Hot desire rushes through my body. My breathing hitches, and I manage, "Lily, I would prefer you come first and often before me."

She raises an eyebrow, as if my words weren't a warning for her to stop. Molten heat bubbles at the base of my shaft. She doubles her speed, sets her hot mouth on my chest, and continues until I burst onto her belly.

Holy hell! I glance down at Lily and see she has a devilish smile on her face. I rock onto my heels and locate some napkins to clean up. Then I lie beside her and gather her against me, our legs tangled.

"I wasn't kidding, sweetheart."

"As intriguing as your words were, and I'm sufficiently intrigued, I didn't want to stop. I didn't think you were kidding, but I knew you wouldn't stop me. Arguably, now it's balanced. S'mores, then more sexy time later?" she asks.

I laugh. "I'm not even close to done with you for today." For the rest of my life, more accurately. "I need to make one thing clear."

A sliver of doubt cast over her face. "What?"

"I don't want to skip over the exploration of your body and how to make you scream my name and shudder from my touch because we've been best friends forever. It's an important aspect of our relationship."

Silencing Lily has never been a feat I've successfully completed often, but it takes her longer than usual to reply. "No more sexy time today?" she frowns.

"Stella, you're killing me. I didn't say that. I merely want to slow down a little."

"I can deal with a little, but not much."

I groan, kiss her quickly, and push to my feet. When I return with our snack, she has my shirt tied at her waist. Lily has been wearing my clothes since middle school—a hoodie here, my varsity jacket in high school, and shorts once. The possession I feel is more significant in this moment.

"It's wrong to cover up when I only recently garnered the ability to stare," I inform her.

She wrinkles her nose, a quirk she's had as long as I can remember, and it's equally as adorable as the first time I noticed. "You promised I wouldn't get cold, so I stole your shirt."

My shirt that hangs off her shoulder. "Were you cold?"

"Only because you let go."

I never realized before, but Lily is a vixen. She owns her wants in the bedroom, or patio in this case.

"What am I going to do with you?"

She winks at me. "Whatever you want."

I growl, set down the tray with s'more fixings, and haul her between my outstretched legs.

"Better," she notes and giggles softly when I bite down on her exposed shoulder. The muffled moan caught in her throat catches my attention. I tuck the information away for a later time.

We prepare our roasting forks and scoot closer to the flames. She rolls her marshmallow slowly and methodically while I hold it directly in the flames and watch it burn to a crisp. While I wait for Lily to finish hers, my marshmallow starts to droop.

"Catch it, Lily!"

She rests her stick on the ground in time to catch my melted marshmallow in her hands. Her laugh surrounds us, and it's glorious. "Now what?"

I grab a graham cracker in one hand and attempt to scoop the gooey confection from her hands. I fail miserably. Not only are her hands covered, so are mine. Undeterred, Lily lifts my hand to her lips and swipes her tongue along my sticky skin. I think I'm more upset about not thinking of this method of eating the marshmallow before she did.

"You have to share," I demand.

She laughs and releases my finger from her warm mouth. I dip my head and suck the sugary goo from her hands and drag my tongue up her arm until my shirt gets in the way. I skip over the fabric and reach for her lips. Without breaking our connection, she turns and settles with her legs over my thighs. Her heat nestles against my rock-hard shaft. The fabric of her leggings block nothing. Her eyebrow rises, but otherwise she says nothing. Unlike earlier today, we have time to learn each other. I untie my shirt, lift it over her head, and cast it aside.

I retrace a path down the center of her chest with my tongue and snake my hands beneath the waistband of her leggings. My attraction to Lily was well controlled until recently. The sheer notion her panties match the bra from earlier nearly pushes me to hurry. I don't. Instead, I peel her leggings downward as if I'm unwrapping a present—one I have waited to open for at least a decade.

I pause at her hips when I see a tattoo. There is extraordinarily little about Lily I don't know. The ink is new information. It's a crescent moon with a star over the middle and an ornate lotus flower design. I finish removing her pants, hook the side of her lace panties, and lower them to see the entire tattoo on her olive skin. I bend forward and kiss her inked skin. For the moment, I intend to ignore the distinct scent of her arousal and the darker spot on her thong. "When did you get the ink?"

Her eyes glisten with potential tears, but none fall. "Three days after the draft."

I dig deep into my brain and attempt to recall any time between then and now when I could've seen her tattoo and fail. She has had a tattoo symbolizing us on her body for as long as I've shelved my feelings for her.

"Did you go to Keith at The Ink Shoppe in Boston?"

She frowns. "Yeah, how did you know that?"

I drop another kiss on her skin, eliciting goose bumps and a slow exhale. Rocking back on my heels, I lower my joggers and boxer briefs to reveal a remarkably similar tattoo on my upper thigh. The unshed tear from before falls down her cheek. I swipe it away with the back of my hand.

She presses a kiss to my knuckles before I lower my hand. "When?"

"Not long after you got yours."

"Why?"

I exhale sharply. "I wanted to have a piece of you with me wherever I ended up."

"You always had one." Her hand rests over my heart.

"Inwardly, sure. I wanted an outward symbol too. A reminder of where I came from and where I wanted to go."

"Did it work?"

"Yes and no. It was a double-edged sword after Gran. Before she died, the tattoo reminded me you were always with me even if I ended up being traded to San Francisco. It was a small piece of you I could carry with me always, even if I pushed you away."

"And now?" Her tone is soft and hopeful. Her chocolate eyes bore into mine.

I push back and kiss her tattooed skin again and reply, "Now, I want to memorize every inch of you until I know you completely."

Drawing her close again, I kiss her deeply and possessively. I tangle one hand into her silky hair and slide the other down her torso and into her panties. I expected her to be wet, but soaked would be a more apt description. My finger skims over her clit and slides through her folds. I saw back and forth as my thumb draws circles over her nub at the same time. As I slide one finger into her sopping center, she bites down on my lower lip and moans.

Without discontinuing the circles with my thumb, I withdraw my finger earning a whimper from my breathtaking woman.

"Don't worry, Stella." I replace my single digit with two. "I've got you."

Her breathing falters and shallows as her inner muscles pulse around my fingers. Lily claws at my back when the pulses ripple through her entire body, and she shudders against me. I refuse to relent until the waves of pleasure cease. When they end, I redouble my efforts until she shatters again, screaming my name. I gather her against me and lower us to the blankets closer to the warm embers. Aside from screaming my name, Lily hasn't uttered a single word. Rarely can I render her speechless, it seems I've done it twice in one evening.

"You okay?" I drop a kiss to the top of her head. Mind reading would be an exceptionally useful skill right now. Before anything romantic happened, I could read Lily better than anyone. In this moment, I'm still figuring her out.

She nods against my chest and burrows deeper into my arms. I didn't plan on exhausting her propane tank. When the flames fizzle out, we clean up and snuggle into bed until morning.

CHAPTER TWELVE

LILIANNA

Bright and early the next morning, I find myself wrapped in Leo's arms in the center of my bed. He's warm, and his hold on me is tight enough to keep me close and doesn't allow me to slip out of bed. Flashes of the first part of our exceptionally long date tiptoe through my head.

Compartmentalizing my feelings for Leo was difficult over the years. Now having his full-fledged attention is more than I anticipated. Partially accurate, Leo, my best friend, was attentive before Danica. Leo as my other half—still isn't an accurate description—has always been a part of me. Adding in physical affection is life altering, and I haven't even—

"What are you thinking about so hard so early in the morning?" Leo murmurs against my neck.

"You."

"Care to share?"

I twist slowly in his arms and set my hands flat on his chest. "It isn't new information. More like observations of our friendship and how this level is insanely awesome."

"I agree. Part of me is upset—"

"No, no backtracking. Any decision either of us made about our relationship was what needed to happen before now."

"We could've had more time, and I wouldn't be dealing with—"

"Don't you dare. We didn't lose time. We gained a new aspect of our relationship."

"Not completely," he reminds me.

"Being cheeky about making me wait, I see."

He presses a kiss to my forehead and pushes out a harsh breath. "We can't go back after I make love to you, Lily."

"Could you now?"

His silence shares volumes about Leo's thoughts.

"Neither can I."

A little while later, he breaks the silence. "Ready to continue our epic first date?"

I giggle. "Sure. Are we eating here or out?"

"What kind of boyfriend would I be if I didn't get your favorite breakfast for our first date?"

"One who wouldn't know what my favorite breakfast is."

"Fair enough. We may have extensive knowledge, but still… we're picking up breakfast."

"Are you going to share where we're going?" I wonder if he will keep it a surprise.

"I would prefer not to, but I still can't drive, so… our first stop is the Perk. The dress code is exercise clothes."

I smile widely at him. "Oooohhh! I like this so far."

"I thought you might. Get moving, beautiful."

After a quick kiss, I hustle into the bathroom and fuss with my hair. We're backing out of the garage less than forty minutes later. Hand in hand, we stroll into the Perk and pick up our order. As expected, Leo orders my coffee perfectly and makes the best scone choice given the options on the daily menu.

I smile and sink my teeth into the first bite of the strawberry walnut scone.

Leo lowers his mouth near the shell of my ear. "I did good, huh?"

I nod. "You already knew that, didn't you?"

"Of course. Your smile is all the confirmation I need. I've had years to learn almost everything about you. We're working on the rest." He presses a kiss to my forehead, and we make our way back to the car.

He opens the driver door and hurries around to the passenger side. Leo's manners aren't new information, but I appreciate them more given he acted similarly when we weren't dating. *Dating?* It doesn't seem like enough for what we are. I push those thoughts away for another time, set my hand on the shifter, and turn my head in his direction.

"Do you want me to direct you or just tell you now?"

I lean over the console so I'm close enough to kiss him. Before he even tells me, I know without a shred of doubt it will be perfect. "You can tell me. Then I'll kiss you breathless for the perfect choice. Then we can go enjoy your date-planning prowess."

"It isn't prowess. It's using the inside, best-friend information to my advantage."

I tilt my head in anticipation. "So?"

He eliminates all but a sliver of space between our mouths. "We're going to walk Marginal Way and then walk through the village."

I pepper his lips and face with fast kisses before slowing to a toe-curling, bone-deep kiss of love and happiness. "You hate shopping."

"I'll shop with you."

"I see you, Leonardo, and your sweet words."

"Good. It won't change."

I pull into traffic and drive to the parking lot for the Marginal Way. The ride isn't terribly long, but it's long on actions. Leo's fingers are linked with mine, and he didn't change the station on the radio even though I know country isn't his favorite.

Parking in the closest spot to the trail, we silence our phones then meander down the path. It winds along the shore with exquisite views. We pause near the lighthouse and simply soak in the feel of us here as a couple. If we've been here together before, it wasn't memorable, which likely means we were in a group. While the walk isn't long, we take a seat on bench sixteen and absorb the salty breeze and soothing waves.

Taking photos isn't really my thing. I prefer to live in the moment. However, I make an exception now. I pluck my phone from my pocket, outstretch my arm, and take a selfie with my lips plastered on Leo's cheek. After lowering the phone, I snuggle into Leo, and we sit on the bench for quite some time, lost in us and our thoughts. I don't like to compare my past relationships, but I could never just be with anyone other than Leo. He's always the first person who comes to mind when I need advice or consolation, even when either of us was dating someone else.

"Ready to keep going?" He sets a kiss to my forehead.

Sweet mercy! I never realized how intimate those were until he unknowingly kissed me at the hospital. Now it's purposeful and means exponentially more. With our hands intertwined, we casually stroll the rest of the path. Instead of walking the path back, we meander through the village and poke around in a few shops, just being goofy, trying on sunglasses and hats.

As we near the car, Leo pulls out his phone and scrolls through his messages.

"What else are you up to?"

A devilish glint materializes in his jade eyes. I've never met anyone whose eyes express more than Leo's.

"I'm making sure the rest of our date is all set up."

I inhale and smile up at him. "Okay." I wait impatiently for him to elaborate. "And?"

"No details, Stella."

"Okay."

Surprise crosses his face. Nothing about Leo would fall into the pretty category. He's scruffy, scarred, and mine. There's a tenderness about him he only shares with me, and I'm grateful only I know that facet of him.

"You aren't going to push and prod until I cave?"

"No. You don't need to do all of this for me though."

Leo guides me between two of the quaint stores and lifts my hands to his lips. "I know you don't need me to take care of you. Your self-sufficiency is hot as hell. I need you to allow me to care for you because I want to."

I'm frozen in place. "It isn't about taking care of me. You have been for as long as I've known you. I'm a simple girl, Leo. What I want aren't things. I want a man who will stand beside me. I want a man who looks at me like my father looks at my mother. How you look at me. I want you. I want us. The rest is just stuff."

He exhales sharply and looks skyward. Whatever he has planned for the rest of the day is more than simple.

I continue before he can speak. "I appreciate whatever you have planned for the rest of our date. I need you to know being with me doesn't require over-the-top anything each day. You have been giving me what I need for years; it just took us unbearably long to make it official."

"I hear what you're saying, but a man wants to take care of his woman. I need you to grant me the opportunity to do it. I love you, Lilianna. I have since the day we met." Leo curls his arm around me and draws me flush against his body. His lips seize mine in a possessive, no-holds-barred kiss that is barely appropriate for our location. Regardless, we kiss and kiss and kiss some more. I can barely breathe.

I tug his lower lip between my teeth and break our kiss slowly. "I love you, Leo. I have since before I knew what love was."

Silence surrounds us. Not even the tourist crowd is registering in my mind. I'm a private person, but having Leo claim me on a public street is more than I thought it would be.

"Want to get ready for dinner?" Leo murmurs near my ear.

I drop my head in acknowledgment, and we finish our walk back to my car. When we arrive home, I note my sister Lia's car parked outside.

"Why is Lia here?"

"I thought you might want some help getting ready," Leo proudly answers.

He's absolutely right. Also, he knew I would choose Lia instead of my older sisters. Lina or Frankie would've been fine, but I'm closer to Lia. His attention to me is astounding. There was no reason for him to notice this detail over the last twenty-plus years. Yet he did. "Thank you."

"No digging for details. Pip only has what she needs to know. I only shared the necessary information with everyone because you're relentless when you want to garner information." Leo coined her "pipsqueak" soon after they met. He shortened it to "pip" when she was a teenager.

"You know me so well."

He leans over the armrest and brushes his lips over mine. "Yes, I do. You need to be ready by five."

I glance at the dashboard clock. An hour and a half is more than enough time, isn't it? What on earth is he planning? Once we're inside, Lia whisks me away to my bedroom.

"How was your teenage date and early-morning date with Leo?"

I grin at her. "Good. How much detail do you know?"

"Not falling for it, Lily. I want details. Lots of details."

"If I'm sharing, so are you," I state pointedly.

She huffs. "You first."

"We're figuring out how we work... romantically. Are you even old enough for this conversation?"

"Very funny. You know how old I am."

Was I old enough when I was twenty-two and dating Matt? No, but I did it anyway. "At first I thought it would be weird kissing Leo, but it's far from weird. It's like coming home. Part of me wishes I spoke up sooner, but it wasn't the right time for us."

"Awwww. I'm so happy for you. Leo is my favorite brother. It was nice to have a ginormous big brother in elementary school who happened to be one of the best football players in town. Please don't tell Luca."

I pretend to zip my lips shut. "You and Leo always had a special relationship."

"Get in the shower, Lily. Your man has a few more tricks up his sleeve."

My man. I seriously love that. "Fine, going." I step into my shower and hurry along. Then a wave of trepidation slams through me—hard. Hard enough for me to set my hand on the Carrara marble title. Are we really doing this? Despite our slow-down agreement, I could feasibly have sex with Leo at any time going forward. Leo, my best friend for my entire life. *Holy fuck!* Butterflies flutter in my belly, and my heart starts to race.

I never felt this way before or *after* sleeping with…. I push out a harsh breath, add more hot water, and gather my composure. I soap up my legs and shave from my ankle to… everywhere. The water is cold by the time I finish. I don't believe it has ever happened before.

"Lily, are you okay in there?" Lia calls.

"Yes." Got lost in my head for a minute, but I'm going to own my feelings and allow our romantic relationship to proceed. "I'll be out in a minute."

I throw on my robe, and Lia joins me in the bathroom. "Ready for more?"

I lift my eyebrow at her and take her extended hand. Lia leads me into my closet. Hanging beside my mirror is a garment bag from So Elegant.

"He didn't…," I whisper.

"Yeah, he did," Lia whispers back.

I unzip the bag and find a long, fitted-to-the-waist, burgundy silk dress with a plunging neckline, slightly flared skirt, and thigh-high slit. "Wow! Did you already look?"

"No, it's gorgeous. You have a similarly colored lingerie set, don't you?"

"Close enough, yeah." I look down on the dressing bench and find a box with a pair of fancy shoes. How did he get these here so quickly? I pull the heels out of the box and take a moment to gawk at the red soles. I don't need any of this, but damn if it doesn't feel good to be a little spoiled by Leo. "Did you help?"

"No. He did this all on his own with a little help from Kelly and the card with your measurements from Frankie's wedding. Now, sit so I can dry your hair while you do your makeup. You can't be late for your first date."

Blushing and unable to control my smile, I take a seat at the vanity, and Lia gets to work on drying my hair. I apply more makeup than I usually wear, not surprising given I rarely wear any at all. Lia assists me in stepping into the dress. The silk is soft and smooth against my skin.

"You look beautiful, Lily."

"Thanks, Lia. Is this all he has up his sleeve?"

She shakes her head but zips her lips at the same time. Lia grabs her bag and I walk her to the living room. I look around, but Leo is nowhere in sight. As Lia hugs me close, the doorbell rings.

"Have a wonderful time. Love you, Lily," she says, pulling away.

"Thanks. Love you too, Lia."

She grabs her keys. "You should answer the door." She winks at me, then slips down the stairs toward the garage.

Feeling confused but excited, I answer the door, and the sight of Leo dressed in a suit and tie on the other side with a huge bouquet of flowers nearly knocks me on my ass. I'm entranced by him and the weight of this date.

"Lilianna, you look stunning."

"Thank you. You look pretty hot yourself." I reach a shaky hand forward and take the flowers. I inhale the scent before setting them on the console table near the front door.

"Can I come back in?"

A small smile curls up at the corner of my mouth. Then I stifle a giggle. "Yes, please come in."

"No reason to be nervous, Stella. It's just me."

"Just you is precisely why I'm nervous and trying like hell not to be."

As if he knows I need more reassurance, and he likely does, Leo draws me into his arms. I set my hands on his chest when one arm slides over the flare of my hip and rests at the curve of my ass. The other glides under my arm, and his big, warm hand heats most of the exposed skin of my back. The instant his strong arms tighten around me, every fiber in my body calms... or at least the nervous ones. The part of me noticing the effect I have on Leo is another matter for later.

"I know I said this already, but you look gorgeous."

"Thanks. Did you decide on the dress or let Kelly choose?"

He loosens his hold on me slightly and tilts his head downward. "I gave her a loose idea of what I wanted, and she ran with it."

I'm almost afraid to ask but do anyway. "Which was?"

"I asked for a body-hugging, moderate cleavage-baring dress with soft fabric. Kelly has skills."

"Is this why you were worried before? My reaction to the dress and shoes."

"Partially. I'm trying my best not to attempt to make up for lost time. Please allow me a little latitude for tonight."

"I will."

With the added height of the shoes, kissing Leo requires less stretching. I meet his mouth with mine and twist my tongue along his. He lifts my toes off the floor and takes two long strides further into the house. I grip his lapels and melt into him. The consuming surge of desire casts aside the awareness that Leo is kissing me with abandon. It takes restraint not to push his suit jacket to the floor.

I clench my thighs together to slow the flood of wetness. "Leo, we're going to miss our reservation if we don't leave soon."

He sets his forehead against mine. "We aren't leaving here. Matteo will be here in—"

The doorbell interrupts his response.

"Right now?"

Leo laughs softly and kisses the tip of my nose before answering the door. "Hey, Matteo. Thanks for coming."

"You're welcome, Leo. Family first. *Cugina! Sei bellissima!*" Matteo greets me with a kiss on each cheek.

"*Grazie, cugino!*"

"Now go. I'll bring your appetizers in fifteen minutes." Matteo swerves around us and steps into my kitchen. Matteo is a celebrity and athletic chef. He also happens to be my cousin. When I bought my house, it needed work, and I enlisted Matteo to assist in designing the kitchen. It closely mirrors his personal kitchen in his home, which is a few miles away.

Leo offers me his arm. I graciously loop our arms and allow him to lead. My patio looks like a scene from a romantic movie. Twinkle lights hang low enough to cast a gorgeous glow on the round table and two covered chairs that now occupy the patio. Soft jazz is playing in the background. Most notable and much like last night, the privacy screen is set up, though my neighbors aren't close.

"How did you pull all this off?"

"My crew is exceptional. Also, they're rooting for us and have been for a long time—at least that's what they've been telling me."

In a whisper, I ask, "My siblings?"

"Your parents too."

A tear slips over the ball of my cheek. Leo kisses it away.

"When I asked you on a real date, I knew I would need help pulling it off. My boys are great, but none of them live close enough to assist with courting you properly. Although I'm sure they would show up to see me finally give in."

"Who knew?"

"Back in college? Just Mo. They all suspected and respected me enough to stay away from you." He pulls out my chair and sits beside me before continuing. "The first call was difficult, Lily. I was terrified they would shut me down and convince me we weren't going to flourish as a couple."

"Who did you call first?"

"Lina. I would've called Frankie first, but she's not home yet."

Matteo steps through the French doors with a pitcher. He silently fills our glasses and retreats. Leo doesn't continue, as Matteo quickly returns. He sets a sharable plate of bruschetta with burrata and heirloom tomatoes in the center of the table and a second dish with watermelon, prosciutto, and mozzarella skewers on the other. Then he disappears.

I slide a serving of bruschetta onto each plate and grab a skewer. After a huge bite, Leo continues. "I was wrong, so wrong. If I was unaware you didn't share with them, I would've thought everyone knew about your feelings other than me."

I shake my head. "No one knew until a few weeks before I told you. I couldn't deal anymore. I was close to imploding. I spent one of our movie nights in Boston to avoid you altogether. I couldn't bear to be here alone again."

"Why didn't you tell me?"

"You know why. I would never give you an ultimatum." I don't need to add *"like Danica did."* I would prefer to never utter her name again. "I didn't know about your feelings then. You hid them exceptionally well, especially from me."

He takes my hands in his. "I never will again."

With a sweet kiss to my wrist, we return to eating and polish off the appetizers a few minutes before Matteo serves the main dish—seared scallops over a citrus salad with tomato and zucchini risotto. He leans closer to Leo and whispers some instructions.

Matteo straightens and turns to me. "Nice to see you two finally together."

"Thank you, Matteo. Everything is perfect," I offer before he slips back inside. "What was he whispering about?"

Leo winks at me. "He made dessert too."

"Of course he did. Will you share what he made?"

"Nope. You can wait until after the dancing portion of our date."

"Dancing, how fancy." I try to keep a straight face, but I can't.

Relief washes over him. "I was going to corner you at Frankie's wedding."

I set down my fork and verify I heard him correctly. "Meaning?"

"With Frankie's wedding party being small, she asked me to dance with you at the reception. I planned to win you over with our shared history and divulge my true feelings. Circumstances dictated otherwise."

"While I would've preferred to skip the hospital and damaged bar aspect, the time apart may have been a blessing."

"Why?"

"I wouldn't have accepted your invitation if it came any sooner."

His brow furrowed. "Because?"

"I would've been afraid to be a rebound and ruin our friendship."

"Is now long enough?"

"Yes." It's a small, seemingly insignificant word that states volumes.

CHAPTER THIRTEEN

LEONARDO

I set my napkin on the table, rise from my chair, and extend my hand toward her. "May I have this dance?"

Her hand glides along my palm as she stands from her chair. My body craves to feel her curves molded against me again. I press a few buttons on a remote Lia set up earlier. She assured me the music would be perfect. Honestly, I don't need music. All the noise in my heart and mind quiets with Lily in my arms.

With one hand curled tightly around her waist, the other linked with hers bent between us, we move slowly to the music. Time stands still. Her breathing is measured as her head rests on my chest.

A memory from the past crashes into my thoughts. Junior year of high school, we won the state championship for football. The homecoming dance followed the game. I embodied the captain of the football team, popular guy vibe. Yet I refused to date the head cheerleader, although Macie tried her best to make it happen. Instead, I used Lily as a buffer. I didn't bring a date but told Macie I had one. It was the last time I danced with Lily. I realize here and now, it wasn't my smartest move.

"I'm sorry, Lily."

She lifts her head and looks up at me. "For what?"

"You're going to think I'm crazy, but I don't want anything else unsaid between us."

Silently she waits for me to continue.

"I used you as a buffer for the homecoming dance junior year."

A slight pause later, Lily bursts into laughter. Aside from the reason she's laughing at me, her laughter is melodic and glorious to my soul. "Oh, Leo! Girls talk way more than you think. I heard Macie and the rest of her squad talking about how she was going to make you hers at the dance. I knew before you asked me to go with you. I was never under the impression it was an actual date. I only went because you asked. Otherwise I would've gone home after your game and spent the night reading or hanging out with my siblings."

"Seriously?"

"Of course! That all you got?"

"Yeah. You have something you need to share?"

"I can only think of one potential faux pas you may not know about."

"Do tell."

She laughs softly. "In college, Gina came to me and asked me if there was any way I could help her get you to give up football."

"Did you give her ideas?" Levity laces my tone.

"No, of course not, but I never shared with you."

"The irony is we met when she gave the freshman athletes our tour of the team facilities. She knew from the beginning I was there to play football."

"I thought she was brighter than that."

"No, not even close. I think even then it was on purpose to be with the new star recruit."

Lily's eyes flutter closed.

Rather than push further down memory lane, I set my hand on Lily's waist and turn her away from me. The loss of her flush against me leaves me feeling cold and bereft. Once I surround her in my arms again, I dip her and grip her thigh with my hand. I set a possessive, spine-tingling kiss to her lips before drawing her upright again.

"Dessert now or later?"

"Now works. Will you share what Matteo crafted now?" She bats her eyes at me.

If I crack, she'll learn another weakness when it comes to her. Her innocent look is too much to handle. The fact is I'll do anything for Lily until my last breath. I would before we leapt into a relationship. I groan and answer, "Apple tart with almond mascarpone topping."

"Did you request that? Matteo doesn't know my favorite fruit."

"I requested something with apple for dessert. He handled the rest."

She clasps her hands around my neck and goes up on her toes as tall as she can to plaster a grateful kiss to my lips.

"Come on, let's go plate dessert." I take her hand in mine and lead her into the kitchen. Matteo left strict instructions for proper presentation of his magical confection.

Step by step, we follow his rules and plate the tart. I carry two waters and two forks while Lily carries our dessert to the table. We retake our seats and dig in. I watch the first bite of what I know will be a delectable dessert disappear into Lily's mouth.

As predicated, her moan of appreciation says it all.

"Really?"

She blushes fiercely. "What? It's exceptional."

"No moaning about food."

Her nose wrinkles in protest. "They are not the same!"

"Don't care."

She huffs. "Fine." Lily devours the tart mostly in silence with a few glances in my direction.

"What's on your mind? You can ask me anything. You're the only person who can." My assurance has her setting down her fork and her gaze locked on mine.

"It's not time for this conversation yet."

"Never a bad time to talk about anything, Stella."

"I suppose because I know you well, I know you've aged past some of your life goals. Have you amended them?"

When we were seniors in high school, our advisors had us create five, ten, fifteen, and twenty years plans for our futures. "Did I physically create a new one? No. Did I amend the timeline? Yes."

"What did you change?"

"After retiring and buying the bar, I wanted to be with you, but—"

"I was with Oliver."

"Yeah, you were. I guess the same logic applied then as it did for you and Danica. Do you still want a huge bash of a wedding and a bunch of kids?"

She hesitates. "Not so much a bash, but it'll be huge given the size of my family and the friends I would invite."

I note she didn't answer the children aspect of the question. Initially, it makes me wonder the reason for her nonanswer. Then I realize it has to do with me. I shouldn't be shocked. We share each thought, dream, and disappointment with one another. "You didn't answer the entire question, Lilianna."

She inhales sharply. "I know. Can we not talk about the other part of the question tonight?"

"Yes, if you tell me why you don't want to share your answer." I grip the seat of her chair and yank her beside me before hauling her into my lap.

She buries her head into the crook of my neck before responding. "I'm terrified our answers are different." Her reply is muffled but understandable.

"What if they're not?"

She sits up fully, and her expression is a mixture of concern and a dash of hope. Her delicate hands cup my scruffy jaw, and her eyes are trained anywhere but to mine.

With two fingers I lift her chin. "My answer is different than it was in high school and even after I got drafted. I achieved my dream of playing football in the NFL. Was it as long as I hoped? Not by miles. My desire to have a family was directly tied to my career. I didn't want my children raised mostly by their mother, nor did I want to worry about them seeing me injured on television. I want to be a hands-on dad, which I can do now, assuming we can find an excellent executive manager for the bar."

"What?" Her words and her body language don't match in this moment. Lily is bubbling with the potential of having a family with me.

"You always said your number was maybe one child, ideally a boy, after you retired from a lengthy career in the league. Why did you never share this with me before now?"

"I didn't have a reason to. Asking you not to watch me play was a fool's request. You attended every single game my entire career. A silly, though protective, request like that would've derailed our friendship permanently. You were always the first person at the end of the tunnel to check on me most of the time before Gran."

"Please don't mess with me, Leo. Not about this."

"Regardless of your professional aspirations, you wanted to be a mom for as long as I've known you. I would never dangle your dream of motherhood in front of you, only to snatch it away."

"I only ever wanted to be the mother of your children."

"I know, and my circumstances are different now." I lean forward so our lips are a hairsbreadth apart. "I'll give you as many as you want to carry."

The floodgates open, and Lily is peppering my lips with sensual kisses. In a move of flexibility I didn't know she possessed, Lily threads her left leg between us while turning in my lap. One leg falls to either side of me on the chair. The shiny material of her dress is bunched, exposing most of her creamy thighs. My hands slide beneath the material in an attempt to push it higher. When I fail, Lily sets her high-heeled feet on the concrete floor. Not only am I able to caress her hips and perfect ass, but my mouth is level with the valley between her breasts, which I've learned is an erotic zone for Lily.

"Leo." Her voice comes out breathy and dripping with unmistakable lust.

I round her hips and smooth my thumbs over the fabric of her panties. "You're already soaked."

"Yes. You just promised to fulfill one of my life goals with me."

"The idea of having a child arouses you this much?"

"No. The notion of carrying your child arouses me that much."

I grip the strap of her dress and bra and push it down her arm. I tease my index finger along the lacy hem and suck her nipple into my mouth. At almost the same time, I push the fabric of her panties aside and spear her with two fingers. As her inner muscles tighten around the invasion of my fingers, Lily rocks forward and back on the balls of her feet, meeting the thrust of my hand. Her fingers thread into my hair and hold me against her breast. I bite down on her nipple harder than I plan to, and I'm rewarded with a shudder and a whimper.

Learning Lily's bedroom preferences is rapidly moving to my first priority, even before fixing the bar. Fuck. She feels spectacular writhing against me because of the ministrations of my fingers and teeth. As I increasing my speed, she clamps down on my fingers and clutches my bicep with her free hand. All it takes is the swipe of my thumb on her swollen clit to push her careening over the edge of bliss. Desire and orgasm drunk Lily is a goddess.

"Let's go inside," she suggests.

A battle of wills breaks out in my heart and mind. On one hand, this feels exponentially fast, only a little more than a week since I kissed her the first time. On the other hand, we've been friends for over twenty years. With that sheer number in mind, I can overcome the idea we're rapidly approaching the point of no return. I'm already there. Her fierce loyalty, gumption, and unselfishness to put me first cement her into my life. The tattoo is my undoing. Her reasons for inking her supple, flawless, olive skin exemplifies her as the pinnacle of my dream girl. Back then she chose me despite my stupidity and inability to choose her. I didn't answer her yesterday about going back to before; there are no words to exemplify how deeply I love Lily.

She fixes her dress before murmuring, "Still worried?"

"No. Nervous, I guess."

"Why?"

I cup her face in both hands and drag my thumb across her kiss-swollen lips. "If how I feel when your lips are molded to mine with you in my arms is only the beginning, I'm yours until the end."

Without another word, Lily presses a scintillating kiss to my lips, takes my hand, and attempts to lead me inside. I release her to shut off the music and snuff out the candles. After linking our fingers, I guide Lily past the hallway that leads to her bedroom to the front door and open it for Lola.

"We aren't leaving the bedroom until morning. Another ten minutes isn't going to kill us."

"It might," she retorts.

With Lola secured and the alarm set, I draw Lily closer and drag my tongue along the vee of her dress. Blindly, her hands work the buttons of my shirt. With a hunger I've never felt with anyone but her, we dance down the hallway. I pin her to the wall and reach down to gather her dress in my hands. Her bare skin beneath my fingers is heavenly.

Seizing the opportunity of my divided attention, Lily wraps her arm around me as best she can and swivels us to the opposite wall. She grips my hands and lowers them, forcing me to release her dress. She strips off my jacket and tugs my shirt down my arms before turning her back to me. Now her movements make sense, I can't get her dress off without unzipping it first.

With three well-placed kisses on the exposed skin of her back, I lower the zipper. The curve of her ass and the tease of a thong nestled between her cheeks hardens my cock even more. I slip my hands beneath the straps of her dress and smooth it down to the floor. Dragging my fingertips in a ribbon pattern up her body raises goose bumps on her soft skin.

"Nearly naked Lily might be my favorite version of you." Her taut nipples tighten more as I pinch them through the lacy fabric.

Lily's head falls back against my chest, and I slide one hand over her belly and into her panties. I saw my fingers over her from front to back. The overwhelming urge to taste her rockets through me. A momentary blimp of concern surfaces, and I tamp it down equally as fast. Lily and I are chasing an us.

A sense of appropriateness filters into my mind. Before I consider it long, I withdraw my hand. A whimper of displeasure escapes from Lily's lips.

"I refuse to taste you for the first time in the hallway. We're doing this right, Stella." I lead her to the edge of her plush king-size bed. My eyelids close briefly. When I reopen them, Lily is staring at me with unfiltered, undisguised, consuming desire.

She unclasps her bra and pulls it away from her luscious curves and slithers out of the matching lacy thong. "What about naked Lily?" Without another word, she sits on the edge of her bed and spreads her thighs to bare herself to me.

Years and years' worth of pent-up desire, sexual tension, and frustration rumble from my lips with a growl. Within seconds, my pants and boxer briefs join her luxury lingerie on the hardwood floor, and I fall to my knees before her intimate offering.

The first swipe of my tongue exceeds expectations exponentially. Lily is soaked with arousal, and it's mine for the tasting. Her fingers thread into my hair. With each flick of my tongue, Lily wriggles closer to the edge of the bed. I delve deeper into her. She clings to me as I bite her clit and bury two curled fingers into her core.

"Holy… Leo… never stop."

I grin against her and increase the intensity of my masterful lashing of her sex. Lily's breathing reduces to pants, and her body bows as her first climax of the night has her careening over the edge into ecstasy. I squash the swell of pride in my chest. Never thought I would experience a day when Lily was pliant and languid from decadent sensations I caused, despite my yearning for the same. As the shudders decrease, I place lingering kisses upward. I savor her rosy nipples as I climb her body. Surrounding her with my arm, I center her on the bed.

"Lilianna Stellaluna." At my words, her gaze turns to mine. "I want to watch you submit to us. Eyes on me."

As if entranced, her small hands encircle my length and drag the tip along her seam, covering me with her arousal.

"Still on birth control?"

She nods.

I watch the head and the first two inches of my cock disappear into her. Another inch, then another, then I pause when she exhales slowly.

"Damn, you're tight."

"More accurately, you're big and thick."

I arch an eyebrow at the compliment, then in question. A moment later, it hits me. "How long?"

"Do you really want to know right now?" Lily allows her thighs to widen, opening more for me.

I push forward slowly until I'm fully buried in my best friend—a title that is surpassed by center of my world, lover, partner, wife, and mother of my children. All of which fall short of love of my life and soulmate.

A few deep breaths later to allow her body to adjust to me, she answers my question. "My battery-operated friend, probably a week. A man... since Oliver. Not a fling kind of girl."

"No, you're not. You're my forever."

Lily's visceral reaction to my response—unequivocal, unconditional surrender. "I need you to move."

At her request, I withdraw and plunge into her again to the root.

"Oh my... Leo. Again."

I lower to my forearms and sweep my tongue into her parted lips as I move inside her more rapidly. She clenches around the invasion of my throbbing penis. I've never been with anyone bare. It's indescribable. Sprinkle in the fact that this is my last first time with a woman, it's fitting.

Lily's fingers dig into my sides deeper with each thrust into her wet, heated center. "Harder." Her gaze is cast downward at our connection.

"I don't want to hurt you."

"You never could." Her body pulses and trembles when I heed her request.

"Look at me, Lilianna."

The moment our gazes meet again, she shatters around me. I've never seen a more magnificent sight than Lilianna splintering from pleasure I provided. I explode with deliberate strokes into her. Making love to Lily obliterates every memory of anyone before her. There's only her until my last breath. I'm ruined for anyone but her. I crush my lips to hers and pour each ounce of love into her—my Stella. She's my North Star. Always has been, always will be.

I roll us onto our sides and gather her into my arms.

"Don't move yet," she requests, her lips moving against my chest.

I didn't plan to, not anytime soon. "I'm not done with you. Nowhere near done."

"We feel spectacular together."

"Yes, we do." Never before has sex filled me so fully. I realize now, I was waiting for her, for us to be real. She was always beside me, but never fully mine until tonight. The others were simply placeholders to scratch an itch. Only once and I'm more satisfied than ever before. Not sated completely, but after a brief respite, I plan to achieve satiation.

Lily requires less downtime than I do. Within fifteen minutes, she pushes me to my back and explores my body from head to toe. Once she's satisfied she has licked, nipped, or bitten the majority of me, she straddles my hips. After two strong strokes with her hands, she impales herself on my cock.

"Damn, Lily!"

"I meant it when I said demanding in here. Did you plan on sleeping?" She sets her hands on my chest and rocks her hips against me. "Don't you worry, I've got this!" She takes my hands and sets one at the curve of each hip. Lowering her hands to the mattress, the angle of her body changes, and I lengthen more inside her.

"You feel incredible squeezing me!"

Lily glides along me in a steady rhythm until she's on the cusp of another climax. She sits up again and plunges down over me, meeting my upward thrusts at a feverish pace. My fingers dig into her hips. Her breasts bounce in time with our movements.

"Don't stop, Lily. I'm close."

I slide my thumb over and rub circles on her clit. Her hands cover her breasts, and she tweaks her nipples hard.

"Come with me," she urges.

Two penetrating thrusts later, a hard climax ripples through Lily's body, driving me to burst forward deep inside her. She rides out the waves of us before collapsing on my chest.

"Is that going to keep getting better?" she murmurs against my skin.

"I hope so."

We clean up and snuggle in her bed, talking about nothing and everything. Hours later, I roll with Lily in my arms, tuck her against me, and cover us. I longed for these moments so many times. Now we're finally one, and I refuse to let anything derail us.

CHAPTER FOURTEEN

LILIANNA

Late summer light filters into my bedroom. I'm deliciously sore in places I've never been before. I slide my arm out and note the sheets are cold. It doesn't surprise me Leo is already awake.

"Don't leave the bed, Lily," he bellows from the kitchen.

How does he know I'm awake?

He appears bare chested at the threshold with two cups of coffee and Lola hot on his heels.

I pull my lower lip between my teeth. *Sweet mercy! That man is mine.*

"Lola was whining to go out again."

I frown.

He saunters into the room. "What's with the frown?"

"I had plans for you this morning." I accept the coffees, and he settles beside me in bed.

"Did you? Well, we don't have a lot of time until we need to go to family dinner." He steals a kiss and then retakes his cup.

I twist to check the clock. It's nearly noon. We need to arrive for dinner around two.

"Are you going to share your plans with me? Did they include more naked Lily time?"

I lift my shoulders. "I'm still naked now."

"Finish your cup, and we'll tangle up these sheets again before dinner."

"Can we be quick?"

After another heavy gulp, he steals my cup and hovers over me. "Only one way to find out."

I laugh softly and submit to his mouth caressing my skin again.

His fingers slip between my thighs. "You're soaked already. What on earth were your plans?"

"You're going to have to wait until after dinner. For now, make me come hard and fast."

He flips me over and draws me up to all fours. After shucking his shorts, he thrusts forward in one deep stroke. As he hammers me from behind, jolts of pleasure twirl up my spine.

"Leo, don't stop."

He doubles his efforts. The instant my fingers flick my nub, the waves of my orgasm crash through me. Almost immediately, hot bursts dart from Leo into me. He sits on his heels and pulls me back as well. He presses a row of kisses along the top of my shoulder blades. "We absolutely can be quick. Think you can keep your hands to yourself in the shower?"

I smirk. "I'll do my best."

"I understand. Now that I can kiss you and touch you, I crave it."

"Same."

He withdraws, leaving me hollow and bereft for the moment. We're coming right back here later tonight and every day after that. *Will he leave after the bar is restored?* A sliver of fear slices through me. It's crazy soon for me to be thinking about living with Leo. *Isn't it?* Yes and no. I push my thoughts away and step into the bathroom. The steamy glass enclosure does nothing to hide Leo's silhouette. Heat pools between my thighs, forcing me to clench them. I exhale and step inside with Leo. My shower is massive, but it feels tiny sharing it.

"You okay?"

"Yeah, why?"

He stops rinsing and surrounds me in his arms. "I'm almost done. What were you thinking about?"

It's heartening and scary as hell how well he knows me. My answer doesn't come fast enough.

"Lily, it's me. You can tell me anything."

"Even if it's insanely soon for me to be thinking what I'm thinking."

"Especially then," Leo assures me.

"I don't want you…." I stumble, but he waits me out. I bury my face into his chest. "I want you to stay."

He pulls back and looks down at me. "Do you think you can scare me off?"

I shrug in response.

"I love you. I have my entire life. Since I've shared my feelings with you, it only grows stronger. You can't get rid of me now."

"I never want to."

"I'm not going anywhere, except out of this shower, so we aren't late. I need to make a good impression on your family."

I shake my head. My family may keep Leo over me some days.

He presses a kiss to my temple and slips out of the shower. I take a quick shower and hurry to get dressed. Before we're out of the garage, my phone has an incessant stream of texts.

Frankie: We're back. What's going on with Leo?

Lina: Was it as good as expected?

Lia: How was your date? The music rocked, right?

Mama: Don't be late, Lily. Leo's presence is required.

Willa: Hey. I want details of your date and after your date.

"Who is messaging you?"

I turn my phone so he can see the messages, then set it down. "Everyone. You aren't going to answer Lina, are you?"

"Worried what I may say?"

He hauls me close and kisses me fiercely. "No, hell no. We are fire in the bedroom. I'm wondering how much you four share, because I know without a doubt you don't share with Luca."

"No, I won't share with Luca. I would prefer you to remain in one piece. You may be bigger, but he's wily. As far as the girls, I'll answer them diplomatically. Which is to say, you blew my mind, but without sharing anything other than broad-stroke details." A severe blush creeps into his cheeks. It's sexy as sin. "You're hotter when you blush. I've never seen it before this very moment."

"What is the most detail you've ever shared with any of them?"

"Clearly, this was before anything happened, but... I told Lina I had a deeply rooted desire to taste whiskey on your tongue."

"That's hot as fuck, Lily. We will make it happen."

My cheeks heat up from revealing the tidbit to him.

"So is the blush rising on your cheeks."

"Well, the last twenty-four hours merely proved my instincts about us were right."

"I agree. Do you have a limit on PDA in front of your family?"

"As long as we don't approach inappropriate, I'm fine. Don't forget about the kids either."

I pull into my parents' driveway as Leo answers, "Understood."

Speaking of the kids, our niece and nephew rush out the front door.

"Yay, Uncle Leo is here," Emilia shouts and runs to Leo with her arms outstretched, ready to be lifted. At eleven, she realizes Leo's hugs are the best. She's a ball of energy unlike her mom.

"What about me, Em?" I feign rejection.

"You didn't get hurt and need hospital rest, Auntie."

"Fair enough."

Em scampers away after my reply.

Leo leans closer. "Well explained, Stella."

"Thanks. No reason to give her unnecessary worry about the best uncle in the world." I wink at him and link our fingers. With the precision of an army battalion, the family files out the front door and lines up on each step. Only my parents remain in the house.

We encounter Ellie and Antonio next.

"Glad you're feeling better," Ellie offers. "I'm sorry about your business."

"Thanks, Ellie. It's fixable, but it'll take some time."

Antonio and Leo fly through a handshake they've been adding to for the last few years. A pang of sadness and guilt trickles into my chest. I stole the last few months away from them.

Before I can admonish myself more, Leo lowers his mouth near my ear. "Stop. Blaming. Yourself."

Silently, I catch his gaze and press a kiss to his cheek. "I'm trying."

"Try harder." He turns my head toward him and sets a chaste kiss on my lips.

A chorus of "awwwws" ripple through my family, who're anxiously awaiting to greet Leo. We greet everyone else in turn as we climb the steps, and they scatter into the house, the kids likely to the playroom. Leo and I make our way to Papa's office.

He's cuddling his newest grandchild. As a dad, Papa is amazing. Papa as a grandpa is mesmerizing to watch. I can't wait for the baby he's doting on to be ours. "Hi, *piccola*. How are you?" Papa sets a kiss on my cheek, and I take Luke from his arms.

"I'm good. You?"

"Never better."

Somehow, I think his demeanor reflects Leo's presence.

"Leo, great to see you here for dinner." They shake hands and bro hug.

"Mama didn't really give me a choice."

Papa offers Leo a nod of acknowledgment, like "get used to it." I note the undertone of "you're stuck with her now." I don't hate it. As luck would have it, Luke starts to squirm and cry.

Papa ushers me out of his office. "Willa warned me he was getting close to feeding time. Why don't you bring him to her and give me a minute with Leo?"

"Okay, Papa." I weave through the hallway and ask Willa for Luke's bottle. Instead, she excuses herself into the guest room upstairs to feed him herself.

I follow the delicious scent of Mama's cooking into the kitchen.

"Lilianna, how are you?"

"I'm good. How can I help?"

She shakes her spoon at me. "You can take a seat and chat with me. How is Leo doing?"

I follow her instructions and sit at the island. A little over six years ago, my father remodeled the kitchen, complete with a chef's stove and double oven. Mama requested a massive island with stools. "You should ask him yourself, Mama. He'll be right out."

I wonder what Papa and Leo are talking about. I make a mental note to ask Leo later.

Mama presses, "How are you?"

"Aside from my work issues, I'm fine. Before you ask, the new head guy wants me to be in the office in Boston each day."

"You don't want to change." Her words are a statement not a question.

"No. I plan to share my counter proposal tomorrow."

"If it isn't accepted?" Mama asks.

"Not sure yet." I know exactly what I plan to do, but I should run it by Leo first.

"You'll make the right choice."

"Thanks, Mama."

Leo and Papa join us in the kitchen.

"Hi, Mama."

She sets down her spoon and steps into his wide-open arms. "Oh, Leo. I was worried about you."

Me too.

"I'm going to be just fine. The bar is going to take a bit longer though." After releasing my mom, Leo sidles beside me with his arm over my shoulders and a kiss to the top of my head.

I don't miss the look of approval passing between my parents. Luciano and Rosalie have a finely honed private language, much like mine and Leo's.

"Can you gather the rest of the family, Luc?" Mama asks Papa.

"Of course, *amore mio*." Papa leaves the kitchen.

Leo and I carry dishes into the dining room where everyone takes their place at the table.

"Uncle Leo?"

"Yeah, Em."

"I put you next to me at this end of the table." Em has been creating personalized place cards for the last few years. She takes his hand and leads him next to her chair. Her tiny hand is dwarfed by Leo's large one. A stab of concern filters through me. Em is still worried about Leo even though he's here, and she put on a good face earlier. "Don't worry, Auntie. You can sit on the other side."

Laughter erupts around the room. Dishes are passed, and dinner proceeds as if there wasn't a gap of a few months where things were rocky between Leo and our family.

Halfway through our meal, Leo sets his hand on my thigh and leans close enough for his crisp, fresh cologne to surround me. "What are you worried about, Stella?"

Containing my physical response to the heat of his hand on my exposed thigh is more difficult than I anticipate, especially as he creeps higher. If he intends to soothe me, he's having the opposite effect. He's stoking my need for him with a simple caress of his fingers. "The inquisition gets closer and closer as the end of dinner beckons."

"They love you. I'll rescue you ten minutes after they abscond with you into the backyard."

"Deal." I press a kiss near his ear and whisper, "I love you."

He turns his head so no one can read his lips and replies in kind. The rest of dinner passes far too quickly for my liking.

"Respite is up, Lily. Time to chat." Lina hooks my left arm, and Frankie hooks my right arm.

I gaze over my shoulder at Leo. He offers me a curt nod. I have no choice but to allow my sisters and sister-in-law to lead me outside.

"Spill," Frankie demands.

"You first," I challenge.

"Fine. Our honeymoon was spectacular. Our accommodations were luxurious, and the water turquoise blue."

Lina asks, "Did you leave your luxurious accommodations?"

Frankie blushes. "Not much. Now you, Lily. Have you and Leo—"

Lina interrupts, "We're your sisters. Please tell us if it was amazing or terrible!"

"I'm dying here, Lily!" Willa adds.

I can't help but laugh. I choose my words carefully. "After an awkward start, it was better than expected."

"Woo-hoo! Now we need to find a suitable man for Lia," Lina throws down a challenge. "How is it going with your hottie classmate?" Her question is directed at Lia.

"It isn't. School's over, we graduated, and we both have real jobs now. We kind of lost touch."

"Did you ever find out the deal with the little girl?" Frankie inquires.

"No, I didn't. Look, he wasn't interested in me as more than friends, and it's fine," Lia answers. Her posture sinks. She's interested in him though, or she was.

"Consider the sister squad officially on the prowl for a guy for Lia," I announce.

"No, thank you. I'll find my own guy," Lia counters.

As promised, Leo appears on the back porch. "Time for dessert, ladies."

My sisters and Willa file past Leo one by one and return to the dining room.

His arms collapse around me, and he hauls me close. "How did it go?"

"I'm considering it a success. I didn't overshare, and they didn't press." I glance around his body on both sides to verify my sisters have gone inside. "Our blazing sheet time is safely between us."

"Well done," Leo praises me and lowers his lips to mine. His touch sends spikes of desire to my toes, and I can't help but lean into him.

I slide my hands up his chest and cup his face. My lips part, and our tongues twist until we're interrupted by a thunderous round of applause. I drop my head onto his chest and shake it back and forth. "Go away. We'll be right in."

"I merely wanted evidence, not anecdotes," Luca states.

The rest of our family agrees and files away from behind us.

"Our family is amazing," Leo mumbles against my head.

"Yeah, they are." I lift my lips to his again before leading him inside. We spend the next few hours laughing and devouring Mama's desserts before our hour-long goodbye.

While we climb into bed, I remember to ask about his conversation with Papa.

"What were you and Papa talking about after I left?"

Leo takes a deep breath. "I won't lie to you, Stella. He reminded me of a conversation he and I had a long time ago, but I would like to keep our discussion then and today to myself a bit longer."

I consider his request. Leo would never keep anything from me that may hurt me. "Okay." I snuggle deeper into his arms and allow sleep to claim me.

CHAPTER FIFTEEN

LEONARDO

Wide awake in the wee hours of the morning isn't an unusual occurrence for me. Lily is snuggled into my side with the top of her head framed by my arm. A conversation from my past is replaying in my mind in addition to snippets from a conversation earlier today.

"Leo, how are you truly?" Papa asked.

"Physically, I feel fine. My new injury was to a different part of my brain. Repairing my bar is going to take some time." I purposefully left out the part where Danica, or whatever her name is, duped me. The extent of her scheme is still unknown.

"And my *piccola*?"

I was silent for a few moments.

He continued, "Do you recall a conversation we had about Lilianna soon before the draft?"

"Yes, sir. I asked for your permission to date Lily."

Papa clasped his finger in front of him on the desk. "Yet you never asked her. Why?"

Lily already knows I shelved my romantic feelings and why. Sharing with Papa wasn't a betrayal. I settled my nerves and explained my reasoning for not chasing Lily back then—the risk of losing her family after losing all I had left of my own.

Papa is a thoughtful, careful man. "I see, and now?"

"When I shared with Lily, she made me see if she and I didn't make it, you, Mama, and the rest of the family would never cast me aside. However, her selflessness, she also saw what losing the only family I had left would do to me. Lily is an amazing woman, and we decided to be a couple now."

"Lilianna is wise beyond her years, always has been. You came into our family when you were eight years old. Rosalie and I will always have a seat for you at our table."

"Thank you, sir. When the time comes, I would.... I assure you, it won't take a decade this time." I inhale sharply. "Sir, I would appreciate your blessing to marry your daughter."

Papa grinned. "Which one?"

I laughed.

"You have my blessing to marry Lilianna, if she'll have you."

"Thank you. We should get out of here before they ask questions," I offered.

"Too late. Both Rosalie and Lilianna are detectives and quite perceptive."

I smirked. "Truer words." We exited his office to the kitchen.

Lily stirs beside me, pulling me out of my thoughts. "Morning, Stella."

She presses a kiss to the side of my chest. "Morning. How early is it?"

"A little before six."

"Want to take a walk with me and Lola before I clock in?" Lily pushes up to sitting.

"Sure. What time is your call with your boss?"

"The call is at ten. Then we have your appointment with the building inspector, fire marshal, and Scott, right?"

"Yeah. Are you sure you should be skipping out on work given their request? I understand if you can't come with me."

"I'll share with you what I'm thinking while we walk."

I nod, and she's on her feet.

Within fifteen minutes, we're strolling down her driveway with Lola scampering a bit ahead at the end of her teal leash. Lola is part Cavalier spaniel and part poodle. She'll be medium sized when she's fully grown.

"Tell me your plan, please," I ask.

"I'm not moving to Boston, nor do I plan to commute there each day either. I'll offer another day or two a month in Boston, but no more. If my work doesn't speak for itself for whomever the new person is, so be it. I'll give my notice and take all my vacation time. Then search for or create a new job for myself."

"Good for you." Given how well Lily handles my finances, I would assume she's equally secure with her own.

"Thanks. It makes no sense to me why I would need to change anything."

"New management always make changes."

"True, but it's been five years. I'm not the only person with a remote arrangement."

"That should be part of your presentation as well."

"It is."

"Will you let me know how the meeting goes?"

"Of course."

We reach the edge of her gated neighborhood and turn around. Our trudge back uphill is harder than I anticipate. My breathing is labored, and my legs feel like lead.

"Leo, are you okay?"

"Yup, need to slow down a little though. Apparently, nearly three weeks without a workout is catching up to me."

Lily slows her pace and takes my hand. Our walk turns into a causal stroll back home. "I'm sure Dr. R will clear you at the end of the week to work out again."

"I hope so."

When we arrive at the house, Lily hurries straight to the shower while I prepare breakfast. When I finish and make my way to the bedroom with her coffee, she's clasping her bra.

"Damn! I'm too late."

Lily giggles and turns to face me. Her lingerie leaves nothing to the imagination, at least not this set. It's sheer nude lace and the panties barely cover her. "You can take it off later."

"Promise?"

"Absolutely." She accepts the coffee and takes a heavy sip. "Thank you. What did you do differently?"

"I added a dash of cinnamon to the grounds before brewing."

"It's amazing." She steals a kiss and retreats into her closet. All too soon, she's fully dressed and headed into her office. "I'll be done in time for your meeting."

"Okay," I reply and watch her walk out the door. Her shoulders slump and her pace slows. This request is weighing heavily on her. The bigger question is which aspect is bothering her. The fact they want her to go back to a work-from-the-office format, or an underlying accusation her work isn't up to par. Frankly, it can't be the latter. She's a rock star despite working from her gorgeous home.

I shower and dress before starting a second cup of coffee. I slip into her office and give her a fresh one too. She scribbles a thank you on a small notepad as I drop it off. I blow her a kiss and wink at her over my shoulder. Her smile is thanks enough.

With a hot cup, I take my phone onto the porch and reach out to Smithson.

"Morning, Leo. You were on my call list for this morning. How are you feeling?"

"Good. Any updates?"

"We cobbled together video footage, and I took an investigative trip to Portsmouth. Danica's landlord was helpful. He provided a copy of her rental agreement, which gave us her social security number and date of birth. Her real name is Shelby Woods. She does in fact work for Midland Construction. The reason she left those voice mails for you and the connection to the gas leak are still undetermined."

"At least one thing she told me was true," I retort.

"Has she reached out to you?"

"No."

Smithson replies, "Good. We're working to gather more information about her and connecting the dots. I'll reach out when I know more. Also, the investigative report from the YFD is complete."

"Thanks for the update. Iris from YFD sent it a few days ago. I have an appointment at lunch to start on the estimates and timeline. Let me know if you need anything else from me," I offer.

"Will do. Good luck, Leo."

I end the call and mull over his revelations. Shelby. Her name is Shelby. It isn't a horrible name. There must be more to it, something deeper, more sinister. Moving on to more important topics, I focus on allaying the fears of my bottling contracts and tamping down my optimism for pulling off the rebuild at least until later today. I'm confident it'll take longer than I would like. Choosing to run a bar after retirement was a blow. Yet I was successful and have turned a decent profit for the last few years. I merely hope I can hold on to my staff and customers during the rebuild.

Lily emerges from her office. Her demeanor indicates her meeting didn't go as planned.

"That bad?"

She shrugs. "My boss didn't decide either way. He indicated I need to present my request to the new VP personally for consideration."

"Seems odd, but when?"

"On Friday afternoon."

My phone vibrates in my pocket, but I ignore it.

"Do you have an update from Smithson?" she asks.

I share the information he provided.

Thoughtfully, Lily asks, "Looking back, does anything strike you as odd about her behavior?"

"Not really, aside from me never going to her place. With my hours, it made sense at the time. She didn't lie about having an apartment in Portsmouth, just about everything else."

"Ready to start moving forward with the repairs?"

"Yes. Also, can we talk about my finances with respect to how much I have to close the insurance gap?"

"Sure. I can run the numbers for you."

"Thanks." We make our way to the bar and arrive at the same time as the inspector but after Scott.

Scott did the refurbishing and buildout when I first opened. He came highly recommended from a few people we know well, including the Barnetts and the Morgans. He owns his company and only hires exemplary subcontractors when necessary. Scott also recommended a colleague so Lily could have her kitchen done sooner. "Great to see you again, Leo and Lily. I'm sorry it's under these circumstances."

"Me too," I reply.

They provide us with hard hats, and we enter the building. I survey the damage with Lily close to my side. Inexplicably, she reaches for my hand the instant my emotions start to bubble to the surface and catches my gaze. The unspoken words in my glance are enough to satisfy her fears for now. Her gesture isn't so I won't feel; it's so I won't crumble alone. Lily has seen me at my highest and lowest points. Not once did she ever make me think how I felt was unacceptable or too much. Lily walked beside me through nagging injuries and serious concussions when I was young and now today. It exemplifies who she is, and I'm grateful she's mine.

Lieutenant Foster follows closely behind the building inspector and Scott who asks pointed questions about the repair.

"The exterior structure remains relatively undamaged. The interior is another matter. Will building and zoning require a full rebuild of the damaged south wall or repair?" Scott asks.

The inspector consults a small notebook. "Since the building was fully refurbished when Mr. De Gaetano opened his establishment, only a repair will be required."

Silently, I cheer, squeeze Lily's hand, and draw her closer. For the next hour plus, we walk through the damaged portion of the building with our escorts and discuss the extent of the damage.

"Another full inspection of the boiler system will not be necessary, as it was clear the mechanism was tampered with," Lieutenant Foster states.

Rage explodes within me. "I would never—"

Lieutenant Foster expeditiously cuts me off. "I apologize. You have been cleared of any wrongdoing, Mr. De Gaetano. If we suspected you or Miss Cappelli, you wouldn't be here right now."

"My apologies as well. Do you have any idea how and when the system was tampered with?"

"YPD is working to determine the culprit or culprits. However, given your consistent accounts of your whereabouts and the reasoning Miss Cappelli has a set of keys, we're working on other theories."

"Such as?" Lily asks.

"I would prefer not to discuss the investigation any further at this time. We have cleared both of you and the building."

I keep my thoughts to myself. It's clear they suspect Danica—Shelby—in some way but can't connect her yet.

Lily answers on our behalf. "I appreciate your candor and accommodation. Determining whoever is responsible for Mr. Santos's death, Leo's injuries, and the property damage is our intention as well."

Foster nods and continues following Scott and the inspector through the final damaged area—my apartment. We navigate through the bar. Luckily, a restoration company was able to handle the water damage the day after my injury. Lily wasted no time in protecting my business interests at the same time as she was caring for me. We climb the interior staircase. My bedroom is mostly intact, as is the master bathroom and second bedroom I used as an office. My kitchen and living room are a few stories below my feet.

"I can rebuild the floor plan exactly the way it was, Leo, if you wish to maintain the apartment up here," Scott states.

"Yes, I want the apartment to be rebuilt."

Lily tenses and attempts to remove her hand from mine.

I refuse to let her pull away. I lean closer so only she can hear me. "Breathe, Stella. I want it back the way it was, so I don't have to wrangle with building and zoning for a change to the structure. I meant it when I said you can't get rid of me."

Her body relaxes, and her head drops as I lift her hand to my lips. We wrap up our discussion, and they're ready to leave. The building inspector steps to the side with Scott. After a few minutes, the inspector excuses himself.

"Can I pack up a few things in here before I go?" I inquire of Lieutenant Foster.

He checks the time. "I have about thirty more minutes before I need to head out. Whatever you can accomplish beforehand is fine with me."

Lily turns to me. "What do you need?"

"My clothes, shoes, and Gran's albums in the closet."

With a quick kiss, Lily pulls my luggage from the closet and sets it on my bed. I fill it while she packs Gran's albums.

"Do you want the memorabilia too?"

"If we have time." I retained a few boxes of awards and plaques from each year of football, starting when I was about twelve. For my senior year of high school, Lily created a collage and booklet of my accomplishments, both football and otherwise, for Gran. It's tucked away in my closet. That piece will have a new home at Lily's as soon as she can hang it.

Lily shakes her head and increases her speed. She has no intention of leaving without each item I want.

"Can I have your keys?" Scott asks Lily.

"You don't have to assist with this?" I inform him.

"We're friends, Leo."

"Thanks."

Lily hands Scott her keys, and he begins making trips down to her car. With only a few minutes to spare, Lily and I exit the building with the last of my necessary personal belongings.

"Thank you for your time and waiting, Lieutenant."

"You're welcome. Good luck with the refurbishment. Detective Smithson or Jones will keep you informed regarding the investigation."

"Much appreciated."

I join Lily and Scott, who are chatting near her car. "Thanks for the assistance, Scott. It's above and beyond."

"No problem at all. I'll get you an estimate and time frame in the next few days. Please let your insurance company know you hired me. If you need copies of my licenses or whatever, reach out to my office. Either Jodi or I can assist you."

"Will do," I reply, knowing Lily is mostly working with the insurance company on my behalf. After opening her door, I round the car and take my seat.

"Dunne's?" she asks. Dunne's is a family-owned ice cream shop with amazing flavors. Although the name has changed, it has been around since I was a kid.

"Don't you need to get back to work?"

She shakes her head adamantly. "Nope, I'm taking the rest of the afternoon. I have over six weeks of vacation time. This afternoon seems like the perfect time to play hooky."

"Yes, let's get some ice cream." As she drives, my phone vibrates with an incoming text.

I pull it out.

Mo: How you feeling? Let me know when you can chat about the reunion.

Me: I'm good. Let's talk soon. I need a timeline for the bar to be fixed.

Mo: Sounds good. Later.

I notice that I also have a missed call and a voice mail, but I don't recognize the number. It isn't abnormal. Vendors call from unsaved numbers frequently. I key in my password and listen to the voice mail.

Danica's voice pierces my eardrum. Shelby, her name is Shelby. Ugh! *"Leo. Where are you? I can't find you. I need to see you to explain.*

Please call me back at this number. I'll be in town on Wednesday for a few days."

Without another thought, I forward it to Smithson. Then I stare out the window and ponder her words. Not even the gorgeous scenery is going to pull me out of my now crappy mood.

Lily sets her hand on my forearm after shifting into park. "Who was on the phone?"

"Mo texted and there was a voice mail from Danica."

"*Oh*. Want to talk about either?"

"I need to work out the timeline with Scott before I can answer Mo. I would like to hold the reunion at the bar, but if Scott's dates are too long…."

"You can host it at our house."

Our. I love how *our* sounds. "Maybe. I don't want the guys traipsing through the house."

"The guys are awesome, Leo. We aren't talking about when you were all young, immature rookies. Almost 80 percent of you are now retired from the league and most have families."

"True. I'll think about it. I'm not sure I want to share our life with all of them. Mo and Monique, maybe. The rest, not so much."

We order our ice cream and take a seat at the green picnic table facing Lily's car. As expected, she opts for her favorite checkerberry while I choose cookie dough.

After arriving home and immediately letting Lola out, I start a load of laundry. Unnecessary, maybe, but it'll only take a few loads to wash my wardrobe before putting it away. Lily vanished into the bedroom as soon as we got back.

"Leo, could you come here?" she calls.

I find her in the middle of her huge closet. There's more than enough storage, and it was separated and organized for her when I pulled out my suit for Miguel's funeral. "I'm set now."

"Meaning?"

"I shifted my dresses and suits over here and moved my heels over there." She points to different sides of her closet. "You can have this side."

A rush of unfettered happiness courses through me. The notion of living with Lily in the abstract is one thing, but for her to make room for me is something else entirely. I clasp my hands around her waist, lift her into my arms, and pepper her with kisses.

"It's just a closet, Leo."

"No, it's more than that. We're moving forward together, and I'm crazy excited."

"I can feel that."

My cheeks heat at her insinuation. She isn't wrong. My erection is straining against the fly of my jeans.

"Should I not point out the obvious? Blushing is hot as hell on you."

"You too. Let's see if I can make you blush too. Your sheer lingerie needs to be examined thoroughly."

She raises an eyebrow. "You mean removed, right?"

"Yes." I lower her to the floor, and Lily whips off her top and wiggles out of her jeans. "Your lingerie makes your sexy-as-hell body look like a present for me to unwrap each day."

"Awwww. That's sweet, and I'll remind you of those words when you learn how much it costs. Right now, I need you to make love to me, Leo."

She doesn't have to ask me twice. Lily and I spend the rest of the afternoon trading positions and control with delicious and satisfying results. Before we dress for dinner, I ask, "How much are we talking?"

"Approximately—"

"You know what, never mind. It's worth every penny."

CHAPTER SIXTEEN

LILIANNA

The week has passed quickly, and Leo and I have been working on living together peacefully. Thankfully, he's neat and a decent cook—both attributes I appreciate immensely. I love him fiercely, but if he were messy, it would spike my need for order. Despite Mama's attempts otherwise, I can't cook as well as she does. I never truly paid complete attention when I lived with her.

My meeting with my boss is set for four. Leo has been pacing in front of my desk, waiting for the appointment to start.

"If you don't sit down and promise to be silent, you need to leave," I inform him.

He raises his hand in mock capitulation and takes a seat as if he were my client.

I purposefully dressed for this call from head to toe. Typically, I work in casual clothes, but for this call, I'll look as serious as I should. The teleconference indicates I have been admitted to the call.

"Good afternoon, Lily. Thank you for joining me."

"You're welcome, sir."

He twists in his chair to address someone else in the room. Then he returns his attention to me. "Unfortunately, there has been a scheduling issue and the new VP isn't available this afternoon. His next appointment isn't until next month."

"That isn't acceptable, Jerry. I will not agree to the changes to my employment contract until I speak with the new VP personally."

Jerry shakes his head. "I'm not sure I can set a meeting before you need to be back in this building."

My anger is increasing with each sentence Jerry utters. "I won't be back in the building except as already required until I get a legitimate explanation for the requested changes to my employment contract."

"You can be easily replaced, Lily," Jerry reminds me.

"If you believe that, then the VP wouldn't have agreed to this meeting he didn't show up for." I've got him there, and Jerry knows it.

"I'll see what I can do about rescheduling sooner."

"Have a lovely weekend, Jerry." If there was a way to end a video conference call like slamming a wall telephone, I did it to end this one.

Before I take a step, Leo is hauling me into his arms. I allow him to absorb most of the tension wracking my body.

"This makes no sense at all."

"No, it doesn't. Why don't I get dressed, and we can go to Morgan's for dinner?"

I shake my head against his chest. "How about pizza, wine, and a movie?"

"Deal. You need another hour or two?"

"Nope. Jerry blocked this off for two hours. In my opinion, my weekend starts right—"

My declaration is interrupted by my doorbell ringing. I pad out of my office to the front door with Leo right beside me. I don't have uninvited guests. Leo's protective side is smoking hot. Alpha vibes I haven't seen since before he retired ripple off his frame.

I open the front door, wondering if I ordered something I forgot about. Instead, I'm faced with someone I'd prefer never to see again. "What are you doing here, Oliver?"

The circles under his eyes are pronounced, and his skin is pale. He looks tired and worn down. Yet he's dressed in an expensive suit and tie. "I wanted to talk to you. I knew you wouldn't take my call, considering you haven't responded to my emails."

I filter his emails directly into my trash folder. I haven't seen an email from him since a few months after his transfer. "I have nothing to say to you. You made your feelings clear when you treated me like a brainless accessory for your career."

Leo silently and unnecessarily stakes his claim by narrowing the gap between us and setting his hand on my hip. Oliver clearly doesn't see Leo's actions in the same way. Then again, he never seemed to worry about my friendship with Leo or the amount of time we spent together while we were dating. Then it dawns on me that Oliver didn't see Leo as a potential challenger for my heart. Oh, how wrong he was.

Oliver scrubs his hand down his face. "Even if I admit you were right? I miss you, and how I treated you is unacceptable. I need you back in my life."

"Even then. Please leave."

Oliver looks over at Leo. He has done nothing Oliver would notice aside from his possessive hold on me. I can feel the tension and anger simmering from his fingers digging into my hip.

"Lily, I need a second chance," he begs.

"I'm not interested in giving you one. I've moved on. You should to. Please leave." I slowly start to close the door.

Unfortunately, Oliver sets his foot onto the threshold. Leo shifts beside me and starts to lean forward.

"Easy, Leo," I whisper. "Move your foot, Oliver, or I will call the police."

"Your brother hated me."

Rightfully so. He doesn't know Luca isn't with the YPD anymore, and I don't plan on sharing. "He judged your character better and faster than I did. Leave, Oliver, and don't come back."

"I won't give up on us, Lily," he restates before moving his foot.

"You're fighting an unwinnable battle," I retort as he retreats and lock the door. With a gentle shove, I push Leo into the living room. "Please sit."

He complies. I walk over to the window and verify Oliver has, in fact, left my property. Then I take a seat on the tufted ottoman in front of Leo.

"I know letting me handle him was difficult for you."

Leo blinks once.

"I appreciate you not losing your temper despite him deserving whatever you would say to him." I set my hands on Leo's and catch his gaze.

"He's not worth any words, especially yours," he murmurs.

From the very beginning, Leo understood me better than anyone else. He knows when to push, when to pull back, and when to allow me to handle things like he did with Oliver today. "No, he isn't, not anymore. I'm not sure he was after the first year or two either. Regardless, let's forget about him and get to our movie night in."

Leo doesn't move or speak another word. I decide to wait him out. As well as Leo knows me, I know him. Oliver's appearance reminded him I have a dating past like he does. Given how long it's been since we were together, I'm surprised it bothers Leo so much. The only explanation is, unlike Matt, Leo saw Oliver as having the potential of whisking me away from home and from him.

As if he's finished dissecting my interaction with Oliver at the door, Leo offers, "Why don't you change, and I'll order the pizza."

"Okay. Are you sure you can order correctly?"

He winks at me. "I'm sure my extensive knowledge gleaned from our years and years of friendship will yield acceptable pizza delivery results. Plus, Scott inadvertently loaded two cases of wine into your car from the bar, including your favorite."

"Which favorite? The crazy expensive one or the middle-of-the-road one?"

"Middle-of-the-road one."

I kiss him slowly and deeply before shedding my suit jacket on the way to my bedroom. Releasing a cleansing breath, I rehang my suit and tug on shorts and a tank top. It's been a long time since Oliver and I have spoken. Why is he begging for another chance now? As soon as the question is in my mind, I shove it away. Aside from having no interest in Oliver, I'm building a life with Leo, one I've wanted as long as I can remember.

When I return to the kitchen, Leo is pouring the wine he uncorked. He wasn't lying; I know the label anywhere—Kistler Chardonnay 2017. I accept the glass, swirl it twice, and take a healthy sip.

"Thank you."

"Pizza should be here in twenty minutes," Leo shares.

I nod. "Any update about the repair time or from the insurance company?"

Frustrated, Leo grasps the back of his neck with both hands. "No, not yet."

I set my hand on his thigh. "Everything will work out. Your workers will come back. As painful as it is, you should set up an ad to replace Miguel. Then he or she will be ready when the repairs are complete."

A sadness casts over his face. "Yeah, you're right. Consider the task added to my list for tomorrow."

"Please say that again," I demand.

"Don't get used to it, but you're right."

I grasp the front of his shirt and tug him closer. I murmur with slight exasperation, "I would never," and sear his mouth with a blistering kiss.

His huge hands surround my rib cage, and he sets me on the island. My tank top floats to the floor.

Much to his surprise, my bra is nowhere to be found. "You took it off?"

"I can put it back on if you would prefer to remove it yourself."

He groans and latches onto my nipple with his teeth and then soothes it with the warmth of his mouth. I sneak my hands beneath the hem of his shirt. His muscles contract when my cold hands graze his warm skin. Leo travels down to the waistband of my shorts. Setting my palms on the granite, I lift my hips to allow him to shimmy my shorts and skimpy panties off.

He grasps the inside of my thighs, spreading me wide open for his perusal. Wetness gushes forward from the carnal look in his emerald eyes. With two fingers, he forms a V and teases me without touching my clit.

"You're mean," I accuse.

"No, taking my time. I want to savor every second I get with you, Stella. I have time to make up for."

"We're both at fault." A prickle of heat streaks from my core to my head and back down to my toes.

"It was more me than you." Leo continues to fluster me. The instant the heel of his hand contacts my clit, the doorbell rings. "Don't move, Lilianna."

I whimper softly. The loss of his hands on my body leaves me yearning for more. Mentally, I picture the approach to my home from outside with relation to my state of nakedness and the probability of being seen through my front windows. If anything, it would be my back on display. Content the tinted glass and location of my driveway is private enough, I lift my glass to my lips and wait.

"Thank you. Have a great weekend."

I overhear Leo accepting the pizza. His voice and demeanor are cool and subdued regardless of the fact I'm waiting for him spread wide and naked on my granite island. He sets the box on the stove and returns to the exact same spot he was before. "I told you not to move."

I purse my lips, dip my finger into my glass, and draw on my skin. I trace an L onto one breast, dip my finger again and add an E on my belly. Leo's hungry gaze is fixed on where I will drip wine next. Finally, after another dip into my glass, I draw an O starting at my pubic bone, down between my thighs, and around my swollen nub.

A hearty growl escapes his throat, and Leo traces the first letter of his name on my breast with his mouth before moving on to the second letter on my stomach. Each time we're naked or my tattoo is exposed, Leo touches it or kisses my inked skin, as if it has become his touchstone of proof we were meant to be after all this time apart and fighting for different aspects of family—Leo for keeping his together and me for wanting to include him more fully.

He pauses briefly with his tongue hovering over the last letter. Rushing away, he releases every window treatment in the living room and returns. "Turn around."

I twist as requested, facing the now covered windows. He spans his hand across my chest and nudges me to my back on the cold surface. Gripping beneath my ass, he pulls me to the edge of the counter and sits on the stool eye level with my dipping folds.

"You like challenges, Moon?"

"This kind? Fuck yes! I'm going to make you scream my name repeatedly with my tongue and fingers, and then I'm going to make you pulse around me until you're hoarse."

A gush of arousal pools between my thighs before the first swipe of his tongue. "Holy hell."

The point of Leo's tongue rolls over me from top to bottom, and a shudder washes over me. His words coupled with the intense surge of pleasure has me clutching the edge of the counter. My first orgasm builds in my lower belly, its arrival hastened by the nip of his teeth on my clit at the same time as he plunges two curled fingers. The instant he hits the magical button within me, my release uncoils like a spring.

My knuckles turn white as I scream his name repeatedly. As if one quaking orgasm from his masterful tongue isn't enough, Leo sucks my nub into his mouth and brushes his fingers back and forth, teasing my tight hole.

With gritted teeth, he asks, "Has anyone ever?"

I push up onto my elbows and look straight at him. "Only me."

Satisfied with my answer, Leo rises, wraps my thighs around his waist, and inches into me with agonizing precision. My body contracts around him until he's nestled fully inside me. The more we share, the more I crave.

With determined strides, Leo carries me to my bedroom. Pinned between Leo and the wall, I slide up and down over him, pushing off his shoulders.

"Lily, slow down if you want me to last."

"I need you to fill me, and then we'll do this again in a different position for the rest of the weekend, unless you have better plans."

Rather than answer, Leo pistons upward and meets me as I sink over him. Pleasure flares in my body as he lengthens and throbs inside me. With one hand on each hip, Leo burrows deeper until he flies over the edge of bliss with me. Clinging to him as the heavenly pulses subside, I slow my breathing with my face nestled in the crook of his neck.

Adding some space, Leo asks, "All weekend?"

"I have no other plans. Do you?"

"None at all other than being beside you." We clean up a bit and eat lukewarm pizza naked in bed.

After a brief respite, we choose a movie we don't watch and continue learning about one another in bed. As promised, we don't leave the house and test new positions on almost every available surface imaginable.

CHAPTER SEVENTEEN

LEONARDO

Lily has already sequestered herself in her office to work for the day. Her work ethic is off the charts given the turmoil with her boss right now. I have a list of things to tackle as soon as I finish walking Lola. When I return, I set a fresh cup of coffee on Lily's desk and earn an air kiss as a reward because she's on a call.

Then my phone starts ringing off the hook for the day. "Morning, Scott."

"Hey, Leo. Do you have a few minutes?"

"What do you have for me?" I hear rustling papers, and I hope it's the plans to fix my building.

"I pulled the old drawings from the buildout and had them reapproved by the town to repair the current damage."

"That was fast," I admit.

"The nature of the damage and the fact there has been an investigation allows the building department to more efficiently approve the necessary repairs. Also, I'm sure they don't want to run into weather issues in the fall or winter. All that said, I've coordinated with the framers and mechanical contractors. They will be getting started as soon as the materials arrive."

"Okay. What's the approximate timeline? I won't hold you to the fire. I'm trying to see how far out I need to rebook events, etc."

"I understand. The framing and exterior will be completed within a month."

"Will I be able to host events in the building once framing is complete?"

"No, because there won't be complete and working electrical or plumbing. Also, it won't pass the health department without running water."

I figured as much. "Okay. What do you need from me?"

"Lily put me in contact with the insurance company and informed them I would be making the repairs. I need a payment to cover the cost of materials to get started." His request reminds me Lily and I didn't talk about the liquidity of my assets yet.

"Send me an invoice, and I'll get it paid. I appreciate how quickly you're working on this. Your reputation is stellar, Scott."

"Thanks, Leo. I need my favorite craft whiskey distillery back up and running before my stash runs out."

I laugh. "Understood," I say and end the call. I walk toward Lily's office to grab her empty cup. Unfortunately, it's untouched and cold. I lift the cup in question. She mouths, "No, thank you." Retreating to the kitchen, I wash both cups and answer my phone, which is now ringing again with a Boston number—a call likely from Dr. Rothstein's office to schedule my follow-up.

"Hello."

"Leo. Oh my God! You answered."

Fuck!

Her voice grates on my nerves. How did I allow her into my life? *Idiot!* She was exactly the opposite of Lily, that's how.

"Not intentionally. I have nothing to say to you. Goodbye, Danica." I end the call and internally vow not to answer any calls from a number not in my contacts.

A second call from the same number rings through. I send it straight to voice mail and block the number. Rage bubbles inside me. Probably against the rules, but I hustle downstairs to Lily's finished basement and throw open the door to her home gym. While she hasn't been working out since I've arrived, I know she generally works out instead of eating lunch.

I tug on a pair of boxing gloves and hit the heavy bag relentlessly until my arms feel dead and heavy. I fall to sit on the cushioned floor and hang my head. The urge to hurt someone, specifically Danica, is intense and overwhelming right now. Never once have I considered harming a woman before now. Channeling my anger was simpler knowing in my head and in the abstract Smithson is handling her.

The notion I shared my bed with her tastes bitter. The extent of her betrayal is still unknown. However, without a doubt I was taken for a fool by Danica Ryder aka Shelby Woods. My inclination to rail against her ultimatum should've made me more introspective of her intentions. Yet the deeper I investigate her actions, nothing stands out. That realization pisses me off further. She didn't take or make secretive phone calls or texts. She didn't ask for information about my business or finances or spike my concern for privacy in any way. She was never alone in my apartment or my bar. At most, she was unsupervised in my apartment for ten minutes tops while I showered every now and then. Usually, she was sound asleep or left after.... With newfound rage and, consequently, energy, I throw a few more punches at the bag until I get lightheaded and stagger to the wall to hold myself upright.

A small set of hands grasp my flanks. Lily is bolstering me too. "Are you out of your mind?" Lily yells too loud for how close she is to me. She guides me to the floor again. "What happened?" She waits longer than I expect before asking, "Are you feeling okay?"

Slowly, I lay on the floor. Lily lies beside me despite my sweaty, smelly body. I turn my head and look at her. "I accidently answered a call from Danica."

"Accidently?"

All I can do is chuckle. It sounds ridiculous. "It was an unknown number. I answered because it was from Boston, and I thought it could be Dr. R's office."

"How did answering the call lead to you sweaty, lightheaded, and working out despite doctor's orders otherwise?" She takes a beat before continuing. "I don't want to discuss how our fiery sheet time could also be construed as against doctor's orders as well because it's too phenomenal to skip."

"Completely agree. Merely hearing her voice made me boil with rage. I needed to let it out. With each punch, I went over the time I spent with her. Unfortunately, I didn't recall anything helpful."

"Despite not wanting to hear anything you considered, what did you eliminate?"

I share my thoughts with Lily. It isn't until I get to Danica being alone in my apartment or office does she interject with questions.

"You don't think ten to fifteen minutes unsupervised is enough time to do something sinister?"

"Not really. I mean... I never saw anything out of place or missing. As you taught me, my bar office is always locked."

"What about your personal office?"

"Unlocked, but again nothing was in my personal office other than schedules and invoices. Neither of those would be helpful if she's involved in the tampering."

"You truly think she isn't involved somehow?"

"Not sure. She definitely lied to me daily. Did she tamper with the gas supply to my building and bear responsibility for Miguel's death? I don't know yet."

She cups my face. Her expression is a combination of concern and love. "Are you still dizzy?"

"No."

"Please sit up slowly."

I comply. She removes the gloves from my hands and casts them aside. We pause there for a few minutes before she guides me to my feet.

"Let's get some food." She attempts to lead me upstairs, but I thwart her efforts.

"I'm sorry for the lost time, Stella."

She shakes her head vehemently. "No, we didn't lose time. We built a solid foundation of trust, loyalty, friendship, and platonic love and learned what we didn't want before adding physical intimacy and romantic love. No more looking back for fault."

She's right, of course. I allow her to lead me upstairs and prepare a midafternoon lunch. While she makes our sandwiches, I fill her in on my call with Scott and the other calls I need to make this afternoon.

"Where are you thinking of hosting the reunion? I was going to suggest Harborside or here. My concern is needing to decrease the guest list for here," I inform her.

"I hadn't thought of the number of guests as a potential issue. Whatever you want is fine. What is Mo's opinion?"

"I'm going to call him this afternoon."

An incoming video call sounds from her office.

Her head tilts to the clock. "Crap! Sorry about the mess."

"Go, I've got this."

She steals a fast kiss and hustles back to her office. I clean the lunch mess, take a shower, and tug on fresh clothes. With my furry shadow, I slip outside onto Lily's master balcony and call Mo.

"Hey, man! How you feelin'?"

I don't plan on sharing my stupidity from earlier today. "I'm pretty good. How are Monique and the girls?"

"Good. Getting big. So are you going to dish the details, or do I have to ask?,"

"Yes, Lily and I are dating although the term is wholly inadequate as a description for how long we've known one another."

"About time, man!"

"No kidding."

"I'm happy for you. You deserve it."

"Thanks, bro!" I share the details for the restoration of the bar and get his thoughts on Harborside.

"Does Harborside have an outdoor area we can use? I agree about not using Lily's house. The guys are great, but there's a lot of us."

"I believe so. Lily knows the banquet manager through Luca. We'll reach out."

"Sounds good. Keep me updated if we need to shift the date."

"Will do. Later." I end the call with a productive feeling. With a deep inhale, I dial Smithson. My call goes straight to voice mail. I leave a message. Hoping to end my calls on a good note, I call Harborside at Morgan's.

"Good afternoon. Thank you for calling Harborside. How may I direct your call?"

"Maggie Washington, please."

The hold music is brief before she answers. "Hi, this is Maggie. How can I help you today?"

"Hi, Maggie. It's Leo De Gaetano. I'm an acquaintance of Luca Cappelli's."

"Hi, Leo. Nice to hear from you." After a brief explanation of what I need, she indicates Harborside has a second location nearby that would meet all my needs for the event. Without another thought, I give her a deposit and set up a meeting for a tasting and venue set up.

Feeling accomplished, I take initiative and schedule my appointment with Dr. Rothstein. Afterward, I stand in front of the refrigerator and note we don't have anything for dinner. I pull out my phone and place a grocery order, complete with ingredients for Lily's favorite summer dishes.

While I wait, Smithson calls. "Hey!"

"Hey, what can I do for you?"

"I may have messed up."

"Meaning?"

"I accidently answered a call from Danica."

Smithson laughs. "How does one accidently answer a call?"

"Very funny. I answered the call intentionally because I thought it was my doctor's office. She was calling from a different number."

"What did she say? What did you say?"

"Nothing of note short of surprise I answered. Considering she tricked me into doing so…. Anyway, once I realized it was her, I told her I didn't have anything to say and ended the call. She immediately recalled. I blocked the number."

"Okay. What was the number?"

I rattle off the number and indicate I won't answer any unknown callers anymore.

"No worries, Leo. I'll add this to our file."

"Any updates?"

"Theories and strong suspicions but nothing concrete yet."

Progress. I can work with progress. "Can you share?"

"Shouldn't, but I will say you don't appear to be her only victim."

Interesting and curious. "Thanks, Smithson. Let me know if you need anything from me. I may be able to keep my cool for a short time in her presence, but not very long."

"I'll keep it in mind."

Victim. I've never considered how I would be labelled in this situation. If anyone should be labelled a victim, it's Miguel. I suppose I am as well. I dig deeper into his words. *You don't appear to be her only victim.* Meaning… she has more aliases, she duped more men, or something worse? Content I can't let my mind fall into the abyss of possibilities, I put the finishing touches on dinner and knock on the doorframe of Lily's office. "Just about done?"

"I finished work about an hour ago. This is for you. Scott sent over the initial invoice. I was weighing the accounts and interest rates to determine how you can pay him and cover some carrying expenses for the bar."

"I appreciate it. Did you receive the payout from the insurance company too?"

"I didn't receive the check, but they provided a proposed settlement amount. We can go over it later."

"Okay. Can you break for dinner?"

"You cooked? We don't have any food."

I love when she says *we*. "We do. I took care of it. I used the local delivery."

"Nice. I'll be right out after these print."

Over dinner we discuss the options to cover future expenses and which accounts she suggests I use first. I've already given Lily carte blanche for my finances, and her advice is sound. "Please pay Scott and then move whatever you need to maintain my contracts."

"No problem. What else is bothering you?"

It took monumental resolve to bury my feelings for Lily all those years ago. Now I'm an open book to her. I share the small glimmer of progress Smithson offered earlier.

"I see why you wouldn't term yourself the victim, but you are despite how hard it is to use the word."

I shrug.

"Let Smithson do his job. You're moving forward with the repairs and maintaining everything else for your livelihood. That's something, no?"

"It is. Containing my anger is harder than I anticipated."

"Hence the overly aggressive, irresponsible boxing session earlier." A statement, not a question. Her concern for my well-being is evident in her pointed words.

"I wasn't thinking clearly. Still not. I keep searching for something, anything, a clue I missed. A frozen moment over the last year plus where she messed up… and I can't think of one, not a single time."

"Assuming Smithson is right and you aren't the first business owner, what is different about you?"

"Maybe it's not me but the result of the damage."

She wrinkles her nose. "I don't understand."

"Her voice mail… she said no one was supposed to get hurt, meaning no one got hurt the other x number of times. Miguel's death is the difference."

"You should share that with Smithson. Maybe it'll help. Then you're going to sit in the jetted tub."

"My head is fine, Stella."

"Please." Her plea is laced with more worry than I would like.

"I will if you join me."

"Relaxing only. No sexy time in the tub."

A frown mars my face. "None tonight?"

"Not necessarily."

"Fine. No sexy time in the tub… tonight. I reserve the right to use your huge soaking tub to contain naked time with Lily in the future."

"I accept your conditions," Lily concedes.

We wash the dishes and take a short evening stroll with Lola. Then, as requested, I soak in her huge tub. I've never allowed myself to imagine what a life with Lily would be like. I mean a relationship, not a friendship. A relationship with Lily exceeds expectations beyond measure.

CHAPTER EIGHTEEN

LILIANNA

A trip to my office in Boston is the last thing I want to do. My professional life is still unresolved. Despite efforts otherwise, I have been unable to schedule a meeting with the new VP. Ideally, I can steal some time while I'm in the city today. The VP transfer from Chicago to Boston was complete over a week ago.

Dressed for the office in a tailored suit and my fancy new shoes from Leo, I slip out of the bedroom. It's crazy early, but my siblings have sent well-wishes overnight and this morning. Luca is the most likely texter this early. Luke is still working on his sleeping skills. Once my coffee is prepared, I leave Leo a note and set up his first cup of the day. It isn't until I get within forty miles of the city does traffic come to a halt

I use the talk-to-text feature in my car to respond to my text messages from my family.

Luca: Good luck today.

Me: Thanks. How's Luke?

Luca: LOL. Wide awake, much like his badass auntie. How's Leo?

Me: He's fine. Figuring out Danica's involvement, not so much.

Luca: Smithson will get it done. There's always Jacob as an option.

Me: Didn't think of that. Worth a call?

Luca: I would if it were me. His guy has more access than Smithson.

Me: I'll talk to Leo tonight. Kiss Luke for me. LY.

Luca: Will do. LY2.

Next up is Lia from the wee hours of the morning.

Lia: How is Leo? How are you and Leo?

Me: Everything okay? You were up late.

No answer, as I suspected. She's probably still sleeping.

Frankie: Hey there!

Me: How's married life?

Frankie: Pretty freakin' awesome! How is newly dating life?

Me: Same, but dating doesn't seem like enough with our history.

Frankie: Makes complete sense. You two have been through a lot.

Me: True.

Frankie: Can you give me a call about Lina's wedding?

Me: I'll call you when I'm on the way home from the city.

Frankie: TTYL.

Lina and Gugliotti are getting married on New Year's Day at the stroke of midnight. The majority of our friends simply believe they're invited to a party, not a wedding. It's perfect for them.

With plenty of time to spare, I pull into a spot in the parking garage and grab another coffee on my way through the lobby. I boot my laptop on my desk and pull my reports for the day. Before they even load, my phone is ringing.

"Good morning, Lily speaking."

"Miss Cappelli, this is Delores. Jerry would like to see you in his office before the quarterly meeting."

"I'll be there in ten minutes. Thank you, Delores."

"You're welcome."

Once the reports finish, I lock my laptop and make my way to toward Jerry's office. I knock on the door and wait for him to reply.

"Come in."

Shock doesn't begin to describe the myriad of emotions flooding my system right now. Clad in a suit with expensive cuff links, Oliver rises from the sofa in Jerry's office.

"What are you doing here?" I ask.

"I work here," Oliver responds.

Surprise takes residence on Jerry's face before he composes himself to speak. "Oliver, how does your fiancée not know about your promotion?"

I'm dumbfounded, but manage, "His what?"

"Promotion," Jerry repeats.

"Oliver, you better start explaining right now."

"Jerry, could you excuse us?" Oliver requests.

Incredulous, I put a hand up to hold Jerry in place. "No, he stays. I want a witness to this conversation. How could you?"

"Corporate intimated I needed a wife to rise up the ladder in the company," Oliver offers quietly.

"Instead of being honest—"

He interrupts, "I made it seem like we never broke up and we're engaged to be married."

"Are you serious right now?" I take his nonanswer as acquiescence to my words. I'm seething right now. "You led the company to believe we've been a long-distance couple for the last four years? How could you do this to me?"

My fists clench and unclench at my sides. "Oh, I understand more clearly now. You need me to sign the waiver. Corporate requires a notice and waiver for each interpersonal relationship between employees to prevent lawsuits for harassment. When we weren't in the same department or the same state, it wasn't a big deal. Lying and betraying me wasn't a big deal. Now with your new promotion, here in the Boston office, you're my boss. Dragging me back here full-time is a power play to make you look legit."

Oliver acknowledges my statement by dropping his head. Jerry is stock-still with wide eyes.

"We aren't a couple anymore and haven't been for a long time. You showed up at my house to protect your promotion instead of sitting in on the call for me to 'meet' you and discuss my remote work arrangement." He pushed me off until after his promotion was official before revealing himself to me as my new boss.

"Yes. No. I miss you. I want you back. I want to rekindle our relationship."

I turn toward the window and take a few moments to gather my composure before adding, "Perhaps my dismissal of you at my home wasn't clear enough. Your lie about our long-distance, long-term relationship is no different than your invitation for me to follow you to Chicago." Stifling my laughter is harder than I anticipate. "You want me to be your arm candy again. No, I will not. I'm madly in love with someone else."

Oliver clenches his jaw while Jerry listens, his mouth agape.

I shift my focus to Jerry. "I will not return to this building to make his promotion stick. Nor will I be a subordinate to him given the circumstances. Please consider this my notice. A formal notice will be provided by the end of the week. I'll utilize my vacation time fully and then resign." I turn toward the door. Before leaving, I address Oliver, "Do not follow me, do not call me, and do not return to my home. A second visit won't be viewed kindly by my—"

"Leo? I thought you weren't interested in him."

I don't dignify his words with a response. With hurried steps, I return to my office and pack up. There aren't many personal items in my corporate office, but I toss them into my tote anyway. Within thirty minutes, as the elevator door closes, the quarterly meeting begins and I'm not sitting at the table.

Half of me is petrified, and the rest is relieved. I make my way to my car and fall into the driver's seat. Inexplicably, I'm not ready to bawl. I'm comfortable and confident with this choice. I shall see how the rest of it plays out before I officially submit my resignation. Before I leave the garage, I send an email to HR indicating I'll be on vacation effective immediately. I mute the notifications for my work email on my phone and make my way to a special place I share with Leo.

It isn't until the moment when I park in front of the bakery in our college town does the memory hit me. Every Sunday morning in the off-season while we were in college, Leo and I would make our way to Anzetti's Italian Bakery. Three generations run the bakery. When we were in college, Lucia and Guido were stepping aside for their children, Lucy and Peter. The final time we were here pulls to the front of my mind.

We were up all night and caught the sunrise at the highest point on campus. He had already been drafted, and we knew our time seeing one another each day was running short.

"Isn't it gorgeous?"

"Yeah. I'm going to miss you." I shared.

"I'm always going to be with you, Stella."

"Not really, Moon."

"We may not be able to see one another every day, but you're my best friend and always will be."

I recall leaning into him, and he held me tighter that morning. Little did I know we both got tattoos and how the years in between then and now would play out. The rush of sweet-smelling confections assails my nose as I step inside and returns me to the present. I scan the case three times before narrowing down my choices.

"How can I help you?"

When I look up, I recognize her. "Hi, Lucy. Nice to see you again."

"You as well, Lily. Where's Leo? You two were attached at the hip."

I smile. "We still are, but we live in Maine now. I'm here for work."

"Please say hello for me and my family. What can I box up for you?"

She boxes my order, and I start the trek home much sooner than I originally planned. Shortly after one, I pull into my garage. Leo is standing with his hands on his hips with a look of concern and confusion on his face.

He greets me with a toe-curling kiss that renders me breathless. "Is everything okay?"

"No, but these will help."

Sheer glee glows on his face when he sees the Anzetti's box. "Why didn't you call me? What happened?"

"I needed time to stew and manage my anger and emotions about the whole situation. The new VP, my new boss, is Oliver."

"Your ex? Wait, what?"

"Yeah."

"I'm going to need more as an explanation." He relieves me of my bag and the box of pastries and guides me inside.

We curl up on the couch with bottled waters and the pastry box.

"What did you order?"

I wink at him. "Our Sunday morning order, plus a few extras."

"You're the best ever!"

A smile grows on my face in response. He opens the box and pulls out pasticciotti and sfogliatella. I take the cannoli and put them in the fridge for later. By the time I return to his side, most of his sfogliatella is gone. I share the happenings of my day and my intention to resign.

"He's slimy, Stella."

"Yeah, I never saw it until he asked me to move with him. Condescending, chauvinistic, and content with keeping the male hierarchy in place, sure. I never considered he would stoop this low to climb the ladder at the firm."

"Are they going to allow Oliver to keep his job?"

"Probably. If he was smarter, he would know it isn't a prerequisite to be married for any position in the company. If anything, the person who led him to believe that would more likely be fired than him."

"Are you sure you want to resign? You love your job, and you're exceptional at it."

"True and thank you. Absolutely. I can't have Oliver as my boss."

"I agree. What are your other options?"

I consider his question. Honestly, I have been mulling my options since the request to come back into the office. "I can open my own brokerage and manage portfolios for private people or small companies. I could also search for another in-house finance manager, remote of course."

"Do you want to go private?"

"Private is where I'm leaning."

"How much time do you have to think about it?"

I chuckle. "I have six-plus weeks of vacation, which I'm using as we speak. However, I could not work for some time and be fine."

"I'm proud of you, Lilianna. Whatever you decide, I'm sure you will crush it."

"Thanks."

"Are you up for a field trip, or do you want to stay here and wallow?" Leo asks.

"Surprisingly, I'm not wallowing. What are you thinking?"

"A trip to the Wiggly Bridge with Lola for some fresh air and a longer walk."

I smile. My big, burly man including my tiny, fluffy fur ball is adorable. "Sure, let me change. Remind me, what time is your appointment tomorrow?"

"Ten at the hospital annex building. Dr. R actually lives closer to here than to Boston."

"Sweet. I'll be out in a few."

After a short ride, we walk the length of the bridge and trail a few times. As expected, Leo is silent as we stroll along the shore and tourist attraction Wiggly Bridge. His arm securely around my waist is not only possessive but a reminder he's here and mine. He knows better than anyone my need to think and overthink every decision. It's a trait that annoys most people but makes me exceptional at my chosen profession.

While outwardly it may seem I've decided on leaving the corporate world, inwardly not so much. Starting next week, I plan to see what other options are available for me in the corporate setting and research the requirements for owning my own brokerage.

CHAPTER NINETEEN

LEONARDO

The first time I met Dr. Rothstein was scary as hell. My first documented concussion was during sophomore year of high school. Gran was adamant I see the best neurologist possible, regardless of the lost wages and travel into the city.

"Ready, Lily?"

She comes out of her closet fully dressed. "Yeah. Nervous again?"

Lily being able to read me shouldn't be a surprise. Gran didn't fight her on tagging along. She has been beside me for every appointment since the first one. Gran knew before I did Lily is the only woman for me.

"Always am."

She steps into my space, rises on her toes, and kisses my concerns away for the moment. "Are you concerned because you're having issues or the mere fact you need to see him again so soon?"

"Mostly the latter."

"If you feel fine, there's no reason to be worried, right?"

My response takes too long for her liking.

Lily hops up on the dressing bench, which makes her slightly taller than me, her hand on her hip and her index finger pointed close to my face. "Leonardo Dominic De Gaetano, spill now!" she demands. Her tone and posture are sexy as hell and shouldn't cross my mind right now but monopolize my attention anyway. "Leo, have you been hiding post-concussive symptoms from me?"

"No."

"Moon." The endearment falling from her lips sounds hurt and distraught at the same time.

"Maybe."

Instead of demanding more, she throws her arms around me and pulls me closer. Fear and tension roll off her frame in waves. "What? Headaches? Dizziness? Memory loss?"

I inhale her—her scent, her comfort, her concern, and most importantly her love. "My eyesight isn't the same. Not sure it's worse, but focusing for too long is harder."

She pulls back to add some space between us so she can look down at me. "Why didn't you tell me?"

"You have done some much. With the issues at your job and working to help me, I didn't want to add more."

"No, none of those things matter. True, my professional life is currently in turmoil, mostly by choice. The rest isn't a burden. It's what you would do for me if I needed you too."

Damn! She's completely right.

"Is it only your vision?"

I rest my head against her shoulder and reply, "Yes."

"Let's share with Dr. R and see what we do next."

I hold her closer. "I couldn't do this without you."

She exhales and smiles. I feel the muscles of her shoulders lift. "Good thing you're stuck with me then."

"Not stuck. Never stuck. Choosing to be still and beside you isn't stuck. It's deeply rooted love. I love you."

"I love you."

The ride to see Dr. R isn't long, but it's tense. Our hands remain linked the entire ride and as we walk to his office. The receptionist shows us right into the exam room.

He joins us almost immediately thereafter. "Hello, Leo. Hi, Lily. How are you doing?"

I share my concerns, and he completes his exam. He makes a few notes and checks something on the computer before sharing. "Good news, the area of your brain from this injury appears to be healing well. Not so good news, the new injury has hurried the deterioration of your occipital lobe a minor amount."

"Meaning he needs to start the vision therapy sooner than we discussed when we were here a few months ago?" Lily asks.

Was that only a few months ago?

"Correct. I recommend an eye examination with a specialist, and then she can determine whether you need new glasses, vision therapy, or both."

"That's all?" Relief floods my body. Getting my vision checked twice a year has been a fixture since my second concussive injury.

"That's all. You were worried?" Dr. R looks back to me.

"Yes."

"Given your history, you're where you should be or perhaps a smidge early. Nothing to be overly concerned about." He instructs me to schedule with the specialist and maintain my follow-up with him in two months.

I stand and extend my hand to him. "Thank you." We leave the exam room and stop at reception to get the specialist's contact information. It's then I notice a voice mail from an unknown number and one from Smithson.

"You okay? The visit wasn't terrible."

"Yeah, it isn't that. I'm okay with Dr. R's recommendations. I have a voice mail from an unknown number and Smithson. Worried, I suppose."

"Play it. We can handle anything together."

I prepare myself to hear her voice again and input my password. The sound of her voice grates on my nerves now. Lily threads her fingers through mine.

"Hey, baby. I miss you so much. Why won't you at least hear me out? This wasn't my fault. I only did what he asked. Just like the last…. I need to talk to you. I need to make this right. Please call me back at this number."

I mull her words and get stuck on "what he asked."

"Breathe, Moon. You have every right to feel how you do, but she isn't here right now, and Smithson is on it."

"Still pisses me off. My friend is dead, and she's nowhere to be found."

She lifts her free hand to my face and turns my gaze toward her instead of my phone. "I know it's hard. Maybe Smithson has an update. Listen to his message."

Smithson's voice fills the air between us. "Leo, give me a call. I want to set up a time to meet with you to discuss the case. Thanks."

"See. Call him back. We're free for the rest of the day." Lily bolsters my confidence in the process a bit.

Truthfully, it hasn't been long. The torture of not knowing where Danica is and the fact she isn't being held responsible for Miguel's death is hard to fathom. The damage to my building is one thing, but Miguel losing his life because… I don't even know her motivation.

"Stop blaming yourself."

"I'm not… exactly." I scrub my hand down my face. "I'm wondering why. Why me? Why my bar? Why Miguel? He did everything right with his second chance, and yet it wasn't enough."

"Your feelings are legitimate and understandable. Miguel's death isn't your fault"

"Yes, it is. I hired him and dated Danica."

"Frankly, we don't know whose fault it is. Mostly, it's her fault, or at least we believe it's her fault."

I heed Lily and call Smithson.

"Hey, Leo. Any chance we could meet today?"

I scrub my free hand down my face. "Yeah. Where would you like to meet?"

"I can stop by Lily's near the end of shift if that works. I'll be in the neighborhood this evening."

"Sure, we'll be there." I wonder why Smithson will be nearby but don't ask. I share with Lily.

"Okay. What should we do now?" she asks.

"Let's go to Harborside for lunch to see the outdoor space for the reunion," I suggest.

"Sounds good." Lily walks to the passenger side of her car and hands me the keys. "You drive. It isn't far from here."

I open her door, steal a tender kiss, and walk around the hood. I'm not nervous about the mechanics of driving, only my vision, but Dr. R didn't say I couldn't drive.

"You can always pull over if you need to," Lily reminds me.

With my nervousness sufficiently tucked away, I pull out of the parking spot and ease into traffic. I successfully park at Harborside, and we tour the exterior party area before a nice, late lunch on the patio.

Near the end of our meal, Maggie Washington stops at our table. "My staff indicated you were here." Maggie is married to one of Luca's former YPD coworkers.

"Hi, Maggie. Nice to see you again," Lily greets her.

"Hi, Lily. Leo. You as well. Is the patio area large enough for the reunion?" she inquires.

"Yes, it's larger than we need, and the view is spectacular." Harborside rises to its name. The building is along the lower edge of the harbor with a stunning view off to one side and a marina to the other.

"Great. The menu is set per your request."

"Thank you, Maggie. I appreciate your assistance with this. The guys and I look forward to getting together each year. Now it's only six weeks away."

"You're welcome. Hopefully you'll be up and running again soon. My husband's whiskey cabinet is looking barren."

I chuckle quietly. "I understand. Email me what his poison is, and I'll check the barrel room the next time I access the building."

"Sounds good. Have a lovely afternoon."

Lily replies, "You as well, Maggie."

We pay our bill and make our way back to Lily's. Soon after we arrive, Smithson does as well.

Lily greets him at the door with a hug and leads him into the kitchen.

"Hey, Leo. Thanks for agreeing to meet here."

"No problem. Why are you in the area, if you don't mind sharing?"

Smithson waves his hand. "Scarlett is caring for Emme and Bennett while Sam and Savannah are on a business trip."

Lily fills in the rest. "Sam and Savannah live a few streets over."

I nod. "Makes sense. How can I help you?"

"I don't want to say I have a break in your case, but I have uncovered a pattern and filled in some of the pieces."

"Okay." My voice cracks, and I take a seat.

"Danica Ryder neé Shelby Woods has three more aliases, including Molly Johnson, Emily Middleton, and Olivia Jones. There are three cases similar to yours that we can trace back to Danica. Each time she dates a business owner, something happens to the business. As Molly, she dated the owner of a pub in Maryland, and it flooded. Foul play was found as the water supply to the business was tampered with, but the authorities were never able to pin it on anyone specific. The building was gutted and needed major repair. Molly was with the owner for just under six months. Posing as Emily, Danica was engaged to a restaurant owner with three properties. Within four months of dating, the original location in Philly was destroyed by fire. Arson was suspected, but they never found the perpetrator."

As he speaks, my foot bounces on the lower rung of the stool, and I zone out as he continues sharing about the third alias. It isn't until Lily sets her hand on my thigh do I realize I'm doing it. The heat of her hand on me draws me to the conversation rather than the spiraling thoughts in my mind.

Refocusing on Smithson's words, I hear, "With you it appears she played a long game. If I recall, you were dating for more than a year, correct?"

I grit my teeth and reply, "Yes." Not interested in walking down his reasoning, I ask, "What's the connection?"

"Each company used Midland Construction to repair the damage."

Barely above a whisper, Lily observes, "She's creating work for her company by sabotaging these businesses."

"Yes. However, there's no way she could pull it off alone. Two of her voice mails to Leo indicate as much. Those are the pieces I'm still working on. Who else was involved, when, and how much did they pull the strings?"

"Are there any connections or similarities between the owners?" Lily asks.

Smithson lifts an eyebrow.

"What?" I ask him.

"I was initially surprised, but then I recall you're Luca's sister. Your question is on point and worth digging deeper into. We haven't found any connections but are still working on similarities."

"What can we do to help?" Lily asks.

Smithson answers, "Right now, exactly what you are doing. Ignoring her calls and sending the voice mails and phone numbers to me."

"Please don't take this personally. I realize it hasn't been long at all, but the fact my friend is gone weighs on me daily. He's dead because I gave him a second chance. I'm not because I had a wedding to attend. Is there anything we can do to speed this up?"

Lily shudders beside me, and not the kind of pleasure-filled shudder I coax from her willing curves.

"I understand your frustration, Leo. Whether due to roadblocks or lack of leads, these other three cases are unsolved. They are connected with yours through Danica. I assure you, I won't give up until Miguel's family has some kind of closure and peace. You as well. Will it be jail time for Danica? It isn't for me to decide. I'll compile an accurate and evidence-based case to hold her responsible for her actions and anyone else who assisted or coerced her."

Anger boils in my veins. "No, she clearly knew what she was doing. She shouldn't get a pass because she's a lower person on the food chain." The woman took advantage of me, attempted to at least, and I need to know why.

"While I agree with you on a larger level, it's not how our system works. You know that."

"I suppose so, but I don't like it at all," I grumble at him.

"I know. If I need to enlist outside help, I'll loop in Captain Ramirez. He has connections in other departments, but also some gray ones if I need them. Right now, I'm staying firmly in the black."

Lily hasn't asked another question or moved the slightest bit since I mentioned the wedding or fact I could be dead instead of Miguel.

"Thank you for the update. Whatever you need, just ask." I extend my hand to Smithson.

"Thanks, Leo. Bye, Lily." Smithson shows himself out. Aside from the occasional family dinner when he would show up with Luca, I don't know him well. However, his observation skills are finely honed.

I take Lily's hands in mine, lead her to the couch, and sit beside her with one knee bent between us so I'm facing her. "What do you need right now?" Lily isn't generally hard to read. I know why she's upset, just not how she wants to deal with it. I'm not sure if she wants to beat the hell out of the heavy bag downstairs or bawl her eyes out. Frankly, I was wondering when she would lose the tight grip she has on her emotional control. It's been more than a month since my unplanned hospital rest.

Her eyes lift from our hands to mine as she climbs into my arms and buries her head into the crook of my neck. Hot, wet tears streak down my skin to the collar of my shirt. Body-shaking sobs overtake Lily. I tighten my hold on her and draw one hand down her back and return to the top. The pain of hearing Lily cry, knowing it's my fault but not truly my fault, is a gut punch. A hurting Lily shreds me. Untold minutes pass, her heaves lessen, and she lifts her head. "I'm sorry."

I drag the pad of my thumb over the balls of her cheeks. "Nothing for you to be sorry for. You are the strongest person I know. I knew you would crumble at some point. I just didn't know when. I'm not going anywhere anytime soon, Lilianna." *Ever, if I have anything to say about it.*

"I was so scared, Leo, and you weren't even mine."

Hers. "I know. I would've been in your position as well. Hell, it wouldn't have taken this long for me to lose control of my emotions."

Her shoulder lifts toward her ear. "Dr. Rothstein eased my concerns this morning, despite the vision specialist recommendation. This injury was the first time I genuinely thought I might lose you, by you not waking up or you not being you when you did. I'm not talking about us as a couple. I mean you. I was willing to be on the sidelines of your life if you were truly happy. Following Dr. R's advice was the second hardest thing I've ever done."

I probably could surmise the answer, but I ask anyway. "What was the first?"

"Choosing me. Driving away from our bench when I knew you were coming to talk."

"I understand why you didn't stay then. Please don't shut me out ever again."

Lily presses her lips to my cheek. "I won't."

"Pinkie promise?" I offer my hooked pinkie between us.

She closes hers around mine. "Pinkie promise."

I drop a kiss atop our intertwined fingers. "What do you say to an old-school evening?"

Intrigued, she bites her lower lip.

"Do you have any idea how sexy that is?"

She shrugs, but the sparkle in her eyes tells me she knows exactly what the move does to me. The kicker is she does it unconsciously. Hell, she can probably feel me hardening beneath her. "What are you suggesting? How old-school?"

"If you gather the blankets, I'll get the pillows."

"We haven't built a fort in—"

"No, let's do it." I kiss her hard and smack her booty after I set her on her feet.

With a sweet yelp and a look of "I can't believe you just did that," she walks down the hall.

Within ten minutes, we reconvene in the living room with more fort-building supplies than we could possibly need. I drape the blanket over the back of her couch and attach it to the top of the stools from the island. Lily creates a row of pillows on the carpet; then she pushes the chair from the other side of the room closer to anchor the other side. We work silently. The next time I look up, Lily is gone.

Confused, I pause and wait. When she returns, her arms are full of crayons and coloring books, and she's also pulled her hair up into a ponytail.

Her long hair tied in a long ponytail makes heat course through me. It was the first part of her I ever touched. The strands felt like silk in third grade. They still do. "You still have coloring books?"

"Of course, for Em."

I grin at her. "Right, for Em. If I open a random page, it won't have an LC in the bottom right corner of most of the pages then?"

She scrunches her face. "Maybe."

I lift open the door and follow her inside. We curl up and color a few pages before Lily says, "This was a great idea."

"Anything to make you smile."

"When is the last time we built a fort?"

I exhale slowly. I know exactly the last two times I built a fort. "You and me or me?"

"The last time you built a fort was at Lina's with Em and Antonio after Derrick's short release."

"Yes, and you ran out of there faster than I could blink. Did you already share with your sisters by then?"

"Yeah, but that isn't why I ran out.... I was torn. Seeing you teach them brought up the last time we built a fort, and I couldn't squash my feelings very well."

"Please explain," I urge.

"Do you remember the last time we built a fort together?"

I think back and fail. "No, I can't pinpoint the exact time or age."

"Okay, the last two were the day Gran died and the day before the draft. After everyone left the house, I was searching for you. I found you in your childhood bedroom with armfuls of supplies. We built a fort and fell asleep, effectively postponing dealing with Gran's death for a bit longer. The night before the draft was similar as far as the situation."

The fort is our little private space, just her and I. "We were dealing with change, fighting to keep us together with the upcoming change," I observe.

"Exactly."

"What's changing now?"

"Everything," she whispers.

CHAPTER TWENTY

LILIANNA

Building a fort with Leo has been our thing as long as I can recall. It's our own private space we create to shut out the outside world.

"What's changing now?"

"Everything."

He opens his arms to me and pulls me across his lap.

I feel safe in Leo's arms, always have. The world could crumble, and he would protect me at his own expense. The reverse is true as well, at least the protective aspect at my expense. "Every time before, I was afraid to lose you or, at least, our relationship would change for the worse. I'm not afraid to lose you this time. Are you?"

"No. Things may be unsettled outside of our cozy, cotton sanctuary, but as long as we're facing an obstacle together, everything will turn out fine."

A stray thought flashes in my mind, but I push it away, or try to at least.

"You need to share the naughty idea in your head."

Feigning innocence, I lie, "I have no idea what you're referring to."

"Uh-huh. I know you better than you know you. What did you realize, Lily?"

"This is the first time we've built a fort as a couple."

He tilts his head in question, pushing me to keep talking. Instead of talking, I twist, straddle his lap, and work his shirt over his head.

"I love your thinking, Stella."

With haste, we cast our clothes aside until we're both naked in our living room fort. With painstaking precision, we alternate kissing one another. I press a kiss to the hinge of his jaw and then the crook of his neck.

Leo grabs my ponytail and tugs hard, but not enough to cause pain, baring my neck to his mouth. The heat sears my skin for the rest of my life.

Stifling the moan is impossible.

"You like that, huh?"

I exhale. "Didn't know until right now." Secretly, I love that he's the only man who ever learned this preference and the only one who ever will. Each traded touch and kiss ratchets my desire exponentially higher until I can't take anymore. "Leo, I need you filling me now."

"Thank God! I'm losing my mind with every flawless inch of you on display, poised to be caressed and kissed."

I giggle. Shifting back a bit, I drag the head of his length through my arousal before taking him deep in one thrust.

"Damn! Still snug around me."

"You feel perfect." I rock forward and lift before slamming back down over him.

Leo curls his arms under mine and grips my shoulder from behind as his thrusts meet mine with a steady rhythm. The coil of pleasure tightens in my low belly and threatens to break. I clench my inner muscles to stave off my climax.

"Again, Lily," Leo demands.

I comply, and he groans. Once more I squeeze him inside me. Leo latches onto my nipple and bites down. "Again, Moon."

He bites down with slightly less force this time.

The contrast of pleasure and pain careens me over the edge of bliss. A few more hard, downward slides, and Leo bursts inside me, his head falling back onto the couch cushions.

Encircling his neck with my arms, I settle against his rising and falling chest with my head on his shoulder. "Will we keep getting better at that?"

I feel him smile against the top of my head. "I certainly hope so, although if it doesn't, we exceed my expectations as is."

"Agreed, but…." My response is muffled against his neck.

"But?"

I drag my tongue up to his earlobe. "We should do it again to make sure."

"We will, but I need some more time, gorgeous. Then I'm going to lay you out atop our pillow flooring and ravage each inch of your soft skin until you scream my name repeatedly."

"Oh my… hell yes!"

Nearly twenty minutes later, Leo lowers me to the floor and begins his quest at the top of my foot. Each flick of his tongue draws me to the edge of distinct and palpable pleasure—a degree that no man has ever met before. The sheer fact he has been my best friend my entire life matters. The level of trust runs much deeper than with anyone else. Sex with your best friend is mind-blowing. He spreads me wide and drags his tongue from bottom to top. Intense, unfiltered nirvana beckons me. Leo's tongue should be labelled as a weapon. The delicious pleasure he can coax from my willing body is unparalleled. Each flick, matched with the curl of his fingers, overwhelms me. At least I thought it did, until he soaks a third finger in my wetness and calls my name.

"Lily?"

Preparing myself to add more to our already pulse-pounding sheet time is heady. I lift my head, catch his green eyes with mine, and consent.

He swirls his fingers in my arousal, and with his eyes trained on mine, he pushes one thick finger into my ass.

The width doesn't hurt, but his fingers are more than mine. Once he's confident I'm comfortable, Leo's mouth reseals over me and works in tandem with his finger to bring me to another body-shattering climax. Once my body calms, I push up to my elbows. His strong jaw features a cocky, smoldering grin.

"Yes, your tongue exceeds the one before."

"One?" he questions.

"Yes, one."

"Part of me feels the need to teach your exes a few lessons, but the other animalistic, carnal, possessive part that is rooted in a future for us is enthralled at your revelation."

I tuck my lower lip between my teeth.

"Lilianna." My name sounds like a warning. What is he going to do? Go for another round, yes, please. But not yet.

"Now, lie down. It's my turn."

He shakes his head. "Not now. I need you pulsing around me as soon as humanly possible."

He secures my wrists over my head with one of his hands. I widen my thighs more as he settles between them more fully and pushes forward in slow, measured increments. The potent, raw passion of him burrowed deeply inside me will never wane. In fact, it gets stronger each time. The surge of another orgasm spreads over my body. Each time we're together, I feel untethered in my response but more deeply tethered to him, and I wouldn't want it any other way.

With our breathing even and measured, I turn us onto our sides and snuggle into Leo's chest. Safely cocooned against him is the only place I want to be anymore. Here everything is fine and nothing outside us matters. I suppose what he said was true. We can handle anything together.

Leo's stomach growls louder than I've heard in a long time.

I giggle. "Takeout or cereal for dinner?"

"Cereal for the win, assuming you still have my favorite."

"What kind of best friend and girlfriend would I be if I didn't have your favorite cereal in my pantry?" Leo's favorite non-sugary cereal is Honey Nut Cheerios. His sugary cereal of choice is Lucky Charms.

"Not mine?" he offers.

"Good answer. I would never fail to have at least one unopened box."

"Even when I wasn't stopping by?" Leo mumbles.

"Especially then."

We dress and crawl out of our fort of naked fun. I grab the bowls and spoons while Leo rummages in the pantry.

He sets his hands on the edge of the tall cabinet. "Lily, you don't have my favorite cereal in here," he accuses.

"Yes, I do." I duck under his arm and wiggle my way between him and the shelving. I hinge at my hips and push him back a little. Ignoring his hardening length is difficult. You would think I would be satisfied. I am, more than I have ever been. Yet I would still go for another round or two despite the soreness it'll cause in the morning. I lean down more and pull out a box of Cheerios.

"Fine, but that isn't my all-time favorite."

"Untrue. You have two, and I have both." I reach in again and pull out the Lucky Charms. "No one knows you as well as I do."

He tilts his head in my direction. "I guess you truly are mine."

"I always was. We just weren't ready to be on the same page."

After dinner, we clean up our fort and turn in for the evening.

Over five weeks has passed since I gave my notice at work. I'm ensconced in my office, researching and clearing my responsibilities. I take a break and gawk at the view from my office window. It isn't as spectacular as the master balcony, but it suits fine during the workday. My exit memo is nearly complete. I would hope so, it's due in a week. My search for a new corporate position isn't yielding acceptable results. Either the position is woefully undercompensated or located clear across the country. I would consider working in an office, but not one three thousand miles away from my home and family. Not only did I search for a new corporate position, but I researched the necessary steps to open my own firm. Building a client base will take some time, but I would be my own boss, create my own hours, and be fully in control of the culture of work should I need staff at some point.

While I've made progress, Smithson hasn't yielded any significant results in locating Danica/Molly/whatever her name is, other than determining she was working with at least one of her coworkers at Midland named Kyle Oaken. He's her supervisor and creates the orders and handles paperwork with the municipalities for the clients she duped. Smithson indicated he has clients above and below board, which means he has legally obtained clients as well as illegally obtained clients.

Danica is involved with each of the illegally obtained clients. Either she's not bright or has some other motivation to dupe unsuspecting men when their businesses suffer losses aside from money. It's the only possible reason to act how she did with these men and Leo.

A notification pulls me out of my thoughts.

Frankie: How is it going?

Me: It's going. Work is almost done. Leo is making progress.

Frankie: Did you find a new job?

Me: No, I'm leaning toward my own firm.

Frankie: From one boss babe to another, woo-hoo!

Me: LOL.

Frankie: Let me know if you need any guidance.

Me: Such as?

Frankie: Attorney? Contacts with the tax office.

Me: Thanks. I'll share with the family on Sunday.

Frankie: No worries.

Me: How's married life?

Frankie: Phenomenal. I didn't think the sex would get better, but…

Me: Ooookkkkayyy! On that note.

Frankie: Nothing to share?

Me: Nope, nothing to share.

Frankie: Come on, Lily!

Me: Nope. What happens between my luxury sheets or on my island is between Leo and me.

Frankie: The island sex is always hot.

Me: Frankie! Done with this topic for now. LY.

Frankie: LY2.

My ringing phone pulls me out of my thoughts. "Hello."

"Good afternoon, Lily. This is Jerry."

"Good afternoon. To what do I owe the pleasure of your call, Jerry?"

He clears his throat. "I wanted to update you on the changes here at the office since you took your vacation."

"No, Jerry. I resigned."

"Semantics. Oliver is serving an administrative leave pending an investigation into his behavior and the impact it had on you and whether his misconstruction of the facts assisted in him gaining the promotion to the Boston office."

Semantics? "I appreciate your attempt to protect the company, Jerry."

He huffs. "Lily, the board would like to speak with you about returning to your position. With Oliver on—"

"Nope, I refuse to clean up his mess. Not only did he toy with my life for four years, leading the company to believe we were in fact engaged to be married, but he played the board and each of his supervisors repeatedly to garner a promotion using my reputation to do it." *Unknowingly on my part, but still.*

"All they want is a sit down with you to discuss options. You won't find another commensurate position in this market."

"Jerry, that actually sounds like legitimate concern for me instead of the company. I'm flattered."

"So you'll consider taking a meeting with the board?" Jerry presses.

"No, I won't. My exit memo will be forwarded to you no later than noon on the last day of my commitment to this company. Good luck, Jerry. You're going to need it."

Jerry begs again, "Lily, please reconsider."

"No. It dawned on me amid this debacle, I'm the best portfolio manager the company has. Not once in four years did someone consider speaking to me about the lies and misinformation Oliver was sharing in Chicago. No one wondered why I never visited my alleged fiancé? No one wondered why Oliver never hopped an early Friday flight to visit me? Not once was I actually considered for a higher position, despite applying three times. Now I understand the true reason behind it. Corporate didn't want so much control consolidated in one couple. An investigation into Oliver and how best to prevent the company from being duped again is fine, but it isn't enough for me to regain my confidence in the company with regards to its staff. It has been a pleasure, Jerry. Give my best to Lauren and the twins."

I end the call and receive a round of applause from Leo. He turns my chair and hauls me into his arms. "I'm insanely proud of you, Lily. Not only for standing up for yourself, but you pointed out the problems to him and refused to capitulate."

"Thank you. I can't go back to the company who doesn't value my expertise or feel the necessity to vet applicants for supervisory positions more thoroughly."

"When do you open the doors for your own firm?"

I smile up at him. "I need to work out a few more regulatory things and transfer my licenses. Soon though."

"Good. How much more time do you need in here?"

"Why?" I ask, my question laced with intrigue.

"I need to finalize a few things for the reunion next week in person."

"I thought the menu was set?"

Leo nods. "It is. I need to finalize the desserts with Kelsey at the Perk and pick up an auction item from Marco."

"Nice, Marco donated again this year?"

"He always does because we shared a stadium, and his team supports the same charity we're supporting with this reunion."

"Sure, give me ten minutes."

Leo kisses me breathless before slipping out of my office. I was dreading the final call from Jerry. Seeing my professional life with my almost old company boxed up and ready to be shipped off is surprisingly more cathartic than I originally thought.

CHAPTER TWENTY-ONE

LEONARDO

While I hoped to put off meeting the vision specialist a bit longer, here we are. Dr. Sarah Alves is the preeminent doctor in her field. She has worked with numerous patients of Dr. R's, and I'm grateful she could fit me in quickly.

One of her associates performed a battery of tests on my vision, rated my focus, and mapped my eyes with a specialized tool. Generally, my nerves don't get the best of me. For this, I'm anxious, and Lily is keenly watching me.

"The solution could be simple, Moon. Once she evaluates you, we'll progress from there." She nods once tightly. "Okay?"

"Yeah." I link our fingers and wait for Dr. Alves to join us.

"Hello, Leo. Pleasure to meet you. I've looked over your file from Dr. Rothstein and your exam from this morning. I assure you, your vision issues can be managed if not cured. You have accommodation issues, which means your ability to see an object clearly and your ability to shift focus between objects at different distances is misfiring."

I exhale sharply, and Lily squeezes my hand.

"The combination of your old concussions and the most recent injury has hastened our meeting." Dr. Alves goes over a few exercises for me to complete daily as well as an updated prescription for stronger glasses.

"Please make a follow-up appointment for two months. With these exercises, you'll be better able to focus in no time."

"Thank you." I extend my hand to her, and she takes it.

"You're welcome. Have a nice day."

We make our way into the lobby. I select a new frame, order new glasses with expedited service, and make my next appointment.

It isn't until we're in the car that Lily says anything. "Her recommendations weren't terrible."

"No, not at all. Dr. R referred us to her, so I'm confident in her skills."

"Same. Ready to check out Scott's skills?"

"Hell yes!" I reverse out of the parking spot and make my way to Endzone. I try not to focus on the time passing from Miguel's death to now. Truthfully, I've been dragging Lily to Endzone almost daily after the crew finishes for the day. I trust Scott completely, but I'm restless. I feel as if I owe it to Miguel to get back up and running as soon as possible.

On the way to the bar, my phone rings. "Hey, Smithson."

"Afternoon, Leo. I wanted to reach out. I don't have anything new, and it's frustrating. I wanted permission to speak with Jacob Blackthorne. We have worked with his firm before. He has a consultant who can access deeper information than I can."

I can read between the lines. He needs to get into the gray to find Danica. "I understand. Whatever you need to do to find her, do it. Please have Mr. Blackthorne send me an invoice."

"Will do. I'll call when I have an update."

I end the call and drive toward the bar.

"Smithson needs Jacob's assistance," Lily states.

"Yeah. Anything I can do for progress, I will."

She squeezes my hand and replies, "I know."

I park in my spot and gawk at Scott's progress. The exterior of the building is framed, and at least half of the masonry work is complete.

"Wow. Scott and his crew are exceptional," Lily states.

"No kidding."

Scott joins us on the south side of the building. "Hey, guys!"

"Your progress is incredible, Scott!"

A proud smile graces his face. "Thanks. This crew works well together. Want to check it out from inside?"

Subduing my gleeful response is harder than I anticipate.

"I'll say it for him, yes, please!"

Scott laughs and leads us inside. "The exterior is complete except for the masonry. Saul should be done tomorrow by end of day at the latest. We restored the second-floor beams and put down the subfloor. Once Eddie finishes running the electrical, I'll have the inspector come out to check both parts."

I'm speechless. The same feeling came over me when I first refurbished this building. It certainly took much longer the last time.

Scott continues, "I need you to select countertops and appliances for the apartment kitchen and tile for the bathroom. There are a few outstanding invoices for materials. I copied you, but if you could follow up with the insurance company."

"Uh-huh."

"I'll make sure he does it in the next few days," Lily informs Scott.

"I get a kick out of you two every single time I see you together. I would be ecstatic to find a woman who gets me like you two get one another."

"Thanks, Scott. You'll find her when you least expect it."

I notice Lily's smile as I pull myself completely back into the conversation. "Your crew is on point. Does their progress impact your estimated timeline for completion?" Scott estimated it would take about ten weeks or so to complete the project. Either way, we're hosting the reunion at Harborside. It would be nice to have Mo and Monique over to the bar before they head back home with the girls.

"They're right where I thought they would be. The building inspector impacts the timeline the most."

"Understood. I appreciate your hard work."

"You're welcome, Leo. It's our pleasure."

"Any reason I can't move a few things around in the barrel room before I leave?"

"Not as far as I'm concerned." Scott glances at his watch. "You have a solid hour before we're done for the day."

"Thanks, man."

"Don't mention it." Scott walks out through the side door.

Excitement is bubbling in my veins. Soon this chapter will look like a mere blip in my story.

"How can I help?" Lily asks.

"I want to check on the whiskey and see if it's ready to be bottled."

"Okay. I thought longer was better." She follows me into the barrel room.

I draw samples from the eight barrels, which are technically overdue. "There's some truth to that. However, given the orders I needed to fulfill, these batches should be done."

"Got it."

I test the samples and determine half need to stay a little longer and the rest are ready to be bottled. "I'll be right back. I'm going to see when Scott and his crew will arrive tomorrow so I can bottle this."

"Okay," Lily replies.

I catch up with Scott and confirm he will be working tomorrow and inform him I need to bottle four barrels. He agrees it'll be fine, and I return to Lily.

She's sitting on one of the benches in the barrel room staring off into space.

"Stella?"

Lily turns her gaze in my direction. A smile grows on her face. "Yeah."

"Everything okay?"

"Can you do something for me?"

I tilt my head in question. "Anything, you know that."

"Drink this." She extends a glass in my direction.

Why would Lily suggest I drink more? Then I recall her words to Lina. *I want to taste the whiskey on his tongue.* Eliminating the space between us, I draw her flush to me. "I lack restraint when it comes to you. I don't want to hurry in any way. Can we postpone your request until we get home? It'll be worth the short wait, I promise."

Lily smiles, releases me, and selects a bottle from the undamaged inventory. "Time to go home. I have a whiskey tasting to attend." She drags her free hand up my thigh, grazing my restrained, hardening length.

"Stella!"

"What? You didn't say I couldn't tease you the entire way."

Damn, that's hot!

With a quick wave, we hurry out of the bar to her car. In this moment it dawns on me, I haven't used my truck since the morning of the…. *Is her box still in my truck?* I reel in my brief panic. Lily will notice, and I'm not ready to share my plans for the box with her yet. But I need to discretely verify it's still on the floor in the passenger seat footwell.

The ride home passes expeditiously. Within minutes of Lola retreating to her doggie bed, Lily has stripped down to her luxury bra and panties. I shake my head, lift two tumblers with my hand, and grab the neck of the LD Star whiskey and join her in our bedroom. Only two sips of whiskey on my tongue is all it takes before I'm naked and climbing over Lily.

CHAPTER TWENTY-TWO

LILIANNA

"Leo, we're going to be late. You know how Mama gets if we're late for dinner."

He rounds the corner, shaking his head. "It isn't my fault you decided to have a replay of your whiskey tasting two nights in a row."

My cheeks heat up, even though it's only Leo here. Images of the last two nights crash through my mind. Before we were together, creativity was not an aspect of my sex life. "Was that a complaint? I didn't hear any complaints when I was licking maple-flavored whiskey off your—"

"Not a complaint, Stella. I will never complain when you want to be frisky and creative with me. I'm ready to leave and have been for the last fifteen minutes. You, however, are fussing with your clothes for dinner with your family. Why?"

"Not sure. It's another normal family dinner."

He hauls me into his embrace and kisses the top of my head. "Nothing to worry about at all. They're family. Will there be fights about the wedding? Probably. Lina will follow the prescribed maid of honor plan. She won't choose one."

How he gets right to the core of my worries is heartwarming and scary as hell. "Thanks."

"Always." Leo hurries me to my parents', and he's happily surprised we aren't the last to arrive.

Ellie rushes out the front door first. "Hey." She hugs both of us before asking, "How are you feeling, Uncle Leo?"

I love that she calls him "uncle" already. Ellie has been an amazing addition to our family. Even better, Tess comes to family dinner now too.

"Much better."

"The new glasses are fire!" Ellie gushes.

"Thanks, Ellie." She smiles and attempts to ask something else but pauses. "What's up, Ellie?"

"Can I ask about how the construction and investigation is going, or is that a difficult topic for you?" Ellie asks, her voice soft and barely audible. She's astute for a fourteen-year-old.

"Construction is moving along as expected. The investigation is moving, but slower than I would prefer," Leo informs her.

"Wow. Cool, I didn't think you would answer me." She hugs him again and dashes back inside.

"Very diplomatic answer, Leo."

"I told her the truth without details, and it was enough for her."

"I'm saying, well-handled."

He tucks me into his side, and we step over the threshold of my parents' house. Within moments, Leo steals Luke from Willa.

"Good to see you guys. How are you doing, Leo?" Willa asks.

"I'm great. What about you? You look amazing!"

"Thanks. I could use a bit more sleep but overall feeling well." Willa glances at me and smiles.

I return her smile with my own and silently answer all her burning questions. Yes, Leo looks sexy as hell with Luke tucked in the crook of his beefy arms. Yes, I can't wait for it to be our baby. Yes, we talked, and we'll get there eventually.

We laugh and leave Leo with the guys. I make my way into the kitchen. "Hi, Mama."

"How is Leo?"

I drop my head. I'm taking it as a vote of confidence. She's more worried about him than me growing a business in private portfolio management. I greatly appreciate it. "He's making progress and will be fine."

"I worry about him," Mama adds.

Same.

Leo's voice precedes him into the kitchen. "No need to worry about me, Mama. Lily won't let me quit on my exercises or fixing the bar."

"I never doubted her for a moment. Could you take these to the dining room?" Mama instructs me.

"Sure, Mama." I set the rolls on the table as the front door swings open and Emilia and Antonio bust in with their dogs closely behind. We never had pets as kids, but only one of us doesn't have pets yet... Frankie.

After welcoming the kids and their parents, we sit down to eat, and the wedding discussions begin.

"Have you finalized everything yet?" Willa asks while passing the pasta bowl. Luke is passed out in his bouncy chair on the floor between her and Luca.

"Sort of. We're pushing the wedding up," Lina replies while glancing at Gugliotti at the same time.

"To when?" Frankie asks.

Gugliotti replies, "The third Saturday in September."

"In five weeks?" Luca questions.

"Yes," Lina answers.

"Are you pregnant?" Frankie asks.

Lina giggles, "No, not yet."

Sweet, another niece or nephew.

"Did you change your mind about the type of wedding you want, Lina?" Mama asks.

"Yes. I don't want anything big. I've learned it isn't about the party but the marriage. We're opting for a small and elegant ceremony in our backyard with everyone here plus a few of Santino's coworkers," Lina replies.

"Wonderful. A toast to the soon-to-be newlyweds," Papa adds. Everyone raises their glasses and takes a sip.

Then the real discussion begins, which turns out not to be a discussion at all. "What do you need from us?" I ask my oldest sister.

"I need each of you to find a dress in a shade of blue you love and that works for you." Lina turns to Tess. "Ellie too, if you don't mind."

Tess nods and smiles. The guys are chatting about baseball and some massive trade the local team proposed. It's then I realize Lia is suspiciously quiet. I catch her attention and motion for her to clear her plate with me to escape the dining room.

Within a few minutes, our plates are washed, loaded into the dishwasher, and we escape out the French doors to the porch.

"Spill, little sister," I demand.

"Nothing really to spill. I took your advice."

"And?"

"Asher said he isn't looking for a girlfriend right now, but we could hang out as friends."

Ouch! "Okay. Then?"

"I set up a time to hang out with him and Nell, but we're already friends."

"You want more than friendship with him despite Nell?" I gently push.

"Yes, I do. It hurts more than I thought it would. The rejection. Although I suppose it isn't a complete rejection. He doesn't want anyone; it's not just me."

I ponder the best advice to give my younger sister. "I would suggest hanging out with him and also allowing me to set you up on a date or finding your own date."

She wrinkles her nose. "Do you already have someone in mind?"

I shake my head. "Not yet. I won't set you up with a weirdo, Lia."

"Don't make me regret this. Okay, you can fix me up, but no one else knows."

I mime zipping my lips shut. "I'm on it." I open my arms to her, and she steps into them. "Don't worry, sis. These things have a way of working out… eventually."

She snorts. Then we both break out into a fit of laughter. "You're the best sister ever. If you share I said that, I'll deny it until the day I die."

"Deal."

"How is it going with Leo?"

"He's making progress. The reconstruction of the bar is well underway, and most of his vendors were understanding. He's worried about restaffing his bar. Some of his employees had no choice but to move on. He has to replace Miguel as well, which is an unwelcome and heart-wrenching task for him."

"And the woman?" Lia asks.

"The Danica issue is weighing on him, but he knows Smithson is working on it."

"I appreciate the update, but not what I meant, sis."

"Oh, okay…." I read into her words again. "Ohhhh! Well, I should give you the party line, it's good and end my reply there."

"But?"

I wink at her. "Since it's you and we share more with each other than everyone else… it's mind-blowing how in sync we are and feels off-the-charts exceptional."

"So the friends-first thing worked for you?"

I see where she's going with this. "It's an option, Lia. However, Asher already said he isn't looking for a girlfriend."

"True, but that doesn't mean we can't get there one day."

"I would suggest you temper your thoughts, but you won't. Don't let yourself pin your hopes on him completely. Promise me you'll go out on a few dates too."

"I promise, Lily."

The French doors open with a flourish only Leo could manage. He clasps his arms around my waist from behind and kisses the top of my shoulder. "There you are. Time for dessert."

Dessert passes with some more discussion of the wedding before we head home. After a long walk with Lola, we curl up and watch a few episodes of *Yellowstone* before falling asleep.

It's barely light out, but I'm alone in bed. Leo doesn't sleep much. Though my worry level is higher than it would be prior to his injury. When I find him, all I can do is laugh.

He turns toward me. His face is covered with flour, there's a huge mess on the island, and the sink is overflowing with dishes.

"What on earth are you doing?"

Leo shakes his head. "I was trying to make you breakfast in bed, complete with crepes, ricotta pancakes, bacon, fruit, the works. However...." He gestures toward the island and hangs his head.

Crepes are my favorite non-American food. I tiptoe over to him and wrap my arms around him. "Oh, Moon."

He catches my gaze and frowns.

"We'll see what we can salvage. Coffee first?"

With a kiss to the top of my head, he releases me to brew coffee. I grab some paper towels and swipe paths along the gooey mess on the marble island.

"I'm so sorry, babe."

"Nothing to be sorry for. I appreciate the effort. What were you doing though? There's flour everywhere."

He laughs. "I was sifting it per the instructions on the tablet. Lola jumped on my calf, and it gave out. Then I knocked over the bowl, which hit the measuring cups of milk and oil, then who knows."

"I love you for trying."

Leaning closer, he brushes his lips across mine and returns to brewing coffee. We're interrupted by a knock on my door. It's still before eight in the morning. Worry and fear courses through me. My phone didn't ring last night, and someone would've called me if there was an emergency.

"Breathe, Stella. I'll get the door while you wash your hands."

I heed his words and wash my hands. Then I dash into the bedroom for a hoodie. I don't plan to entertain company in a threadbare tank top and leggings.

Harsh, pointed words float in my direction. It takes me a minute to place the voice. Oliver.

"Lily was clear. She doesn't want to see you again."

"What are you doing here so early?" Oliver asks.

I continue to eavesdrop on the conversation.

"I live here."

My heart increases in size exponentially. Sharing about us, especially to Oliver, is huge for Leo.

"No, you live above the bar."

Leo chuckles. "I did. Now, I live here. Lily has nothing to say to you, Oliver. Please leave and don't come back."

"No. You don't speak for her," he accuses.

Leo's jaw clenches, as do his fists. "I do have the right to speak for her, but I won't mislead people. That's your MO."

"She told you?" Oliver's voice trembles, as if he believed his subterfuge would be kept under wraps.

"She did."

Silence passes between the open space. It isn't until Leo starts to close the door that Oliver continues. "I messed up big-time. I need her help."

It's only then, after his confession and plea, do I approach the front door. I thread my fingers with Leo's. "Oliver, I have nothing to say to you. I will not help you regain your reputation when you clearly don't understand what it takes to build one legitimately."

"I'm going to lose my job. Lily, please help me," he begs.

"No. You used my reputation to garner power and success within the company we both worked for. You lied and misled our boss for nearly four years. I will not continue to work for a company who fails to properly vet those they choose to promote. I was passed over three times for promotions. Now I know why. The company didn't want so much power consolidated into one couple—a couple I didn't even know I was still part of. Not only have I moved on professionally but personally as well. I will not help you restore your reputation when you destroyed mine to build it in the first place. Leave or I'll call my brother."

"Lily, please reconsider," Oliver pleads.

"She asked you to leave," Leo reiterates.

"I'm sorry, Lily. I never meant for it to get out of control."

I drop Leo's hand and grab the door. "Goodbye, Oliver." I close the door and walk triumphantly back into my kitchen.

"Well done," Leo comments and restarts making coffee.

"I could say the same to you. I appreciate your control with your words and not slamming the door closed in his face."

"He sits near the top of my list of people I have beef with. Harming him would cause you pain, and I refuse to add to what we're going through for the small satisfaction I would garner from punching him."

"Same actually. What do you say to finishing breakfast?"

"I'm in after we clean up this mess first."

I laugh and return to cleaning before restarting breakfast. We end up with pancakes, fruit, and well-done bacon. Overall, I'm grading it a successful meal. "What do you need to accomplish today?"

He polishes off his second cup and shares, "I need to talk with Maggie and swing by the bar to bottle what I can."

"You didn't finish on Saturday?"

"No."

"We could've skipped dinner to bottle. Mama would've understood."

"I know. I didn't want to skip dinner."

"Okay."

Leo asks, "What about you?"

"I have a few more follow-ups with Attorney Kramer about the company formation. It should be approved today or tomorrow. Once she gives me the go-ahead, I can open some business bank accounts and tackle my website. I have a few inquiries from three potential clients too."

"How did that happen?"

"Antionette mentioned something about a notice for a new financial management company in the paper. Two of them are principals from companies I managed with Upton Gerber."

"Fantastic! Poach all the principals. I'm insanely proud of you."

I laugh. "Thanks. Me too."

We finish cleaning our dishes and dress for the day.

"I'll be back as soon as I can," Leo offers.

I set my hands on his chest. "No rush. I'll be here."

"Love you, Lily."

"I love you."

He bounces down the stairs leading to the garage and pulls out in his truck for the first time since his injury. I step into my office with a sense of renewed pride and progress. Being my own boss, like my sister, is going to be phenomenal.

CHAPTER TWENTY-THREE

LEONARDO

While I've been referring to this get-together as a reunion, it started out as an annual charity event while I was in the league. Each year the PR department would host a charity event at the team facility. We didn't take it over exactly, but we kind of did.

"Ready, Lily?" I call down the hall.

She was still muttering to herself in her closet when I left. "Yeah, I'm ready." Lily rounds the corner wearing a black pencil skirt with a floral blouse.

"You look hot as f—you need to change."

"Possessive much? Not a chance, Moon. By your own admission, I look hot, and I'm not changing."

"You do, which is precisely why you need to change. I don't have time to fend off my dirty-minded colleagues."

She laughs. "We waited a long time for us. All the guys have seen me dressed similarly before today. They also know you would cut off their manhood for looking at me sideways. It has always been that way even when I wasn't yours."

"Say that again."

She winks at me and repeats, "I'm yours."

I grumble, kiss her breathless, then lead her to the garage, noting my acquiescence to her assertions. Each one is wholly accurate. I gawk at her toned legs as she sits in the passenger seat. Even in our garage, I open her door for this exact reason. More time to ogle her privately. With a quick glance at my watch, I calculate how long it'll take to drive by Endzone before going to Harborside.

"There isn't enough time, Leo. We can drive by afterward."

She owns me, mind and body. "I came to the same unfortunate conclusion."

"Besides, I'm anxious to see Mo and his family. The girls must be tall by now." Mo and Monique have twin girls, Minka and Mellie, who are eight.

I smile. Lily has always been a constant in my life, and I love she's comfortable in all situations with the guys and their families. "Me too."

The outdoor space at Harborside is set up to my exacting specifications. Maggie and her staff have exceeded my expectations, and the event hasn't even started yet.

Maggie greets us once we step onto the patio. "Hi, guys! Everything is set." A young man steps beside her. "Perfect. Keith will be your liaison for the event. If you need anything, please let him know, and he'll handle your needs."

"Pleasure to meet you."

"The honor is mine, Mr. De Gaetano."

The kid looks familiar. "What is your last name, Keith?"

"Duckworth, sir."

I recall playing with a set of brothers with the same last name and recall meeting this young man quite some time ago. "Which of my teammates is your dad?"

A sadness passes over his face, but he recovers quickly. "Kenneth was my dad." Kenneth was a junior in college, and his brother Kevin was a senior on the team in high school. Kenneth died in a car accident that year, leaving behind his bride and young son.

"It nice to see you again. Do you still have the game ball?"

Joy replaces the hint of sadness. My high school teammates and I honored Kenneth at the homecoming legends game later the same year he died. "Yes, I do. The day you gave it to me is etched in my memory forever."

Lily squeezes my arm and excuses herself with Maggie.

"What have you been doing the last few years?"

"I finished my degree in hospitality management. Then I moved back here to be closer to my mom and younger brothers."

"What is your long-term goal?"

"I want to open my own brewery," Keith replies.

He would be perfect to replace Miguel, but I should discuss it with Maggie first. I don't want to poach her employees. "A strong goal. I happen to know someone in the business. When you're ready, give me a call." I hand him my card.

"Thank you. I'll be near the rear of the patio if you need anything today."

"I appreciate it." Second chances have always been my thing. Perhaps assisting Keith isn't exactly a second chance, but it's close enough in my mind. Ideas and potential ways to bring him on board at Endzone flood my mind. I set them aside for now and seek out Lily. I'm not happy when I find her.

Billy King, my former teammate both in high school and college, an outrageous, cocky, and talented wide receiver, has his arms around Lily. He's the only one of our classmates still active in the league. I approach from the blind side and state a little louder than necessary, "King, get your hands off my woman!"

Lily shakes her head and glowers at me.

"Relax, Leo. I've known Lily as long as you. Hell, Frankie tried to fix us up back in the day. I was congratulating her on LCD Investments. She was offering well-wishes for my upcoming nuptials."

"You're settling down with one woman?" Levity and disbelief lace my words. King has never been with the same woman more than twice. I surmise it hasn't changed.

"Yes, I am."

"Happy for you, man. Is she here?"

King shakes his head. "No, she's filming a movie directed by Ellis Barnett in California."

Ellis is married to Kelly, who designed Lily's dress for our first date. "Friends or not, hands off my woman."

King laughs. I slide my arm possessively around Lily. We chat with King for a bit longer. Then we greet Mo and his family as they arrive. I take Mo's hand, and we bro hug. Afterward, I crouch a little to greet the girls.

Monique hugs Lily tightly as they jump up and down. "It's been so long since I've seen you."

"Same here," Lily replies and shifts over to hug Mo. "Hi, Mo. Looking svelte."

"Why thank you. Monique has me on a meal and exercise plan. It's working, and I'm not starving, so no complaints. I hear congratulations are in store for you as well."

Lily tilts her head in question, then looks at me.

Mo continues, "Big man finally came around, huh?"

Lily laughs heartily. "Yeah, he did."

"How is it all my fault?"

Mo drops his head. "Happy wife, happy life, dude. It would be wise of you to remember that going forward."

I laugh and reply, "Understood." Soon I'll make the wife part of his statement ring true.

"What do you need from me?" Mo asks.

We discuss the schedule again and mingle for a bit longer until the silent auction and meal service begin. I leave Lily and Monique walking along the silent auction items, which range from a spa day to an all-inclusive vacation to Tulum, Mexico to tickets to every home game for our former team. Mo and I head off to the side to talk more privately at his request.

Worry ramps through me. "What's going on, Mo?"

He glances around us nervously. "I'm not going to be able to come back from this injury."

"I'm sorry, bro."

Mo tore his rotator cuff and broke his ankle last season. "Me too."

"When you need to grouse, call me. I'll listen."

"I will. The good news is I have a coaching job lined up, and we'll be closer to each other soon."

"You're moving here?"

"New Hampshire."

I grin at him. "Where?"

"It's a small division two school."

"Congrats, bro! Why didn't you tell me before?"

"Lots of reasons, but mostly I was—"

"Still holding out hope the doctors were wrong," I supply.

"Exactly. They aren't wrong. Therefore, my agent is recommending securing my assets for the long term and focusing on the girls' future. Who manages your money?"

"Funny you should ask. Lily has been doing it since day one as a personal favor. However, she's officially opening her own private brokerage next week. Give her a call and set up an appointment."

"Seriously?"

"It's a long story, but yes."

Mo visibility relaxes. "I was keenly worried about making a mistake here. Monique will be overjoyed."

"Glad she can help. What do you say we get some grub and drum up donations for the woman's initiative charities and the league's long-term health and safety charity?"

"We need to beat last year's numbers."

"Yeah, we do!"

We rejoin our ladies at the table before pulling names for the auction. Unbeknownst to me, Lily bid on and won the trip to Tulum, and Monique outbid everyone for the spa day for the girls. Lily and Monique deliver the auction items and collect the donations from the attendees.

Nearly three hours later and slightly more than thirty thousand dollars raised, we bid farewell to our friends with the expectation of at least monthly dinners after their big move. We surpassed last year's donations by nearly ten thousand dollars. I'm stoked.

"Congrats on a successful event, Leo."

"Thanks, Stella. I couldn't have done it without you."

She smiles up at me and steals a kiss before replying, "Perhaps."

I laugh and lead her to the car. The ride to Endzone is short. I'm floored when we arrive. Scott and his crew are finishing up for the day. I didn't realize they were working on Sundays as well. We hop out of the car and walk the exterior of the building. When we reach the rear entrance, Scott emerges from inside.

"Hey, Leo. Do you come by every single day?" Scott ribs me.

"Mostly," I admit.

"I probably would too if the situation were reversed. The structure is complete, and the apartment is almost complete. We need inspections from the building department before the finish work and your final punch list. I'll set up a meeting after the inspection for a walk through with you."

"I can't thank you enough, Scott. You've made this process seamless and mostly stress free."

"You're welcome. I appreciate it."

"Have a good evening, Scott. I look forward to your call." I link my fingers with Lily's and lead her to the car again.

She waits until I settle into the driver's seat before speaking. "Are you as excited as I am?"

I laugh. "Yes and no. Excited doesn't begin to cover the speed of Scott's progress and the ability to get back to work soon. Aside from the whole Danica aspect, losing my livelihood was difficult. Thanks to you, I have invested wisely and lived within my means. Endzone was my second chance. This is a setback for my business. Until today, replacing Miguel was proving to be a difficult task."

"Keith?" Lily whispers.

"Yeah. Do you remember him?"

"I recall the story and the game where you and the team honored him, but I wouldn't have recognized him, only his last name."

"I'm going to talk with Maggie tomorrow before offering him a chance to interview for Miguel's job and rent the apartment too."

"A wonderful gesture. Did you talk to Smithson too?"

I hang my head briefly. "He's due to give me for an update tomorrow or the next day. I've done everything I can to assist him. Jacob's guy has only been on the case for a little more than a week. I'm not expecting a miracle simply because he walks the gray line."

Lily squeezes my hand. "I know. One would be appreciated though for your peace of mind."

I lift her hand to my lips and kiss the back. "Finding Danica would be amazing for my well-being and demeanor. I need to know... why me?"

"I understand. I would too."

"Where to, milady?" I say silly things merely to hear her sweet laugh and to make her smile. She loves me fiercely, and I'm grateful.

"Home. There's a nice bottle of wine and a cozy hammock with our names on it."

"As you wish."

She shakes her head at the *Princess Bride* quote but doesn't call me on it. Within fifteen minutes of arriving home after a successful event and a positive update for my bar, we snuggle up on her couch instead of the hammock, given the sudden onset of a thunderstorm. Once we finish the bottle, we relocate to our bed and fall blissfully asleep wrapped in one another.

CHAPTER TWENTY-FOUR

LEONARDO

The inspection yesterday went well. With a sprinkle of luck, I should be able to schedule a soft reopening within the next two weeks. When I spoke with Scott after the reunion, I intensified my efforts to replace my staff. Keith was eager to move into a position more closely tailored to his career goals. Maggie was gracious in her understanding and encouragement of Keith to take this step toward his dream job. I reached out to my employees. Most of my staff will be ready to return as soon as I get my certificate of occupancy. Unfortunately, Butch moved on to a day shift job and doesn't wish to return to nights. I completely understand.

The good news is I'm able to enter the building and bottle the product to maintain my contracts. While it takes a bit longer alone, Lily is meeting with her attorney to finalize all the paperwork for her firm. As I wrap up, I get a text from her.

Lily: I'm set here. Do you need help?

Me: No. Wrapping up. Take out from the Inn?

Lily: You know what I like.

Me: Yes, I'm learning each time I get my hands on your lush curves.

Lily: Oh, Moon! That wasn't meant to be dirty.

Me: Perhaps not, but my brain can go there now, and I did.

Lily: You know what I like from the Inn and in the bedroom. Fair?

Me: Fair. Love you.

Lily: See you in a little bit. Love you.

After I finish moving the newly bottled and labelled whiskey into the main area and lock the barrel room. Tuesday morning, they will be picked up after I arrange the time. I verify all the locks, and as I make my way to the coatroom, I see a familiar car parked beside my truck. Rage, frustration, and intrigue rush through my veins. I don't want to see her, but I also need answers. She needs to be held accountable for her actions, whatever they may have been. The last thing I want is a face-to-face confrontation with Danica alone.

I pull out my phone and dial. "Hey, Leo."

"Smithson. I'm at Endzone, and Danica is waiting for me beside my truck in the lot."

"I'm on my way. If possible, don't engage with her."

"I'll do my best." I end the call and consider whether calling Lily right now is the right choice. It is, but I don't want her to see Danica again if possible. I dial Lily and gather my thoughts while it rings.

"Everything okay?"

I scrub my hand down my face. "I want to be clear. I'm physically fine. I was about to leave the bar, but Danica is leaning against my truck. Smithson told me to stay put until he arrives."

"Does he have a plan?"

"He didn't share one with me, but he asked me not to engage her if possible."

"We also don't want her to bolt either." Lily has a point. This is the first time Danica has shown her face since the hospital. This may be our best chance to take her into custody.

"She's knocking on the door. Please wait for me to call you again before you go anywhere. I don't want you near her."

"I'm frankly not a fan of you being near her either, but I know you need to stall her. Be careful, Leo. I love you."

"I love you, Lily."

She won't listen, but at least I tried to protect her from danger and seeing Danica again. I consider Smithson and Lily's words and opt to answer the door. At a minimum, she'll be contained in the building.

Danica rushes inside and throws her arms around me. "Thank God! I was truly worried."

I grip her forearms and unclasp them. "Don't touch me."

She frowns and takes only a small step backward. "I was so wrong, Leo. I was jealous of your relationship with Lily. She was able to spend more time with you because I'm always travelling for work. I miss you so much!"

My phone vibrates with a text.

"Excuse me a moment." I read the text.

Smithson: I'm outside with backup. Is the rear door unlocked?

That was fast.

Me: Yes. We're inside to the right.

Smithson: Thanks. Keep her talking.

Me: Will do.

"You were saying?"

Danica smiles. "I want you back. I miss you. I miss this place."

"I'm not interested in rekindling our dysfunctional relationship. You didn't trust me. Your ultimatum about Lily truly gave me pause and made me reflect on what I'm looking for in my life. It isn't you."

"Leo, don't be like this. We could be great together again."

"No, I'm not interested. I need to get my business running again and replace Miguel."

I hear the door creak but keep her talking. Ideally, she won't notice. I didn't take Danica as a genius. Then again, she's done this before. Someone is clearly looking out for her.

She continues, "The place looks great."

"My guy did an excellent job."

"It was fast. I don't think Midland could've pulled this off as quickly."

I nod. "Right, the company you work for."

"Repairs like this are a huge portion of the business. It's why I was away so long. I'm working on a huge project in Maryland."

"I see. Like I said, I need to replace Miguel."

"Yeah, I'm sorry about your friend. No one was supposed to get hurt."

I glance over her shoulder. Smithson, Jones, and one other person are waiting. Smithson gives me a signal to keep her talking. "What do you mean 'no one was supposed to get hurt'?"

"Exactly that. All I did was follow instructions."

I press forward with my questions, despite my desire to strangle this woman. "Whose instructions?"

"My boss, Kyle. He sets up these schemes."

"I see. You know I lived here. How could you be sure I wouldn't be home?"

"You mentioned the wedding several times. I knew you would be out of the building. I couldn't get all the schedules because your office was always locked. What do you mean 'lived'?"

I won't answer her question. If possible, I won't share about Lily and me either.

Smithson ends my questions when he says, "Shelby Woods, you're under arrest for accessory to murder, fraud, conspiracy to commit fraud, and false pretenses."

"Leo! Don't do this! I love you! I can explain. They made me do it!" She bursts into tears as Smithson recites her rights.

"You have the right to remain...."

I watch Jones haul her out of my bar and tuck her into the back seat of the police cruiser. The tension in my neck and shoulders is off the charts right now. Every muscle is strung tight.

Smithson calls my name. "Leo?"

"Yeah."

"You good? I called your name a few times."

I shrug. "Not sure."

"Understandable."

"Are you going to question her now?"

Smithson looks confused at my question. "Yeah, why?"

"Just wondering. What do I do now?"

He sets his hand on my shoulder. "Let me finish this case. Grab a bottle of your favorite vintage, pick up dinner, and go home. I'll call you later tonight or first thing tomorrow when I have a better picture of what went down."

"Thank you for coming. Resisting the urge to throttle her was harder than I anticipated."

"You're welcome. What happened to ignoring her?"

"I called Lily because I was supposed to bring home dinner from the Inn, and well, she insinuated letting her into the bar would prevent her from rabbiting."

Smithson shakes his head. "Her mind is scary as hell. Financial genius and sibling of a cop make a weird combination of observations and skills."

"No kidding. Speaking of Lily...."

My gorgeous woman drives up and parks on the public side street behind the barricade. The young officer monitoring it radios Smithson.

"Let her through," he instructs.

The second she's close enough, she leaps into my arms, wrapping her legs around my waist.

I add a bit of space so I can look at her. "I told you to stay put. This is the second time you didn't listen," I scold her, somewhat jokingly.

"I'm sorry. I was going crazy with worry. Hi, Smithson."

"Hi, Lily. Good call on letting her inside the building. She probably would've run again."

She smiles. "The last thing I wanted was to allow her anywhere near Leo. However, catching her was more important."

Smithson laughs. "Appreciate the assist either way. I'll call you later or tomorrow, Leo."

"Thanks."

Smithson walks to the cruiser and pulls out of the lot with Danica scowling out the window at Lily.

"What do you say to dinner at the Inn?" I suggest.

"Sounds perfect. How are you feeling right now?"

"Uncomfortable and settled at once. I know those two don't truly mesh." I roll my head around in a circle to ease the tension but fail.

Lily links her hands around me. "They do to me. You're uncomfortable because there are still unknowns regarding Danica but settled because progress has been made."

"Of course you understand my babbling." I lower my lips to hers and follow her to the Inn. The restaurant is right on the water near Short Sands Beach. It's also beneath Lia's old condo. The atmosphere is romantic, and the food is delicious.

"How did the bottling go before Danica showed up?"

I set down my fork. "I finished and moved them to the bar for pickup."

"Good. How does the bar look?"

A huge smile grows on my face. "Scott and his team crushed the repairs, and the inspector signed off. I just need proof in my hands to reopen to the public."

Lily raises her wineglass. "To you, for not giving up when it would've been the easy thing to do."

I touch my glass to hers and take a sip. "Thank you, Stella. I couldn't have done it without your support."

We share a delicious chocolate confection for dessert and stroll the length of the beach a few times before driving up the hill to our home. The walk doesn't take the edge off my nerves.

Lily lets Lola out the back door and waits for her to return. "How would you prefer to relax your mind right now?" Lily's voice floods my thoughts.

My interest is piqued. "What are you suggesting, Stella?"

"We could soak in my huge tub, or I can attempt to massage those knots from your neck and shoulders."

"I'm willing to let you try, but I can't be held responsible for my reaction to your hands all over me."

Lily winks at me, secures Lola, and saunters down the hall to our bedroom. "You coming, Moon? I'll find the massage oil."

"Why did I not know or find this massage oil before tonight?" I ask, rushing down the hall.

Lily laughs and points to the bed. I strip off my shirt and lie on my belly. She straddles my hips, drips the oil on my back, and starts to knead her hands into my tight muscles.

"Damn! Easy, Lily!"

"Suck it up, Leo. Do you remember the last time I gave you a massage?"

I recall vividly. "Yes. It was senior year after the win in the state championship. We went for burgers with the guys, and when we got to Gran's, she chastised me for not taking care of my body. As uncomfortable as it was, you rubbed down my back in the living room."

"What do you mean 'uncomfortable'?"

I shake my head. "Consider how you're sitting right now with your hands sliding along my skin."

"It feels amazing."

I groan as she puts pressure on a specifically tight area. "Yes, but you weren't my girlfriend then. Hiding my reaction to you sitting on top of me and your hands on me in Gran's living room was an impossibility."

The realization on her face in the mirror across the room is priceless. "Oh my… Leo!"

"What? I'm a guy! It isn't something we can turn off. Well, it takes supreme control and effort. Plus, you didn't realize it until now when I told you."

"True. No more hiding."

"I wouldn't dream of it."

Lily tends to each knot in my neck, back, and shoulders. My limbs feel like jelly. I feel much better.

"My turn."

She moves to the side, strips off her tank, and lies on her belly. It takes virtually no time before my hands stray beneath the waistband of her leggings and over the curve of her ass.

"Leo." My name sounds like a prayer for me to continue lower.

Before I follow her implied request, I draw down her leggings and panties and strip off the rest of my clothes too. "Come here, Stella." I point to my lap.

Her eyes widen as she follows my instructions, and we spend the rest of the night lost in one another.

I wake and slide out of bed but not before memorizing Lily in this moment. She's lying on her side with the sheet tangled around her legs and barely covering her breasts. The set of freckles near her tattoo and the single beauty mark near her navel capture my attention. You would think I would know each blemish, freckle, and mark on Lily. Mostly I do, at least the ones visible with clothes on. I'm working on those that were hidden beneath the surface of her body and her heart. With two hot cups of coffee and Lola on my heels, I return to the bedroom.

Lily stirs when I take a seat on the edge of the bed.

"Morning," I greet her and offer her a cup of coffee.

Without a thought, she sits up, baring her chest to me, and takes the cup. "Morning."

"I love how content you are being naked around me already."

A fierce blush creeps onto her skin, and she looks away. "What is your plan today?" she asks before taking a sip.

"Waiting on Smithson to share his findings. I'm meeting with Keith to give him a tour and train him on a few systems this morning and starting a loose plan for reopening in two weeks. You?"

"I have a new client intake at nine and a call with Mo at ten. Did you set that up?"

"No. Maybe. Not really. He shared he needs to retire because his injury isn't healing as well as he would like."

"That's too bad. I'm surprised Monique didn't share with me."

I shrug. "He needs to find a money manager not associated with his agent."

"Not angry, Leo. I appreciate the referral and your faith in me to help our friends."

"I'm crazy proud of you for opening your own firm. You've been managing my money well since I was drafted. I have no doubt, you'll do the same for Mo and every other person who retains you."

"Thank you. Did Smithson give you any idea when he would be reaching out again?"

"No, just today. I'm relieved and less stressed. He can take the time he needs to finish his job. I won't push him more."

"Okay. I would like to come with you to meet Smithson, if possible."

I take her cup, set it aside, and kiss her. "I want you there. Time to get moving. I hear your new boss is quite particular about work ethic and timeliness, but liberal with her dress code for work days."

Lily laughs, steals another kiss, and saunters to the shower. By the time I return with fresh coffee, she's dressed and ready to start her day.

"Have a great day at the office, honey."

She accepts the cup and kisses me sweetly before taking her short commute to work.

I dress, blow a kiss to Lily because she's on the phone, and head to Endzone. As I pull into my parking spot, I notice there's an unfamiliar car in the lot. When I hop out, so does the occupant.

"Morning, Mr. De Gaetano."

"Morning, Keith. 'Leo' is fine. You're a bit early."

A shy grin materializes on his face. "I'm ecstatic about this opportunity. I couldn't sleep."

"Well, come on in."

Hours later, I determine my gut was right about Keith, and maybe chasing my third and final dream will become a reality sooner than I ever imagined.

CHAPTER TWENTY-FIVE

LILIANNA

Once I shake the tug of potential failure, I'm off and running. I consider texting Frankie, but instead I give myself a pep talk and get to work. My doorbell and office phone have been ringing incessantly since before nine. With a new floral arrangement from my siblings and the Barnetts on the credenza in my office, and one fruit arrangement on the island from the Washingtons, I return the three potential client calls from this morning before chatting with Mo.

A small conglomerate, that I worked with at Upton, contacted me about switching to my new company. By lunch, I have signed three new private clients and two corporate clients both from Upton. During those two initial calls, I was upfront about the fact I left Upton. Both new clients were aware and contacted me when they were assigned to a member of the team they didn't know. Jerry informed them I no longer worked there. Both insisted they wanted to continue to work with me and requested a release to shift their business to me. I'm overjoyed. Not only did my hard work pay off at Upton, but it's paying dividends while I branch out and work for myself.

Right before ten, my phone rings and Mo's smiling face appears on my screen.

"Hi, Mo!"

"Hey, Lily. Thank you for taking my call."

"Of course. I'm happy to help. Tell me a little about what you have in place now and what your short-term and long-terms goals are."

I spend a little over an hour talking to Mo. Afterward, I forward him a release and request for financial information for him and Monique to sign and return. One I have those in hand, I can start moving and managing their finances.

I take a break when the doorbell chimes again with another floral delivery. Surprisingly, this one is from Jerry. The arrangement is large but understated. The personal note includes well-wishes and a plea to return to Upton and replace Oliver. I literally laugh out loud and set the flowers on my dining table. All it took was for me to leave for corporate to figure out I'm amazing. Too late to make it right.

Leo arrives home near one. A bright bouquet of flowers, including scabious, ranunculus, mini calla lilies, snapdragon, Limonium, and garden roses, precedes his smiling face into my office. "It appears I missed the memo. Flower deliveries are required before noon."

I laugh and take the flowers from him. "Thank you. These are gorgeous. I don't recall ever sharing my favorites with you. Did I?"

A huge, sexy grin grows on Leo's face. He extends his hand to me, draws me flush against him, and kisses me breathless. Then we settle in the corner of the love seat in my office.

"Despite how it appeared, I have been filing away all sorts of information about your preferences over the years. You did mention two of these varieties of flowers as your favorites."

"I'm impressed. When did I mention this little tidbit of information?"

"Sophomore year in college, spring semester. Mo was desperate to make sure Monique knew she was his one and only. He called me to talk to you and picked your brain for the best flowers, other than roses, to show he was serious about a future with her. While you were chatting with him, you mentioned calla lilies and ranunculus topping your list."

"Uh-huh." I dig into the recesses of my brain, wondering what else I've revealed. "What else might you have heard over the years?"

He winks at me. "Only time will tell what you have divulged unknowingly, Lilianna."

Satisfied with his response, I change the subject. "How did it go with Keith?"

"Very well. My gut was right about him. He beat me there this morning. He's eager to learn and will be a great addition to the team."

"Your instincts haven't failed you yet. Any word from Smithson?"

A flicker of sadness casts over Leo's face. No, it's guilt.

"Your instinct about Miguel was correct. Not only did he deserve a second chance, but he proved you right with his work ethic and turning his life around outside of work. Smithson will set forth a good case to hold Danica and whomever else responsible."

"I understand, but it still hurts. It's hard not to blame myself a little for having him there to cover for me that morning."

"What do you mean?"

"Normally, Butch handled the weekend mornings. While I was waffling over whether to attend the wedding, I gave Butch the morning off. I planned to cover for him. It would take my mind off not attending. Anyway, the time away from you and our family was heartbreakingly difficult—more you, but either way. Miguel called me on it and convinced me I had no choice but to attend the wedding. Not only to be present for my family, but more importantly to reveal my deeper feelings for you."

My heart constricts. "Even if each word is true, the only difference in the outcome would be who didn't make it out of the building. Presumably Butch would've handled the work in the same manner as Miguel. It isn't now, nor was it ever, your fault for making a business decision so you, the owner, could chase your future."

"You never cease to amaze me. No matter how hard I try, you can convince me I have no culpability despite all the evidence to the contrary."

"Not evidence, Leo. You did nothing outside of working your successful business and chasing me. No fault falls at your feet." I tighten my grasp and burrow as close as I can manage.

Leo doesn't speak for a long while. I know it'll take time and reflection for him to completely grasp my assertion. Eventually he will, and then he can truly move forward.

The doorbell summons me to the front door. Turns out it's my brother and Luke. "Hey, Luca! What are you doing here?"

"Hi, Lils. Leo. I heard there was going to be a meeting with Smithson, so we dropped by." He hugs me and bro hugs Leo.

I turn to Leo and raise my hands in question. "Well?"

"We were talking, and I knew you didn't have more appointments today. Smithson will be by in about thirty minutes to give us an update."

"Sweet, plenty of time for me to snuggle the baby. Hand him over, Luca," I demand.

"Nope. Uncle Leo gets first dibs," Luca admits.

"I'm your sister," I whine like a petulant child and barely resist the urge to stomp my foot to make my point.

"Leo is my brother, and he invited me here, so first dibs."

I scowl at Luca. Leo lifts Luke out of the carrier and tucks him into the crook of his arm.

Sweet heaven on earth! That's sexy as hell. I pull my lower lip between my teeth and slowly release it. Leo gloats at me over one of the cutest babies I've ever seen. I would bet only ours will be cuter in my eyes and Leo's. "How is Willa doing?"

"Pretty good. She's tired, but otherwise fine. Tabi showed up for a girls' afternoon complete with a mani-pedis and some charcuterie bar."

"I heard about that place. It's near Barley and Hops. The intent is to offer snack time before happy hour."

"Interesting."

"Thank you for the flowers, Luca."

He raises an eyebrow. "You're welcome?"

I chuckle. "Clearly, Willa handled the congratulatory gift with Frankie, Lina, and Lia. The arrangement is lovely. It's in my office if you wish to see it."

Luca waves me off and takes a seat at the island.

"When do you go back to work?" I ask my brother.

"I'm back in the rotation on Saturday. The extended leave with Willa and Luke was nice."

"What about Willa?"

"She's going to step back in slowly starting Monday. Luke will go to Noelle's center three days a week. The other two days, she's going to work remotely from home with him. I'm not sure how well it'll go with him home, but she's adamant about giving it a shot."

"Of all people, I understand the desire for remote work. Hell, I created my own business so I wouldn't have to go back into the office in Boston. If anyone can pull it off, Willa can."

"It'll be a good example for you to follow," Luca whispers and nudges my attention to Leo fawning over our newest nephew. "What about you? How long until that's your baby?"

As soon as possible is my vote. "Slow down a little, Luca. We barely started dating."

"Bull. You've been dating adjacent for twenty years. He's your best friend. The TMI things brothers and sisters don't discuss are presumably *acceptable*, right?"

I stifle a laugh at Luca's way of asking if my sex life with Leo is good enough. I dip my head in acknowledgment of his assumption.

"No reason for you to wait to make it official and get started on the family both of you strongly desire. You've wanted lots of children from as far back as middle school. You're not getting any younger, sis."

I slap his arm in mock disgust that he would point it out. "You should talk. You're older than me."

"Fair enough. What I'm getting at is your relationship with Leo doesn't qualify as too fast or too short."

"Thanks, Luca."

Shortly thereafter, Smithson arrives.

"Would you like some coffee?" Leo offers.

"Yes. Thank you," Smithson replies.

Leo graciously hands Luke to me before rounding the island to brew some coffee. I pace around the island as the guys take a seat.

Smithson begins his update. "I'm sure you're anxious to hear what I've learned. As expected, Danica started spilling details of the alleged operation as soon as we put her in the interrogation room. As I mentioned before, you weren't the only victim of her feminine wiles. We determined she had four aliases prior to questioning her. Yesterday, she confessed there are three additional ones, bringing the total to seven times she and her partners have pulled this con."

"Damn!" Luca exclaims. "Where did you meet her, Leo?"

"At Endzone. Not important right now, Luca," Leo responds.

Luca raises his hands in feigned surrender.

Leo sets coffee in front of Luca and Smithson before pouring two more. He prepares both cups and moves mine closer. "Please continue."

"To recap for Luca's sake, as Molly, she dated the owner of a pub in Maryland, and it flooded. Foul play was found as the water supply to the business was tampered with, but the authorities were never able to pin it on anyone specific. The building was gutted and needed major repair. Molly was with the owner for just under six months. Posing as Emily, Danica was engaged to a restaurant owner with three properties within four months of dating. The original location in Philly was destroyed by fire. Arson was suspected, but they never found the perpetrator. The other four aliases have similar instances of tampering and destruction of property requiring repair by a construction company. In her voice mails to Leo and when he confronted her at the bar yesterday, Danica continually claimed she was doing as instructed. The ambiguous 'they' she kept referring to is Kyle Oaken, her boss, who we already knew about, his brother Brian, and Martin Woods, her father."

"I can see how Kyle fits in, but what about her father? And how does it connect the victims and me?"

Smithson continues, "With Blackthorne's help, I was able to determine how their victims are connected. Each one is a current or former player in the league."

Leo notes, "That's an odd connection. There are thousands of men in the league and formerly in the league."

"True," Smithson answers.

I ask, "What makes this group unique?"

"Each owns a business or more than one business. Danica dates the subjects and assists with obtaining whatever information is needed to pull off the con."

"What's the con?" Luca asks.

I supply, "She works for a construction company. If she's in good enough with the owners, she presumably could at least persuade them to get an estimate from Midland for repair."

"Got it," Luca replies.

Leo pushes the conversation forward with his next question. "How does it connect to her father?"

"Danica's father works as a janitor with the team you played for, Leo. Beforehand, he worked in Baltimore, Philly, and New York."

Luca adds, "That's how they know who is retiring, opening a new business, or making financial moves. Janitors and service people know everything."

I glance from Leo to our adorable nephew and back to Leo.

"How and when did Danica get a copy of my keys?" Leo asks.

Smithson catches my line of sight and nods in Leo's direction. I take it to mean I need to give Luke to his father or set him down in his carrier. "Danica made a mold of your keys with silly putty. Then she filled the mold with silicone. Her father has access to create keys at his current position as necessary."

I'm on my feet and beside Leo as he processes this development. The last thing he needs is to find another way to blame himself. "When?"

Smithson responds, "Within the first month of your relationship."

Once he answers, Leo nods. There's silence in the kitchen for a solid minute before Leo speaks again. "Why me? All the other 'relationships,' if you will, were much shorter. The longest was—"

"Eight months." Smithson offers the information. "The brother enters the picture here. Brian Oaken, who also works for Midland, had a heated discussion with Danica three months before the explosion. In his opinion, it was taking too long for her to get the information they needed. She felt the need to hurry you along to a more committed relationship in response."

"Which is where the ultimatum about Lily and an engagement ring came into play, right?" Leo surmises.

"Yes, except Danica had already procured all the information they needed to proceed long before her confrontation with Brian. According to her, she had all the information to tamper with the system within the first two months of dating you. She simply hadn't provided it to Kyle and the others."

I'm thinking it and so is Leo, but Luca beats me to ask aloud, "Why Leo? Why the ultimatum? Why wait so long if she had the information?"

The answer feels bitter on my tongue, but I say it anyway, "Danica fell for her mark."

When my words filter through Leo's mind, he tenses immediately. "I need a minute," Leo states and walks toward the bedroom.

"Is there anything else huge you need to share, Smithson?" I ask.

"No. Along with the others, she'll be charged with as many of the counts as possible in each case. For Miguel, they'll attempt to charge her with felony murder, whether it's provable is another matter," he replies.

"I can handle Leo from here if that's it. We appreciate you coming here instead of having us at the station."

"No problem. I didn't want to take the risk of Leo seeing her again. She was waiting for transport when I left to come here."

"Smart. I don't know how he would handle seeing her after hearing more details of her deception."

Smithson rises from his chair, shakes Luca's hand, and hugs me. "Please give my regards to Leo."

"I will."

Luca follows him out the front door after a brief exchange. With two glasses of maple-flavored whiskey—Leo's fave—I make my way to the bedroom. Leo is facing the ocean on the master balcony.

I join him and note his demeanor. The anguish on his face is unbearable. "Want to talk or sit in the quiet with me?"

"The latter, please."

I extend a glass in his direction and curl up beside him on the rattan couch. We sit listening to the waves crashing well into the evening.

Leo offers his impression before we turn in for the evening. "I thought knowing would feel different. I hoped it would make me less angry about Miguel, but… now I know that nothing will. Please don't remind me it isn't my fault. I'm at least a sliver at fault. However, I won't let it derail me. I need some separation from all of this."

"I won't. Dinner or sleep?" I ask.

"Sleep."

I set the glasses on the night table and tuck Leo into bed. "I'll be back as soon as Lola is set."

I take my puppy outside and wait for her to do her business. Against all my rules, she scampers into the bedroom, claws her way to Leo, and curls under his arm. Normally, she sleeps on the dressing bench at the foot of my bed or in her open crate.

"Want me to put her back on the floor?" he mumbles, his eyes fluttering open.

"No need. She feels like you need her comfort too. I'll allow it."

Leo's mouth curls up into a small smile. I join them in bed. A little while later, Lola prances to her spot, and I sidle closer to Leo.

CHAPTER TWENTY-SIX

LEONARDO

Each day I progress away from my idiotic decision to date Danica and the turmoil she caused. Truthfully, my decision to date anyone other than Lily was born out of protecting myself from heartache. I should've given our family more credit—a lesson I learned the hard way. Endzone is reopening in precisely one hour, and I'm more nervous than I was my first NFL game and the ribbon cutting.

"You've got this, Moon. Everything looks amazing!" Lily shouts from behind the bar. She looks hot back there, despite having no bartending skills other than pouring wine and drawing from the tap.

"Thanks, Stella." Given only my staff is here so far, I round the bar and haul her close. "I love you."

She tugs my earlobe between her teeth. "I love you. Go let your customers in."

I heed her words and open the doors. Purposely, I have avoided glancing out the window to see whether a crowd was building or not. The throng of people waiting when I swing open the door is a blessing. My heart is pounding, and excitement for my livelihood renews in my veins.

I greet my family. Mama and Papa are here too. They've visited before, just not when the crowd was expected to be larger than normal.

"Well done, Leo," Papa states.

"Thank you. Hopefully I'm done with setbacks for a little while."

Mama adds, "Only good things for you, Leonardo. Only good things, I can feel it."

I hug her again, and they make their way to greet Lily at the far end of the bar.

My staff is back, and Keith is greeting customers like he has been doing this his entire life. I added an additional server because Cassidy needs to tend bar more frequently than before. She was pleased with the semi-promotion. Server to bartender equals more tips. I consider it a win for both of us.

Nearly an hour has passed when Lily threads her fingers with mine and leads me to the rear entrance. "I have a small surprise for you."

"Lilianna, you know I'm not a fan of surprises." I love the way she melts when I call her by her full name. Yet her reaction to when I call her Stella is more palpable and visceral.

"It's a good one. I promise. Close your eyes please. No peeking."

Reluctantly, I comply. I hear the door open, and she guides me to the right about ten steps.

"Ready, you can open your eyes in three, two, one."

A host of voices shout, "Surprise!" as Lily reaches one.

When I open my eyes, I see most of the reunion attendees outside Endzone clamoring to get inside. I start with Mo and Monique and bro hug and handshake my way through my friends and teammates. They head inside after I greet them. Once I finish the crowd, I lift Lily into my arms and pepper her lips with kisses. "I can't believe you did this for me."

She wrinkles her nose. "I would do anything for you."

"As I would for you."

"Let's go celebrate properly."

I raise an eyebrow in her direction. "Stella...."

"I can't with you. My words aren't always meant to be dirty like you hear them."

I hug her close and whisper, "I'm reveling in my ability to allow my thoughts to go there, and I'm going there for a long time into the future. Wrap your mind around it. It won't change."

"Fine. When we leave here, you and I will celebrate properly."

I wink at her. "Do you mean naked?"

"Yes, Leo. Naked."

I grab her hand and hurry her inside. I don't want the grand reopening to fly by, but given my post-party plans, I kind of do. The crowd starts winding down near midnight. At least my family and friends are mostly dispersed by now. Lily is chatting it up with Monique and King's fiancée, Lara. Within the hour, only the regulars remain with one notable exception, Lia. She's nursing a drink at the far end of the bar. Cassidy chats with her in between refilling drinks.

Lily escorts Monique and Lara out, along with Mo and Billy. When she returns, I point out Lia's presence, and she pulls up the stool beside her sister.

While they talk, I catch up with Keith and Taylor for a quick debrief. "How's it going?"

Keith speaks first. "Good. The table turnover wasn't fast, but it could be because of the occasion. Most people were here for the reopening and stayed longer solely to speak with you."

"I agree. Can we have this type of event more?" Taylor asks before clarifying. "I don't mean the 'needing repair' part, Leo. The themed event party if you will. The tips are insane. There are people in this world who understand if you keep my table longer than an hour, you need to tip more."

"It's a good idea, Leo," Keith agrees.

"Over the next few weeks, why don't the two of you come up with a list of suggestions."

"Consider it done." Keith and Taylor high-five and return to their side work to close the dining area.

I leave them to finish up and make my way behind the bar and chat with Cassidy. Her sentiments are similar to Taylor's, and her opinion of Keith is optimistic as well. I glance up and notice Lily and Lia aren't at the corner of the bar any longer. When I locate Lily, she's waving to Lia by the entrance. She retakes her seat, and I saunter closer to her. "Hey, is Pip okay?" My relationship with Lia is realistic protective older brother. Luca, on the other hand, is restrictive protective older brother.

"She'll be fine. Asher sort of stood her up."

"How does one sort of stand someone up?"

Lily rolls her eyes at me. "Asher said Nell was sick, so he wouldn't leave her with a babysitter."

I consider Lily's statement. "Okay, not exactly standing her up, but Lia's upset about it?"

"Yeah. She's interested in him, but he only wants to be friends. They agreed to meet here tonight."

"Well, I wouldn't worry too much about Lia. Don't you have plans to set her up on a date anyway?"

"Yes, still considering my options."

"Fair enough. I need about twenty minutes, and then we can head home." I lean across the bar and kiss her softly.

During the fifteen-minute ride home, Lily falls asleep in my truck. I scoop her into my arms, tuck her into bed, and join her until morning.

I peel my eyelids open when I hear Lola whining. It's near six in the morning. Slipping out from beneath the covers, I let her out into the backyard.

Overall, the grand reopening was a success. While I'm not a fan of surprises, seeing the guys so soon was a welcome one. Lily isn't a fan either, but she's going to get a huge one soon.

A week has passed since the reopening, and for the most part, the customers, vendors, and bottling contracts have resumed to previous levels. Armed with coffee, I gently wake Lily. It's early, so coffee is necessary to avoid a grumpy Lily.

"It's barely light out, Leo," she grumbles.

"I know, but we need to get going."

She scrunches her face and takes a heavy sip of the coffee. "Did we have plans and I forgot?"

"No, you didn't forget. I made plans for us today. Jeans and a sweater will work."

"Okay, as soon as I finish this cup."

I kiss her forehead and get dressed. Arguably, I don't truly have a set schedule other than beating traffic. I slip a fresh cup of coffee in Lily's hand and lead her to the garage thirty minutes later.

"Are you going to share what you're up to?"

I grin at her. "Nope."

"Will we be back from wherever we're going in time for dinner?"

"Maybe. Don't worry, I'll take the heat from Mama if we're not." I'm not worried. Mama is aware of my plans for the day. We're about halfway into the drive before Lily realizes we could only have one city as our destination.

"Leo, why are we going to Boston?"

I shrug. "You're going to have to wait until we get there to find out."

"Can I make a request?"

Shaking my head, I say, "You can ask, but I may not be able to make it happen. I have plans, Stella."

"Fair enough. Can we stop by Anzetti's before we come back home?"

Anzetti's is our first stop. "I'll see what I can do." The rest of the drive passes with minimal squabbling over the radio and Lily attempting to needle my plans out of me.

"Can you allow me today? Sometimes a guy wants to take care of his woman. What I have planned isn't over the top. Will you think it is? Maybe, but it's for us."

I park down the block from Anzetti's. Lily knows where we are. Excitement bubbles within her. In her haste, she reaches for her door.

One thing Gran taught me was how to be respectful and treat people. Of course she shared specific rules for courting a woman and dating as well. I have been opening Lily's door since we met. Her need to savor buttery Italian pastries almost gets the better of her this morning. I set my hand on her arm. "I'll get your door." Rounding the rear of the car, I open her door and take her hand in mine.

"What are you nervous about?"

Damn! I can't hide anything from her. "Only about whether you'll be angry with me or not when you find out what we're doing here."

"Eating pastries, I hope."

I kiss her temple and laugh. "Yes, we will do that, but there's more."

The sweet scent of pastry and confectionary sugar assails my nose when we step into the bakery.

"Leo and Lily, so nice to see you still together," Peter greets us.

"Hi, Peter. Nice to see you as well."

He smiles. "Ready to get started?"

"Yes?" Lily replies with a question in her voice.

"Perfect. You'll need one of these." Peter hands each of us an apron.

Sheer joy and awe grace Lily's gorgeous face. At this moment, she realizes I somehow made one of her wildest dreams happen. It didn't take much. We spent our Sunday mornings here when we were on campus and stop by whenever we're in the city.

Peter ushers us into the kitchen. "My mother is anxiously waiting for you through the next set of double doors."

"Thank you, Peter," Lily manages.

He leaves, and she turns to me. "How did you remember?"

"I remember every minute detail. Before you ask, I won't share them all at once. I love you, Stella. Let's go learn to make some pastries."

"There are no words. In case I forget later, I had a spectacular day with you. I love you, Moon."

I take her hand in mine, and we push through the double door.

"Ah, splendid. Leo and Lily, wonderful to see you again." Lucia rounds the table and hugs us both tightly. "It's been too long since I've seen you."

"You deserve to sleep in," I offer.

She laughs. It's hearty and nice to hear. "True, but I miss the baking. I took the liberty of preparing the dough for the sfogliatella last night, given it needs to rise at least four hours. We're going to prepare some pasticciotti together."

Patiently and step by step, Lucia walks us through the preparation of the pasticciotti dough. While we follow her instructions, Lucia shares stories of the early days of the bakery and how the family-run business survives even today. "My Lucy wanted nothing to do with waking at wee hours of the morning despite her love of baking for others. Peter jumped in with both feet. Guido and I are most grateful our children want to extend our business. Enough about me. What about you two?"

We finish the dough and set it on the trays for baking. Then Lucia instructs us on cooking the sfogliatella.

"I run a craft brewery and distillery in my hometown. Lily recently started her own investment firm."

"Fantastic! But I was asking more about the two of you together."

A huge smile grows on Lily's face. "It took us some time, but we officially became a couple recently."

"*Aspettare*. You two were not dating in college?" Lucia inquires.

I chuckle. "No, we weren't. We've been best friends since we were eight."

"About time you figured out best friends make the best lovers, no?" Lucia scolds us.

Lily looks up at me with a fierce blush blooming on her face. We reply in unison, "Yes," and burst into laughter.

Forty minutes later, Lucia pulls the pasticciotti and sfogliatella from the oven. While the pastries cool, we fill bags with the custard. Expertly, she guides us through filling the pastries.

"You two are an excellent team," Lucia praises us. "Would you like new jobs?"

"While the offer to learn all the knowledge in your mind is tempting, we must decline," Lily replies.

"Of course, merely a joke. Lucy and Peter might take issue with me giving away our family secrets. Although, I trust you two will guard these appropriately."

"Without question," I reply.

"We should box these for you to take with you."

"*Grazie*, Lucia," Lily thanks her.

"It was my pleasure to spend the last few hours with two people so much in love."

With more pastries than we could possibly consume in the next few weeks and two large coffees, we share our goodbyes and absorb Lucia's warmth again through her words and strong hugs. After a passing gesture of thanks to Peter and Lucy, we make our way down the street toward my truck.

"What else do you have planned for today, Moon?"

I twist toward her in the cab of my truck. "I know you aren't a huge fan, but I do have a few more surprises planned for today."

"Okay."

I frown at my gorgeous woman. "Excuse me? You're simply going to acquiesce, just like that?"

"Yes."

"Who are you and what have you done with my Lilianna?"

She kisses me lightly and pulls back a sliver. "I have been in love with you before I knew what love was. Platonic friendship love is great and allowed us to learn so many things about each other. Romantic love is exponentially greater. I know without hesitation that you and I are meant to grow old together. I resolve to allow you to love me every way you choose and be accepting of the same."

"Thank you. Would you like to know where we're going next?"

She winks and answers, "Surprise me."

I take her mouth in a deep, penetrating kiss that leaves no room for mistaking my agreement with her words. *Soon you will know without question I intend to grow old with you too.* Shifting into drive, I pull away from the curb and follow a circuitous route to our college campus. We're going to share our pastries in our secret spot.

Beyond the football stadium there's a swath of trees that backs up to the nature preserve adjacent to campus. A few members of the inaugural football team carved out and blazed an area for reflection. Is it truly a secret from campus officials? Unlikely. Lily and I came here numerous times while we were in college.

"Excellent choice, Leo."

"Thanks."

We exit the truck with our coffees, pastries, and a blanket. My minions have set up our spot with everything else I need. I link my free hand with hers, and we stroll around the stadium.

CHAPTER TWENTY-SEVEN

LILIANNA

Speechless. No one has ever been able to render me mute other than Leo. Today he has outdone himself. Not only did he arrange for me to learn to bake our favorite Italian desserts with Lucia, but he set up our spot with a comfy and private place to eat them. There's a bistro table with chairs and place settings as if we're having a fancy breakfast here.

"Leo, this is so sweet of you."

He smiles down on me. "Does being a closet romantic fall outside of the best friend knowledge zone?"

"Yeah, definitely."

"Well, now you know. I am in fact a romantic at heart, which I will exemplify more a little later. First, we eat some of our delicious pastries."

The closer we get to finishing our Anzetti's treats, the more anxious Leo becomes. "What's wrong?"

He drops his head. It's classic Leo and tells me I'm spot-on. Something is up with him.

"Nothing's wrong. I have something else for you." He twists in his chair, stands, and spreads the blanket out on the ground. Taking my hand, he leads me over to the blanket, then scurries behind the backdrop and carries a large box over to me. "I started this box after the first dinner with your family. There's a card or note for each event we attended together or each time you pulled me out of my head and forced me to focus on my career. Not all the contents are happy though. There's a copy of your moving obituary for Gran and the video slideshow you created. There are cards from each birthday when we were dating someone else and a few small gifts in here as well. Most importantly, my true feelings are laid out in the notes and cards I never had the courage to give you before today. Well, that's not true. I planned to give this to you at Frankie's wedding."

"You have been saving these all this time?"

"Yes."

I gesture toward the lid of the box. "May I?"

"Please do."

I exhale and prepare myself for the contents of his gift. He would never save something to hurt me, but the fact he saved everything makes my heart melt. "First, I have one too."

"What?" His voice cracks.

"I have a box of us, if you will."

"Really?"

"Yeah, I do. I'll share it with you when we get home." A flood of emotions makes my stomach flip-flop. He has been storing all his feelings for me in this box for years. I unfold one small piece of paper. It reads: "I really dig you." It's a kid's valentine with a digger unearthing a heart. His signature is super cute. I sift through more and find a small box from a jeweler. The contents have shifted a bit because they aren't in order anymore. "Leo?"

"Those were a gift for your twenty-fifth birthday."

I mentally go backward in time. "I was dating Oliver."

"Yes. I may not have liked him at all, but I refused to disrespect your relationship."

I open the small, velvet box and find gorgeous diamond stud earrings. I've always wanted a pair but wouldn't buy them for myself. A single tear rolls over the ball of my cheek.

Leo swipes it away with the pad of his thumb.

"You remembered?"

"I remember everything. You always wanted a pair of classic, diamond earrings to wear everyday but never bought them. You certainly can afford them."

"You need me to say it, Moon?"

"No. I know your reason. You thought it was a gift a serious long-term boyfriend would get for you."

Muffled and teary, I agree with him. "Yes."

"I may not have been your boyfriend then, but I am now."

I sift through the box more and pull out a strip of pictures from a picture booth at the county fair, an old photo from high school graduation, and one with Leo holding me tight while spinning in a circle at college graduation. The look on our faces in that one is mixed. Within a week of that photo was the first time Leo and I were apart for more than a few days. When I look up at him, he's staring skyward.

"Leo?"

"When I left the hospital and I recovered enough, we went to dinner with our family."

"Yeah?" Angst and concern ripple through me.

"I had a private conversation with your father, and you asked me what we discussed."

"Yes, and you indicated you wanted to keep it between you and him." My mind is spinning with possibilities. While it was difficult not to press him, I respect his boundaries.

"I did, and I'm grateful you didn't push me to share before now." Leo continues, "A few days before the draft, we made a trip home to see everyone."

"Right, you wanted to be on campus because we had classes the next few weeks."

"Yes. On that trip, I asked your father for permission to date you."

Shock courses through me. "Really? Why?"

"The same reason that ultimately held me back. I was afraid to lose you and my extended family."

I think back to our tense ride back to campus and the craziness leading to the draft. "You didn't though."

"No, I was terrified you would say no. Then…."

"Gran died," I offer.

Leo nods, inhales deeply, shifts onto one knee, and takes my hands in his. "My conversation with Papa was similar this time. The main difference is I'm not afraid of your answer. Loving you is like breathing.

It's automatic and necessary for my survival. It took me too long to recognize my feelings for you are more than I could've ever fathomed finding in one single person. Most people don't meet their partner and soulmate in third grade, but pulling your ponytail was the smartest move I ever made. Each year since then has only solidified our relationship. True, we took a little detour, but we found our way back to one another. Lilianna, will you marry me and take my last name?"

I capture his lips with mine and kiss him slow and deep. Drawing back, I add a hint of space between us and kiss away the tear on his cheek.

"Stella, you didn't answer my question."

"Yes, oh, Moon, yes!"

He pulls a blue, velvet box from….

My chest tightens when I recognize the logo on the box. I shouldn't be surprised he remembers, but I don't recall when I shared the information or how he could've heard it. "You didn't?" Nestled inside the blue box is my dream engagement ring—a Harry Winston emerald cut diamond with tapered baguettes on either side.

A proud smile graces his gorgeous face. "I did." He slides his ring on my finger, and it's a perfect fit, much like we are. "I love you, Stella."

"I love you, Moon." I kiss him repeatedly until we're both panting. "Do you have any more surprises up for today?"

He lifts a shoulder. "Maybe. What do you want to do?"

"I want to celebrate alone with you." I hesitate a millisecond too long.

"But?"

I wrinkle my nose.

"You want to celebrate with our family too," he offers.

I hold my index finger and thumb apart about an inch. "A little."

The grin on his face says it all.

I jump to my feet and look around. We're the only people here. "Are they here?"

"Sort of. They'll be meeting us for family dinner at our hotel in three hours."

Tears prick my eyes. "Really?"

"Yes. What do you think about checking into our suite, celebrating privately for a little while, and then celebrating with our family?"

I grab my box, hand the pastry box to Leo, and take his hand in mine. "Yes." At a slow jog, we hurry back to his truck and make our way to celebrate our engagement in a posh hotel suite.

We check in and make our way upstairs. The suite has a gorgeous view of the harbor. I set an alarm on my phone to give us time to dress before dinner. It doesn't take long for both of us to shed our clothes and fall onto the plush bed. With slow, painstaking precision, we explore one another as if it's the first time. I suppose it's the first time we chase bliss as an engaged couple. Once the waves of pleasure cease, I curl into Leo's side.

Leo kisses the top of my head. "How long do you want to be engaged?"

"Not long, but it may require decreasing the guest list." A few months seems too long in my mind. I pin my eyes to his.

"How long is not long?"

"The twentieth-fourth of November."

Leo sits up and draws me into his arms. "You want to get married on Gran's birthday?"

The tone of his question makes me pause. "It was just a suggestion."

"I'm not upset. Why then?"

"It's fine."

"Stella, please tell me why?" His words are almost a growl.

"If it wasn't for her, we never would've met. She moved here for you to have a better life. The other option is to wait until September sixth of next year."

"What happened that day?"

I laugh. "You pulled my hair and became my protector for the rest of my life."

"But?"

"I don't want to wait almost another year for the privilege of calling myself Mrs. De Gaetano."

"Say that again," he demands.

"Mrs. De Gaetano."

"Sounds perfect." Leo presses a sweet, tender kiss to my lips.

"It does. I won't say I didn't practice writing my first name and your last name together at one point, numerous times."

"Is that a thing?"

"Oh, absolutely yes." My laughter is interrupted by the trill of my alarm. "Ready to meet the in-laws?"

With confidence, he answers, "I'm set there. Let's go have dinner with our family."

I laugh, and we clean up and dress for dinner. Leo wraps my hand around his forearm.

"Now isn't the time to remind me of your sexy forearms, fiancé."

"I'll push my sleeves up as soon as possible, fiancée."

"Oh, how I love you."

He kisses my temple. "I love you."

We step into a domed pavilion overlooking the water to a boisterous round of applause. Once Leo and I make it through the receiving line, we take our seats and dine on a delicious family meal.

EPILOGUE

LILIANNA

It's been nearly a week since Leo proposed, and I'm still floating on cloud nine. When Lina pushed up her wedding, I was surprised. Now I completely understand.

"Lily, we're going to be late. I refuse to be late this time."

"What are you talking about. I'm ready."

He comes around the corner. Leo is decked out in a suit and tie that matches my dress. "You are gorgeous, Stella."

When Lina indicated we needed a blue dress, I immediately recalled this dress in my closet. "Thank you." My man extends his arm to me, and we make our way to Lina's. Once we park, Leo inhales sharply.

"Talk to me, Moon."

"I'm good. I made it here in one piece. Just relishing in my good fortune for a moment." It isn't the location but the occasion. He rounds the car, opens my door, and kisses me breathless.

"You better make it the next Cappelli wedding in one piece too."

"Don't worry, Stella. I'll be there holding back tears when you make your way to me on Papa's arm."

"I can't wait."

"Me either. Let's get you inside before your sisters have my head." Leo grins at me. The commotion inside the house is more than I expect.

"Divide and conquer. I'll check on the guys, you check on the girls. See you in a bit." He kisses me and ushers me upstairs.

Sobs and tears echo down the hall. "I can't get married without his family here. What am I going to do?" Lina cries.

I reach the threshold and see Lina pacing like a madwoman in the master bedroom.

"I'm open to suggestions. I'm getting married in two hours to the man of my dreams, and his family is stuck at an airport."

"What is Gugliotti's opinion?" Frankie inquires.

"I haven't told him yet," Lina replies.

Oh, Lina!

"Momma, you said this day was about you and Taddy. Whether Gramma and Grandpa G are here shouldn't matter," my niece Emilia offers.

Lina looks at her daughter and smiles. "Thank you, Em. I'm working on how to tell Taddy about the problem."

"I know I'm kind of new here, but isn't your future husband a police officer?" Ellie carefully asks.

Lia answers, "You're one of us now, Ellie. What are you suggesting?"

She continues, "Well, can we arrange an escort for them from the airport? I mean, they'll still be late, but not that late."

Everyone in the room looks expectantly at Lina.

"That's a great idea, Ellie. Lily, can you go downstairs and figure out a place where I can talk to Santino without him seeing me?"

Honestly, the notion is ridiculous considering they woke up together this morning. As I start to move to find a good spot, my phone vibrates in my hand.

Leo: Meet me at the top of the stairs.

I step out of the master bedroom. "What's up?"

"I just got off the phone with Mrs. Gugliotti. They aren't going to make it on time. Does Lina know about this?"

"Yeah, she wants to talk to Gugliotti about an option Ellie came up with."

"Okay."

"Why didn't she call Lina?"

"Apparently, the bride and groom decided phones were off-limits as of nine this morning until after the ceremony," Leo replies.

"Who answered the phone to find out they would be later?"

"I'm guessing Frankie, considering she had Lina's phone and one I don't recognize in her hands."

"Makes sense." I mentally scan the layout of Lina's house. "Will the corner between the office and the living room work?"

"It'll work if Lina puts on a robe over her dress."

"Give me ten minutes, and she'll be down."

"Should I tell him the problem?"

"Let Lina do it even if we'll lose a little time to start working on the solution."

He laughs. "Okay."

I head downstairs with Lina in tow. She and Gugliotti agree Ellie's plan is a good one. Leo offers him a phone, and Lina heads back upstairs. Little does Gugliotti know, he's hastening the arrival of his grandmother for the wedding—a surprise guest Lina arranged even after Gugliotti spoke to her and she indicated she couldn't travel.

Soon thereafter, Lia marches downstairs to get some air. While the others wait in the living room, Lia and I step outside onto the front porch.

"I haven't really talked to you since dinner in Boston. How's engaged life?"

I smile. "Pretty much the same as before except I have a gorgeous ring and a wedding to plan."

"When are you thinking? I won't share." Lia winks at me.

"Soon actually, but we're waiting until after today to share with everyone. How is it going with Asher? How was your date with Keith?" At the grand reopening, Keith asked her on a date. They were classmates in elementary school for a brief time but didn't know one another at all.

"Asher is my friend. He doesn't want a relationship, and I do. Keith on the other hand…." She exhales before continuing. "We had an okay time, and I agreed to a second date."

"But?"

Lia shrugs.

I supply, "You want Asher."

"I do, despite not knowing the full details about the little girl."

"Maybe you should ask him. If he's truly your friend, he'll share with you, right?"

"I would hope so. I met her, and she was with us when we went for ice cream."

"Okay, you need to have a heart-to-heart with Asher. Dig deeper, find out what is truly going on with him and the little girl."

She acknowledges my words. "I will."

I surround her in my arms. "It may not be what you think. It's certainly a good thing he allowed you to meet Nell and spend time with her."

I feel his presence before he says anything. "Hi, babe." I release Lia and turn toward my burly, tattooed fiancé.

He laughs softly. "You good, Pip?"

"Yeah. Guy trouble. Want to offer some advice?"

"Nope. I'm basically your older brother. I'm sure Lily's advice was sound."

Lia smiles. "It was."

"I have an update. Captain Ramirez is set to bring the guests here, and we should only start fifteen minutes late."

"Not bad at all," I offer. We head inside, share the news with the bride and groom, and finish final preparations. Just under an hour later, Lina and Gugliotti are officially married with his grandmother in attendance. We dance the night away and assist with the cleanup.

"How keen are you on going home right now?" Leo asks.

"I'm open to suggestions and sufficiently intrigued. What do you have in mind?"

"Greasy spoon food and then a sunrise field trip."

I sigh. This man gets me, and he's mine. "I'm in." We bid Lina and Gugliotti a wonderful time on their honeymoon in the Bahamas and head to the diner.

The food and the company are amazing. It's been quite some time since I went to a diner decked out in a cocktail dress in the wee hours of the morning. "This was a great idea."

Leo casts a smile in my direction over his coffee mug. "Thanks. Ready for the next part?"

"Sure." We take a short drive back toward… our bench.

We haven't been here since…. "Why here?"

He shifts into park and twists in my direction. "We need to change our last memory of this place to a good one. From here forward, they will all be good."

"I can work with your request."

Hand in hand, we climb the small hill and settle onto our bench. Just under thirty minutes later, the sun peeks over the horizon. Glorious shades of red, orange, yellow, and pink streak across the sky.

Leo draws me against him and presses a kiss to my temple. "Can you promise me something?"

"Anything."

"If you ever need space, come here."

"Why?"

"Then I'll know where to chase you."

I kiss him thoroughly and reply, "I promise."

Thank you so much for reading *Chasing After You*!

I hope you love the Cappelli family. Will Lia find happily ever after too? Order *Chasing Someday* now so you don't miss it!

Ready for a new Blackthorne HEA? Is Alex next to fall? Check out my website for more release date details.

Did you love *Chasing After You*?

Thank you for taking the time to read it. I hope you loved it!
If you liked this book or another one of my books, please consider
posting a review.
A short line or two will be perfect!
I appreciate your support and feedback.

COMING SOON

Two new stories are coming soon!

A York Beach Novel

The Cappellis

Chasing Someday

A Blackthorne Novel

Hers to Protect

MY BOOKS

Protecting Us

MATCHMAKERS' BOOK CLUB
For Love & Coffee

All my books in one place: www.nicolevidal.com/books